KT-226-913

JASON SEGEL
KIRSTEN MILLER

NIGHTMARES!

THE SLEEPWALKER TONIC

~ ILLUSTRATED BY KARL KWASNY ~

CORGI

NIGHTMARES! THE SLEEPWALKER TONIC
A CORGI BOOK 978 0 552 57102 9

Published in Great Britain by Corgi Books,
an imprint of Random House Children's Publishers UK
A Penguin Random House Company

This edition published 2015

1 3 5 7 9 10 8 6 4 2

Penguin Random House is committed to a sustainable future for our business, our readers
and our planet. This book is made from Forest Stewardship Council® certified paper.

Set in 12.2 point Sabon MT

Corgi Books are published by Random House Children's Publishers UK,
61–63 Uxbridge Road, London W5 5SA

www.randomhousechildrens.co.uk
www.totallyrandombooks.co.uk
www.randomhouse.co.uk

Addresses for companies within The Random House Group Limited
can be found at: www.randomhouse.co.uk/offices.htm

THE RANDOM HOUSE GROUP Limited Reg. No. 954009

A CIP catalogue record for this book is available from the British Library.

Printed and bound in Great Britain by CPI Group (UK) Limited, Croydon CR0 4YY

Presented to:
Ms. Patricia Berne

PROLOGUE

It was half past ten in the evening, and the only light in downtown Orville Falls came from the windows of the town's newspaper office. Inside, a young woman named Josephine was still hard at work at her desk.

Every few seconds, her mouth stretched in a yawn. The lids of her eyes desperately wanted to shut, but Josephine refused to allow them. She was far too scared to sleep. For days, she'd assumed she was the only one. Now she knew that wasn't the case.

An epidemic of nightmares was ravaging tiny Orville Falls. Townsfolk reported waking each morning with feelings of dread that they just couldn't shake. One of the newspaper's reporters had even written a story about it. The picture Josephine was sketching would accompany the article. It showed a pair of eyes lurking in the darkness. They were the same cold, heartless eyes that seemed to follow Josephine whenever she drifted off to sleep.

She was adding more ink to the shadows when the chime of a familiar bell told her that the office door had opened. Josephine leaped to her feet, knocking over her coffee. She was sure she'd locked up, but even with her heart pounding loudly, she could hear footsteps crossing the floorboards.

Josephine grabbed the sharpest thing on her desk—a letter opener—and went to investigate. Standing at the front counter was an odd little man.

"Good evening, miss," he said in an accent she couldn't identify. "I apologize if I startled you."

He didn't look sorry, she thought. He looked smug. His thin lips were set in a smile, revealing a set of unfortunate teeth.

"The office is closed," Josephine told him sternly. "You'll have to come back tomorrow."

"Of course," the man said with a bow. As he turned toward the door, Josephine saw that someone was standing in the darkness behind him. It was a little girl. Josephine thought of her own beloved niece, who wasn't much older, and immediately regretted her rudeness.

"Sir?" Josephine called. "I'm sorry. Did you need some help?"

When he turned back around, Josephine saw that the unsettling smile on his face hadn't moved. "I'd like to place an ad in your paper. I'm opening a new shop on Main Street this week."

Josephine forced some friendliness into her voice for the little girl's sake. "Well, you've found the right person. I'm the newspaper's cartoonist and advice columnist—not to mention its entire advertising department."

"How wonderful," the man said. "You certainly *are* the person I've been hoping to meet."

He pulled a sheet of paper from his pocket and slid it across the counter. "This is what I'd like the advertisement to say."

> Take Tranquility Tonic and
> Say Goodbye to Your Nightmares
> ✦ ✦ ✦
> Available at Tranquility Tonight
> Main Street, Orville Falls

"Well, it's . . . clear enough," Josephine said, trying her best not to sound discouraging, "but perhaps I can help you think of something a bit *catchier*."

The man's smile somehow stretched even farther across

his face. "Oh, I assure you, it's quite . . . *catchy* as it is." The odd laugh that followed went on far longer than was comfortable. Then the man turned toward the girl, and his laughter stopped abruptly. After an awkward moment, Josephine broke the silence.

"So, does this tonic of yours really work?"

"Of course," the man replied. "Satisfaction is guaranteed."

"Then I might just give it a shot myself," Josephine said with a yawn. The truth was, she would have tried anything to get rid of her nightmares.

"Well, since you've been so kind . . ." The man reached into his coat and pulled out a tiny sapphire-blue bottle. "Why don't you have some on the house?"

ᴀ CHAPTER ONE ᴀ

THE ZOMBIE FROM ORVILLE FALLS

"Hey, Charlie, I had the *craziest* dream last night," Alfie Bluenthal said. "Want me to tell you about it?"

Ordinarily, Charlie Laird would have answered with a firm *No!* Over the past few months, he'd listened to a hundred of Alfie's dreams. They usually starred Albert Einstein, Neil deGrasse Tyson, or the local weatherwoman, and they seemed to go on forever. If they'd been nightmares, Charlie would have happily tuned in. Nightmares were his specialty, and he considered himself an expert on the subject. As far as Charlie was concerned, there was nothing more boring than someone else's *good* dreams. And kale. Good dreams and kale.

But Charlie happened to be in a generous mood. It was the first hot day of summer vacation, and he and Alfie were lounging on a bench outside the Cypress Creek ice cream shop. A triple-decker cone with scoops of rum raisin, mint chocolate chip, and bubble gum ice cream was slowly making its way into Charlie's belly. He had an hour to kill before he was due back at his summer job, and he couldn't have felt more content.

"Why not," he told Alfie. "Let's hear it."

As Alfie began to talk, Charlie sat back against the bench and let his gaze drift over the roof of the hardware store across the street—and up to the strange purple mansion that stood on a hill overlooking the town. Workmen on ladders had just finished painting the house, covering the dingy grape color with a fresh coat of lilac. At the top of the mansion, an octagonal tower rose into the sky. One of the tower's windows was open, and a kite in the shape of a pterodactyl was riding the breeze outside. The hand that held its string belonged to Charlie's little brother, Jack. The weird purple mansion was their home.

As Charlie listened to Alfie chattering away, he made a game of licking each drip of ice cream just before it reached the edge of his cone, and let Alfie's dream pass in one ear and out the other. A few random phrases managed to lodge themselves in his brain: *cumulonimbus, El Niño, heat wave, high-pressure zone.*

Just as Charlie popped the last bit of cone into his mouth, Alfie's dream finally reached its end.

"So what do you suppose it means?" Alfie asked.

"Same thing as every other dream you've had in the past three months," Charlie replied, still crunching on the cone. "It means you've got a crush on the weatherwoman from the Channel Four news."

"She's a *meteorologist,*" Alfie corrected him, clearly offended that his epic dream had been reduced to a single sentence. "And she has a name, you know."

"Stormy Skies is *not* a real name," Charlie informed his friend.

"How can you say that?" Alfie pouted. Love had turned his once-impressive brain to mush. "Are you trying to tell me Stormy just made it up? I'd like to hear you say that to Mr. and Mrs. Skies!"

Charlie was searching for a way to break the truth gently, when his attention was drawn across the street by the slam of a car door. An odd-looking man had emerged from a beaten-up black SUV. Smoke was billowing from under the hood, and several of its windows were shattered. The man who'd emerged was tall, with messy dark hair. He might have passed for an average suburban dad in his polo shirt and jeans, but something was clearly wrong with the guy. He was shuffling down the sidewalk, his head bent so far to the side that it appeared to be resting on one of his shoulders. As his feet slid forward, the soles of his Crocs barely left the ground. And though Charlie was sitting too far away to tell for sure, he would have sworn that the man's eyes were shut.

Charlie nudged Alfie and pointed. "Check it out. What's your diagnosis?"

Alfie adjusted his chunky black glasses and examined the man across the street. "Hmmm. Let's see. Rigid limbs. Shambling gait. Shocking lack of personal hygiene. And a pretty painful-looking crick in the neck. All things considered, I'd say there's a good chance he's the walking dead."

Charlie sat bolt upright on the edge of the bench. It had been months since

he'd felt such a jolt of excitement. "You think that guy might be a *zombie*?"

Alfie cackled and licked his cone. "I'm *joking*. How could he be a zombie? The portal to the Netherworld is closed." As soon as Alfie said it, the smile slid off his face, and he slowly turned to Charlie. "It *is* still closed, isn't it?" he almost whispered.

"Of course it is," Charlie assured him. "Why wouldn't it be?"

That answer wasn't good enough for either of them. Both boys went silent as their gazes turned to the house on the hill.

The purple mansion where Charlie lived wasn't like the other houses in Cypress Creek. While the rest of the village was as cute as a pack of puppies, the mansion looked more like an enormous dragon perched on top of a rock. It had claimed its hill before Cypress Creek had been founded, and its occupants had been watching over the town ever since.

A man named Silas DeChant had built the mansion, and Charlie's stepmother, Charlotte, was Silas's great-great-granddaughter. For the past one hundred and fifty years, some member of the DeChant family had been in residence at the mansion. It was the family's duty to protect the world from the house's terrible secret.

That secret could be found in the small, eight-sided room at the top of the mansion's tower. The special few who knew about the secret called it the portal. It was a door between the Waking World and the land of nightmares. Fortunately, not many people had ever heard of it. Most humans only visited the Netherworld when they fell asleep, and the terrifying creatures that dwelled there were supposed to stay there.

But the portal had been opened by accident twice in the past. Nightmares had snuck into Cypress Creek, and unspeakable things had come close to happening. If the portal ever opened again and Nightmares entered the Waking World, it would be up to the portal's protectors to round up the creatures and get them back to the other side. For almost two centuries, a single person had always held the job. Now, for the first time, the portal had three guardians living in the purple mansion. Charlie Laird was one of them.

Back on the bench outside the ice cream shop, Charlie and Alfie watched as the zombielike man slammed through the door of the hardware store across the street.

"I should find out what's going on," Charlie said, his heart racing.

"I'm coming with you." Alfie stuffed the rest of his cone into his mouth and tossed his napkin into the trash.

They made it to the store's plate-glass window in time to see the man slap a bill on the counter and then lurch toward the door, his arms laden with cans of paint.

"Hey, mister, don't forget your change!" the clerk called as the door swung open. The man shuffled out to the sidewalk, showing no sign that he'd heard.

Now the strange man was headed in the boys' direction. As the guy got closer, Charlie could see that his eyes *were* open—just barely. But there wasn't much life behind them. A thin stream of drool was trickling from a corner of his mouth. It fed the giant wet splotch that was growing on the front of his shirt, above a small insignia sewn onto his left shirt pocket. The logo looked like a flaming soccer ball.

Charlie and Alfie scuttled behind a parked car and ducked just seconds before the man passed by. A terrible odor trailed in the man's wake, and Charlie covered his face with his hand. Dead or alive, the guy hadn't bathed in a while.

Once the man had passed, Charlie let his breath out. "Did you get a look at the logo on his shirt?" Charlie whispered to Alfie. "I'm pretty sure I've seen it somewhere before."

Alfie squinted. "I can barely see anything. My eyes are

still watering from the smell, and now my glasses are all fogged up. That man was . . . *pungent*. Any idea where you might have seen the logo?"

"Nope," Charlie admitted. He stepped out from behind the car. "It looks like we're just going to have to ask the guy where he's from."

"*No way!*" Alfie yelped as he wiped his glasses. "I'm not going to talk to that man!"

Charlie raised an eyebrow. "What's the problem, Bluenthal?" he asked. "You scared?"

The word *scared* had a magical effect on Alfie. It lifted him up and straightened out his spine. "Yes, I am," he replied without a hint of embarrassment. "Are you?"

"Terrified," Charlie confirmed. "And that's why we have to do it."

"I guess you're right." Alfie sighed, deflating. Their travels in the Netherworld had taught them a lot. The most important lesson, though, was to never run from a Nightmare creature. To make one go away, you had to face what scared you. If you tried to escape, the Nightmare would just feed off your fear. Soon it would start showing up in your dreams every night.

"Good," Charlie said. "'Cause I don't think we want *that* guy paying us a visit after dark. Now hurry up, or we'll miss him." The man had almost reached his car.

"Excuse me!" Alfie called. "Sir!"

"Hey, you with the paint!" Charlie shouted. There was no time to be polite. The man grunted loudly in response but didn't turn around.

Charlie shot Alfie a worried look. It wasn't a good sign. Along with shuffling and drooling, grunting was classic zombie behavior.

"Can we interest you in a nice, juicy brain?" Alfie yelled.

"*Mmmrumph?*" The man's head swiveled toward the boys while his legs kept walking. Suddenly he jerked to a stop and dropped the cans. Blue paint flew everywhere as the man's knees buckled and he fell to the ground in a lifeless heap. A red gash was already forming across his forehead. He'd walked straight into a lamppost.

"Quick, call 911!" Charlie told Alfie as he ran toward the fallen man. When Charlie reached him, he dropped to his knees, took off the button-up he was wearing over his Hazel's Herbarium work T-shirt, and prepared to press it against the man's wound. But the expression on the man's face made Charlie pause. Despite the blood, the guy looked strangely peaceful. He lay there with his eyes closed and a pleasant smile on his lips, as if he were enjoying a good night's sleep.

Alfie squatted beside Charlie. "An ambulance is on the way," he said. Then he noticed the man's odd expression.

"Wow, somebody really needed a nap." Alfie took off his backpack and began searching for tools. "Now that he's out, let's have a look at our specimen."

"The guy may be a zombie, but that doesn't make him a science experiment," Charlie cautioned his friend. "You're not allowed to dissect him, Alfie."

"You can't *dissect* a person until he's dead." Alfie had fished a small flashlight out of his backpack. "I'm pretty sure this guy is still alive, so technically it would be *vivisection*. But don't worry—no cutting." He pried open one of the man's eyelids and shined the flashlight's beam into his eye. "Yep, pupillary reflex is good. Brain stem is working just fine."

Charlie used his free hand to pluck the wallet out of the man's pocket and pass it to his friend. "Thanks, Dr. Bluenthal. Now see if you can find some ID while I search the rest of him."

Alfie riffled through the man's bulging wallet and pulled out a blue-and-yellow card. "This guy really needs to organize his stuff. What the heck is Blockbuster Video?" After a few more attempts, he finally located a driver's license. "Says here the guy's name is Winston Lindsay. He's forty-four. An organ donor. Lives at twenty-seven Newcomb Street in Orville Falls."

"Orville Falls?" Charlie repeated incredulously. Orville Falls was a cute little town nestled in the mountains. It was about half an hour's drive from Cypress Creek, though Charlie rarely visited. "He came all the way here to buy paint? Don't they have a hardware store in Orville Falls?"

"Actually, they have two," Alfie said.

Charlie looked at Alfie. Sometimes Charlie wondered if the kid really did know everything.

Alfie sighed. "Remember the summer my parents sent me to that horrible camp in Orville Falls? The counselors locked me up and forced me to do crafts. I had to sneak out just to borrow books from the library."

"How could I forget," Charlie said, grinning at the memory of the gifts Alfie had presented to his friends at the end of the ordeal. "I still have that macramé owl you made for me."

They heard the wail of a siren in the distance. Within seconds, it had grown to a deafening pitch as an ambulance screeched to a stop on Main Street and two EMTs in crisp blue uniforms leaped from the back.

"Afternoon," said one in a booming voice fit for a superhero. "You the two kids who called this in?"

"Uh-huh," grunted Alfie. For a moment, it seemed like all he could do was stare up at the EMT in awe. Then Charlie nudged him, and the science spilled out. "The subject is unconscious, but his pupillary reflex indicates—"

A second EMT pushed past Alfie and squatted beside Winston Lindsay. "Nice work stopping the bleeding," she praised Charlie as she examined the man's wound. "You boys in the Scouts or something?"

"No, ma'am," said Charlie. He rarely used the word *ma'am,* but this was one of the few adults who actually seemed to warrant it.

Charlie saw Alfie's spine stiffen. "I'm not a Boy Scout, but I do consider myself something of an amateur doctor," Alfie said proudly. "I've studied all the major texts, and—"

"That's great, little buddy," the first EMT interrupted. Then he began to unload the stretcher while his partner examined the patient.

"Pupillary reflex appears to be fine," the partner announced. "But looks like this dude's going to be out for a while. We need to get him in ASAP."

Alfie turned to Charlie and rolled his eyes. Charlie could imagine how annoyed his friend felt. It was hard enough being twelve years old; most adults barely listened to a word you said. Being a twelve-year-old genius had to be particularly frustrating.

The EMTs hoisted Winston Lindsay onto the stretcher, strapped him down, and loaded him into the back of the ambulance. Charlie and Alfie began to climb in after him.

"'Fraid not, little men," said one of the EMTs, pushing them away. "Only family members get to ride in the back."

"But we found the guy!" Alfie protested. "We probably

saved his life!" He didn't bother to add that they were also the ones who'd endangered it by making him run into a lamppost.

Charlie wanted to shout with frustration, but he managed to keep his voice calm. "Sir, we need to know what's wrong with this man," he said. "The situation could be way more serious than you think."

The EMT tapped his badge, which bore the logo of Westbridge Hospital. "Visiting hours are nine to noon." Then he slammed the doors, and the ambulance sped off.

Charlie and Alfie raced back across the street to the ice cream parlor and hopped onto their bikes. Charlie couldn't let the man get away. But the ambulance was already out of sight when he and Alfie finally hit the road, and the sound of its siren was growing fainter and fainter. Charlie began to pump his pedals as fast as he could. Miraculously, the siren began to grow louder again. Charlie looked down at his feet in wonder, and saw Alfie do the same thing. Somehow they seemed to be catching up.

The boys rounded a curve and hit their brakes. In front of them, the ambulance was stopped at a streetlight. The back doors of the vehicle had been thrown open, and the two EMTs were standing next to it, peering into a thicket of trees that lined one side of the road. Both of them wore stunned expressions, and one was sporting what looked like the start of an impressive black eye.

Charlie glanced down. A thin trail of IV fluid led from the back of the ambulance, across the road, and into the trees.

"What happened?" Alfie asked the EMTs.

"Weirdest thing I ever saw," one of them responded as if in a daze. Then he looked at his partner. "We better report it."

The second EMT took out a walkie-talkie. "Dispatch, this is Ambulance Three. Come in."

A voice cut through the static. "Come in, Ambulance Three."

"You're not going to believe this one.

You know that guy we just picked up on Main Street, the one with the head injury?"

"What about him?"

"He just busted out of the ambulance."

Charlie and Alfie swapped a worried look.

"He what? The guy you reported was unconscious with a probable concussion. . . ."

"And I stand by that. He was out cold when we got him. But we had to stop for a red light. The dude broke out of the straps, ripped out his IV, and forced his

way out the back. Gave my partner a pretty sweet shiner in the process. Then he ran off into the woods."

"But how's that even poss—" began the skeptical voice on the other end.

"Hold up for a sec, 'cause I haven't even gotten to the *strange* part yet," the EMT interrupted. "The whole time he was fighting us, the guy barely opened his eyes. I'm not even sure he was awake."

"What do you mean, he wasn't awake?"

Charlie saw the EMT pause as if struggling to find the right words. Then she hit the button and put the walkie-talkie back up to her mouth. "Maybe I'm crazy, but I think he might have been *sleepwalking*."

⚘ CHAPTER TWO ⚘

THE MONSTER BOOK

The portal was shut—that much was for sure. While Alfie had stayed behind to talk to the EMTs, Charlie had high-tailed it to the purple mansion. When he'd gotten there, he'd dumped his bike in the driveway and scrambled up the stairs two at a time until he'd reached the room at the top of the tower. He'd checked the portal; then he'd checked it again. And again—until he'd been perfectly satisfied that the door to the Netherworld was closed.

But Charlie couldn't get rid of the nagging feeling that something was horribly wrong. Winston Lindsay might not have been a zombie, but he hadn't really seemed *human* either. There were millions of creatures in the Netherworld, and no two were the same. They were each as unique as a person's fears. Some slithered, some flew—and some of them shuffled. Even though the portal appeared to be sealed, Charlie had to prove to himself that Winston Lindsay wasn't a Nightmare creature.

Charlie charged back down the stairs and out the mansion's front door. He needed to consult his stepmother straightaway. Not only was Charlotte DeChant a medical professional, but she was the only adult in town who would recognize a Nightmare if she saw one.

As Charlie approached Hazel's Herbarium, he tried to catch sight of his stepmother inside. But there were so many plants fighting for sunlight in the shop's window that it was impossible to see into the store. The feverfew was in flower, and the burdock was covered in large purple burrs. Charlie couldn't help noticing that the skunkweed was looking parched. And the belladonna needed a teensy bit of the special fertilizer he collected from the cow fields on the outskirts of town. Charlie's summer job was tending the plants in his stepmother's shop, and though it was stinky and exhausting—and sometimes downright dangerous—he'd loved it from the start.

The bell chimed as Charlie crossed the threshold of

Hazel's Herbarium. "Charlie, is that you?" Charlotte called from the examination room at the back of the shop.

"Yep!" he shouted.

"Fantastic! Can you bring me that hoary mugwort ointment I made this morning?"

"Sure thing." Charlie grabbed the ointment off a shelf and went to deliver it to Charlotte. He'd barely set foot in the examination room, though, when he hopped right back out again.

"Holy mackerel!" Charlie yelped. "What the heck *is* it?" He'd seen some terrifying things in his day, but few compared to the hideous creature that was lying spread-eagled on Charlotte's exam table in nothing but a pair of tighty-whities. Its skin was bright red and blotchy, and it was frantically scratching itself with both of its hands. And yet, for some reason, the thing seemed to be laughing at *him*.

"*It?*" said a very annoyed woman who was dressed head to toe in white. Charlie hadn't noticed her sitting primly in the chair in a corner of the tiny room. "*It* is my little boy." She turned her glare on Charlotte. "Aren't you going to reprimand your assistant, Ms. Laird? I've never encountered such rudeness!"

Charlie saw Charlotte bite her lip for a second like she always did when she was trying hard to hold her tongue. "My apologies, Mrs. Tobias, but you must admit that your

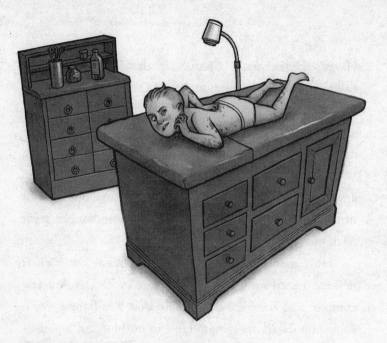

son doesn't look quite human at the moment. This is the worst case of poison ivy I've ever encountered. And Oliver's been to see me three times this summer. Where on earth does he keep getting into the stuff?"

"I haven't the faintest idea," Mrs. Tobias said, backing down a bit.

"Wait a second, is that *Ollie Tobias*?" Charlie asked, stepping forward for a closer look at the creature.

"Hey, Charlie." The boy giggled. Even when he was covered in a rash and stripped down to his underwear, Ollie Tobias could find the humor in any situation. "I was wondering if you were going to recognize me."

"You know my son?" Mrs. Tobias sniffed.

"We go to school together," Charlie answered. He was on friendly terms with most of the kids who attended Cypress Creek Elementary. It wasn't so long ago that he'd helped them escape from their nightmares.

But that wasn't why he knew Ollie. Everyone at school knew Ollie Tobias, because Ollie was gifted. He didn't play any musical instruments or excel at any sports. But you could lock the kid in an empty room with nothing but a paper clip and a box of lime Jell-O, and he'd still find a way to get himself into serious trouble.

Ollie's mother was equally notorious. Kids said she was a genius at inventing cruel and unusual punishments for her exceptionally naughty son. Legend had it that she'd once made Ollie stand on a corner in town wearing a large sign that said I EAT OTHER PEOPLE'S CRAYONS. (Though Ollie had quickly turned the situation to his own advantage by adding SO I POOP RAINBOWS on the other side of the sign.)

On another occasion, Mrs. Tobias supposedly forced her son to wash every car in the school parking lot after he'd been caught writing the words *BOOTY BREEZE* with a bar of soap on his homeroom teacher's car.

Charlie had always figured that most stories about Ollie and his mom were a little exaggerated. Then, the first day of summer break, he'd happened to ride past Ollie's house. Four women in white dresses had been playing croquet in the front yard, and Charlie had seen one of the women knock her ball under the hedges that bordered the property.

"Ollie!" she'd screeched, and the boy had come running. He'd been dressed like some sort of old-fashioned doll—short pants, a striped shirt with suspenders, and a straw hat to top it all off. Bounding behind him had been what had looked like a large, hairless rat.

Charlie had watched Ollie reach the shrubbery, then hesitate. Ollie looked back at the ladies.

"Come on, Mom. Do I have to get it?" he'd pleaded. "There's really nasty stuff growing under those hedges."

His mother swung her croquet mallet like a deadly weapon. She was the kind of woman who could give a kid nightmares. "If you don't like being our ball boy, consider that the next time you decide to shave the dog."

Ollie had simply let out a sigh, dropped to his hands and knees, and fished out the lost ball.

Now, seeing the shape Ollie was in, Charlie was pretty sure he knew *exactly* what was under those hedges. "Have you been playing a lot of croquet this summer, Mrs. Tobias?" he asked innocently.

Ollie sat bolt upright on the exam table as if he'd had an epiphany. He pointed a bumpy red finger at his mother. "The hedges! I told you there's weird stuff under the hedges, and you make me crawl under them anyway!"

Mrs. Tobias had gone sheet white. "I—I—I . . . ," she stammered. Her eyes narrowed as she turned to Charlie. "How would *you* . . ."

"I ride by your house on my bike sometimes. I've seen you and your friends—"

Mrs. Tobias looked like she was about to explode, and Charlotte finally jumped in. "Hey, Charlie," she said, taking him by the arm and gently guiding him to the door. "Would you mind manning the front counter while I finish treating Oliver?"

"Sure." Charlie sighed as he left the room. He was dying to give Charlotte the scoop on the man from Orville Falls, but it would have to wait. There was no telling how long it might take his stepmom to rub enough mugwort onto Ollie Tobias. Charlie would have to start with a little monster research of his own.

He pulled a large black binder out of the bottom drawer of Charlotte's desk and took his place behind the counter. He ran his finger across the title Charlotte had painted in gold on the cover. Then he began to carefully thumb through the pages of the book. As he perused the chapter on zombies, he marveled at the illustrations Charlotte had drawn. Her zombies looked exactly like the creatures he'd encountered during his visit to the Netherworld: Hollow eyes. Purple flesh. Missing limbs. What Charlotte's illustrations *didn't* resemble was the man from Orville Falls.

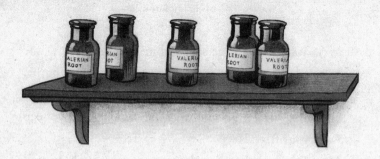

Charlie searched the entire book from cover to cover. There wasn't a Nightmare in it that looked anything like Winston Lindsay.

Charlie turned to the computer beside the cash register. He opened a new window and typed in *clumsy, shuffling, drooling, grunting*. He had no idea what to expect when he finally clicked *Search*.

The first result was a team photo of the 1996 New York Jets. The second was from the website of a hospital so famous that even Charlie had heard of it. He almost gasped when he saw the headline at the top of the page: SLEEP-WALKING: SIGNS AND SYMPTOMS. That was what the EMT had said—the man had appeared to be sleepwalking.

Then the bell above the shop door tinkled, and Charlie made sure a smile was on his face when he looked up from the computer. A confused woman was standing in the doorway, her head oscillating like an old-fashioned fan. "Do you have any lilies today?" she inquired.

"I'm sorry, ma'am, but we're not a florist," Charlie told her.

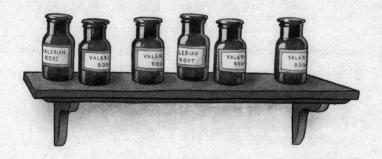

"Oh, fine, then," the woman said with a sigh. She pointed to a vase filled with flowers from the Lairds' front yard. "I suppose those daisies will just have to do."

Charlie didn't bother to tell her that the daisies were nothing but decoration. He wrapped up the flowers, charged the woman five dollars, and tucked the lonely bill into the till.

It was happening more and more often these days. Once, Hazel's Herbarium had attracted customers from all over the state. They'd come for Charlotte's nail fungus remover, teeth whitener, hair straightener, and dog breath freshener. The bestseller had been Charlotte's special tincture of valerian root, a sleeping draught so effective that just a few drops could send an agitated elephant to snoozeville. But these days, the shelves were lined with dozens of bottles of valerian root, all gathering dust. And the people who came through the door of Hazel's Herbarium were usually there by mistake.

Charlotte had done everything she could think of to bring customers back to the herbarium. She offered sales and specials—even advertised a Brew Your Own Love Potion night. But no one came. Charlie had never paid much attention to family finances before. Then one night, during a midnight trip to the bathroom, he'd heard his parents speaking in hushed voices. His dad's teaching salary could no longer cover all the bills. The Lairds needed money if Hazel's Herbarium was going to stay in business. It seemed to Charlie that the only chance they had of making that money was the book he held in his hands.

Charlotte had worked on the book for years, and for the last few months, Charlie had helped. The pages contained everything they knew about the Netherworld. Charlotte had passed through the portal in the purple mansion's tower when she'd been Charlie's age, and the first half of the book told of her adventure. The second half offered tips and advice for anyone who found themselves stuck in the Netherworld—whether in the flesh or in their dreams.

Charlie had read Charlotte's masterpiece at least ten times, and every time he opened the book, it still blew his mind. There was an entire page devoted to "How to Deal with Goblins" and a whole section that covered "How to Have Fun with Your Figments!" He'd never come across another book that was as educational, or as exciting. And Charlotte's remarkable drawings were the best part. The pictures of monsters and ghouls and everything else that goes bump in the night were so lifelike that they looked like they might walk right off the page. Charlie could sit and thumb through the pages for hours. As far as he was concerned, the book was sheer genius. Unfortunately, the publishing community wasn't convinced.

Charlotte had sent copies of the book to a dozen publishers around the country. Only two had bothered to write back. They were both in New York, and they wanted to meet her, so Charlotte was flying to the city at the start of next week. Charlie hoped one of them would bite.

The exam room door opened, and a powerful odor filled the shop. It smelled like a mixture of rotten eggs, baby powder, and cilantro, and it made Charlie gag.

"So rub the ointment all over him three times a day," Charlotte was saying. "I'm afraid there's nothing much you can do about the smell. But the rash should be gone by Tuesday."

"Thank you, Ms. Laird," Mrs. Tobias said, managing to sound completely ungrateful.

"My pleasure. Just make sure Ollie doesn't go rooting around under any more hedges."

The look the woman gave Charlie's stepmother could have killed. Charlotte countered with her most innocent smile.

"I owe you one, Charlie," Ollie whispered, still scratching his rash as he passed.

"No problem," Charlie told him. Thanks to him, Ollie wouldn't be crawling under any more bushes. But Charlie couldn't find the heart to celebrate. Ollie's mother was the one with the money, and she couldn't have been more furious.

"Well, seems like we just lost another customer," Charlotte said, watching with satisfaction as the Tobias woman stomped away. "And for once, I couldn't be happier." She put a hand on Charlie's shoulder. "You did good today. Who knows how many times Oliver would have had to come back if it weren't for you."

Charlie frowned. Mrs. Tobias would never again set foot in Hazel's Herbarium, and it was all because of him. He was hurting the place, not helping it.

But Charlotte didn't notice Charlie's frown. She was busy tidying shelves she'd already tidied once that morning. "So how was your lunch break with Alfie?" she asked. "Was it doughnuts or ice cream today?"

Charlie instantly perked up. He'd almost forgotten. "We went to the ice cream shop, and something really weird happened." That was all he needed to say. Charlotte pulled up a stool across the counter from him and sat quietly while Charlie told her the story.

"I think you can relax," Charlotte announced once

Charlie had finished. "Whatever the guy was, he wasn't a Nightmare."

"How do you know?" he asked. He'd figured as much, but it was best to be sure.

"Well, first of all, you said the man started bleeding after he hit his head. I'm pretty sure Nightmares don't bleed. Second, you said the ambulance guys had him hooked up to all their machines. It would have been pretty clear to them if the guy wasn't human."

She made an excellent case, Charlie had to admit. "So what do you think was wrong with him?"

"Can't say for certain," Charlotte said, tapping the counter as she thought. "He might have been under the influence of some medication. Or maybe he's always been a little bit weird. Who knows?" She paused. "You did check that the portal is closed, didn't you?"

"Of course," Charlie told her.

"Then stop worrying so much!" His stepmom leaned over the counter and pinched his cheek. "There are no monsters in Cypress Creek."

"Don't be so sure about that," said a voice behind her. The herbarium's door had swung open. Charlie's dad was standing in the entrance with Charlie's little brother, Jack, by his side.

No one would ever have guessed that Andrew Laird, with his scholarly glasses and well-groomed beard, was the oddball of the family. But of the four of them, he was the only one who was unable to see the portal. As far as Charlie's dad knew, the book his wife had written was nothing but fiction. He had no idea that the creatures described in it were real.

Charlotte had made it perfectly clear to both Charlie and Jack that she didn't want their dad to know the truth about the house. The portal chose who was able to see it, she said. Some of the chosen called their ability a gift. Others called it a curse. But one thing was certain—it was a lifelong burden. And she didn't want the man she'd married to ever bear its weight.

Charlotte jumped up and planted a kiss on her husband's cheek. "You've seen a monster in Cypress Creek?" she asked playfully, though Charlie could tell she was nervous.

Andrew Laird shook his head. "I don't know if it was a monster, but there's something strange wandering the woods around here. You wouldn't believe the thing Jack and I spotted limping through the forest outside town about an hour ago."

"Werewolf, maybe?" Charlotte forced a laugh.

Charlie tried to laugh too, but nothing came out. His heart was beating so fast that he felt light-headed.

"Nope," Jack said. "If you ask me, it looked a lot like a zombie."

THE DREAM REALM

The second Charlie fell asleep, the zombies found him. He should have expected it. He'd been thinking about the walking dead all day long. It made perfect sense that he'd end up meeting them that night in his dreams.

There were three of them in various stages of decay. One was an elderly lady named Maude, and the second was a teenage boy with a perfectly shaved head who insisted on going by the name Buzz. It was impossible to tell if the third zombie was male or female. The Walgreens name tag still pinned to its shirt read MORGAN. Within seconds, they'd circled and surrounded Charlie. He made a mental note to offer them a few tips on respecting people's personal space.

"Hey, buddy." Buzz offered his hand. Charlie shook it and pretended not to notice when three of the teenage zombie's fingers snapped off. "'Bout time you came to see your old friends."

"We were sure you'd forgotten us," said Maude. Charlie could tell that she wanted to hug him—and probably would have if she'd had any arms.

"I wouldn't worry too much about *that*," Charlie assured her. "You guys are pretty unforgettable. It's just that most of the time when I visit the Dream Realm, I try to spend time with my mom. How's this place working out for you guys, anyway?"

Charlie had encountered the zombies on his adventures in the Netherworld. Since then, they'd retired from their nightmare careers and chosen to become dreams. While humans went to the Netherworld to face their fears, the Dream Realm was where people could relive good memories and experience all of their hopes and desires. Charlie wouldn't have guessed there would be a place for zombies in the Dream Realm, but zombies turned out to be rather popular. Morgan and Maude specialized in Halloween memories, while Buzz's expertise was video game walkthroughs.

"I'd like the Dream Realm a whole lot better if those crazy rabbits weren't always hanging around," Morgan said in a decidedly masculine voice, gesturing toward a bunch of white bunnies that were chomping away at a clump of clover. One turned around as if it had overheard, revealing a head that featured nothing but a gaping mouth filled with razor-sharp teeth. "Boy, those things really give me the heebie-jeebies. Who's ever had a good dream about something like *that*?"

Charlie bit his lip and wondered if the zombie had ever looked in a mirror. Until you got to know him, Morgan was every bit as horrifying as the bunnies.

"Don't mind that old grump," Maude advised. "He always finds something to kvetch about when he's bored."

"Bored?" Charlie asked.

"Yeah, it's been kinda dull around here lately," Buzz told him. "We had a cameo in your friend Rocco's dream last Sunday, but other than that . . ." He ended the sentence with a miserable shrug. "I guess I was expecting a little more action on this side."

"Well, I'm here to see you!" Charlie said, trying to cheer up his friend. "And since I'm here, I could use some advice."

"From us?" Maude sounded thrilled.

"We're all ears," said Morgan, who was missing both of his.

Charlie told them about the man he and Alfie had seen. He even mimicked the guy's shuffling and grunting, but when he'd finished his performance, the zombies were shaking their heads.

"Your stepmother was right. The gentleman wasn't a Nightmare," Maude said. She revealed a rather gruesome wound on her shoulder. "Creatures like us don't really bleed. All the gore that humans see in their nightmares is strictly showbiz."

"Look, no pupillary reflex either," said Morgan, leaning in close so that Charlie could examine a bloodshot eyeball.

"Yeah, and the last thing any self-respecting Nightmare would do if he got to the other side is buy a bunch of *paint*." Buzz's laugh sounded a little crazed, and the look in his eyes would have made most people uncomfortable.

But Charlie wasn't worried. He knew he was perfectly safe. No real harm would ever come to him in the Dream Realm.

"So what do you think was wrong with the guy?" Charlie asked. "And why would anyone drive all the way from Orville Falls just to go to the Cypress Creek hardware store?"

Buzz stopped laughing, and all three of the zombies froze. Charlie could tell that something had taken the walking dead by surprise.

"What did I say?" he asked.

"The man you were describing is from Orville Falls?" Maude asked cautiously.

"Yeah," Charlie said, feeling more on edge than ever. "You guys know the place?"

The zombies traded glances.

"Come with us," said Morgan. "There's something you should see."

Charlie followed the zombies as they lumbered through the magnificent Dream Realm. It was brighter than the sunniest summer day, and everything around him seemed to shimmer and glow with the warmth of a million fond memories. Though his mission couldn't have been more serious, Charlie felt his spirits soar as they cut through Cypress Creek's annual radish festival, passed the giant tree in front of the library as it was being decorated with Christmas lights, saw a pack of little kids constructing an enormous snowman, and watched the sky above them explode with Fourth of July fireworks.

"Did you notice how many people are here?" Morgan asked. "I'd say more than half of your town is in the Dream Realm right now."

Charlie looked around and saw quite a few familiar faces. "Hey, is that Cypress Creek Elementary?" He pointed to a boxlike building in the distance. The playground beside it was alive with little figures crawling up the jungle gym and dangling from the monkey bars. "What's going on over there?"

"It's like that every night," Buzz said. "Since the last principal disappeared, that school has been *rocking*."

"And look. Over there to your left," said Maude.

Charlie found himself peering into the window of Cypress Creek's ice cream parlor. Alfie was perched on a stool inside. In front of him was the biggest banana split ever created.

"It's nice to have your friend Alfie back," said Morgan. "That used to be his favorite place, but we haven't seen him there in a while."

"Let's just say he's been dreaming a lot about the weather lately," Charlie said with a laugh, but none of the zombies seemed interested. Charlie sealed his lips and followed silently as they left Cypress Creek behind. They kept traveling for a while, until Maude suddenly came to a stop.

"This is it," she announced.

"Yep, we're here," Morgan confirmed, taking a place at her side.

Buzz shuddered. "I'm feeling kinda freaked out right now," he said.

Charlie looked around, trying to figure out what was making Buzz so nervous. They were at the edge of a flowery park in the center of a different town. A lovely white courthouse stood at one end, and a fountain shot streams of water into the air. It was the sort of place where people should gather. Charlie could imagine little kids running barefoot through the grass, and picnickers lounging on blankets. But as lovely as it was, there *was* something eerie about it all. Then Charlie realized what was making goose bumps break out on his arms. Aside from the fountain, the place was perfectly silent and still. There were no birds tweeting or katydids chirping. No squirrels scampering up the trees or dogs watering flowerbeds. And there wasn't a single dreamer to be seen.

"This used to be a really popular spot in the Dream Realm," said Buzz. "I mean, come on. Look at the place! It's so cute, I could hurl. Can you imagine how many good memories must have been made around here? And now it's like something right out of the Netherworld."

"The Dream Realm can't exist without dreamers," Maude said, turning to Charlie. "And there hasn't been a dreamer here for at least a week. See how the town is starting to fade?"

Now that she'd mentioned it, Charlie noticed that the edges of the buildings were a little bit blurry. The water in the fountain seemed to evaporate in midair. Even the flowers weren't quite as vibrant as they should have been.

"I don't understand," Charlie said, spinning around to face the zombies. "What is this place? Why did you bring me here?"

"This is the Dream Realm's Orville Falls," said Morgan.

"What's happened to it?" Charlie asked, remembering how busy the Dream Realm's Cypress Creek had been. "Where has everyone gone?"

"We don't know," Maude said. "Nothing like this has ever happened before."

"But I think one thing's clear," Morgan added. "Something's not right in Orville Falls."

CHAPTER FOUR

THE COMETS CRASH

It was Sunday morning, and Charlie was lying awake when he felt the beast pounce on his bed. Slowly, step by step, it slinked over the covers, making its way toward his head. Charlie closed his eyes and remained perfectly still. He waited patiently until the fat, fur-covered monster was just about to take its favorite seat on Charlie's sleeping face. Then, at the perfect moment, he sat bolt upright.

"Ha!" he shouted at the beast. "Got you!"

Caught in the act, Charlotte's evil cat, Aggie, let out an angry yowl, sprang off the bed, and dashed for the door.

Charlie lay back down on the pillows. He'd never been

able to figure out how the cat managed to open his bedroom door. But this morning, he had far bigger concerns than ninja felines. He had to find a way to get to Orville Falls. The town was only twenty miles from Cypress Creek. But Charlie's bike was his main form of transportation, and the road to Orville Falls was all uphill.

Charlotte would have taken him if he'd asked. But Charlie had seen with his own eyes how empty the cash register at Hazel's Herbarium was, and Sunday afternoons were the busiest time of the week. His stepmother was leaving for New York the next morning, and Hazel's Herbarium would be closed on Monday and Tuesday. They couldn't afford a third day of no sales, so Charlie had spent the morning brainstorming reasons for his dad to take him to Orville Falls. But short of announcing that the entire town was in terrible danger, Charlie hadn't come up with anything that stood a chance of convincing Andrew Laird to make the winding, treacherous drive.

Sometime around ten, Charlie got dressed and followed the smell of food downstairs. He was just taking his seat at the kitchen table when the phone rang.

"I'm sorry," he heard his father say, "but we're about to eat Sunday breakfast. I'll have Charlie call you as soon as we're done."

But the phone never left his dad's ear. Andrew Laird's

brow furrowed as he listened to the caller. From across the kitchen table, Charlie could hear the excited voice on the other end of the line.

"Oh, I *see*," said Andrew Laird. "Well, now, that really *does* sound important. *Right*. Yep. Got it." Then he passed Charlie the phone. "I think your friend may be losing it," he said. "Make it quick."

Whichever friend it was, Charlie had no intention of speaking for very long. Even though his stomach was in knots, the broccoli and cheese frittata that Charlotte had just served was beckoning him.

"Charlie!" The voice on the other end of the line belonged to Rocco Marquez, one of Charlie's three best friends. Rocco sounded worried. "You gotta get down here right away!"

"Down where?" Charlie asked, alarmed. There was an edge to Rocco's voice that he'd rarely heard before, and wind was whistling in the background of the call. Rocco wasn't at home.

"The soccer field!" Rocco exclaimed as if the answer should have been obvious. "There's something really weird going on with the other team."

"Weird how?" Charlie pushed his chair back from the table and stood up. He'd just lost his appetite.

"Most of the other team's players are walking around

like they don't know where they are. The ball rolls right past them, and they don't bother to chase it. I'm literally talking on a cell phone while I'm playing soccer, and my team is *still* winning. And the parents watching in the stands all look totally dazed and confused. But the other team's coach is the really freaky one. He's got this giant red cut on his forehead, and he hasn't even put a bandage on it, and . . ."

Charlie suddenly remembered the hardware store man, Winston Lindsay. The logo on his shirt had looked like a flaming soccer ball. The other team's soccer coach was starting to sound a lot like the mysterious stranger from Orville Falls. Charlie's stomach began twisting itself into another knot. "What team are you playing?" he asked.

"The Comets," Rocco replied. "They used to be one of the best in the league, but—"

"What *town* are they from?" Charlie asked, cutting him off.

"Orville Falls," Rocco told him.

The hairs on the back of Charlie's neck were standing straight up. "Call Alfie and Paige," he told Rocco. "I'm putting my shoes on now. I'll be there in less than ten."

When Charlie arrived, the score was 35–0, and there were thirty seconds left on the clock. Two of the Comets chased the ball like madmen, while the rest of their teammates stumbled around the field like a bunch of zombies. Charlie checked the stands. The turnout was light, and the few parents who'd come were drooling and mumbling to themselves. It wasn't a pretty sight.

"So what's the emergency?" demanded a voice over Charlie's shoulder.

Charlie jumped and spun around. Behind him stood Paige Bretter, a tiny blonde with a feisty personality, and she appeared to be rather annoyed. "Did I just get dragged out of bed to see Rocco's team

slaughter the competition? What's new about that? I swear, they're so good that it's *boring*."

"Rocco didn't tell you?" Charlie asked.

"Tell me what? All he said was 'Bring Alfie.' But Alfie's mother wouldn't let him go anywhere. Guess he woke up in the middle of the night and polished off all the ice cream in the family fridge. His mom did not sound amused."

Charlie almost grinned at the thought of Alfie sitting in the Dream Realm ice cream parlor, feasting on a giant banana split. Then a whistle blew behind him, and he was brought back to the soccer game. It was over. The final score was 37–0.

Charlie and Paige watched as one of the Comets' players fell to his knees, clearly exhausted. He stayed there for a moment, his forehead resting on the ground. A short, scrappy-looking kid with dirty-blond hair and freckles,

he was one of the two who'd tried their best to keep the game going. Charlie saw Rocco cross the field and offer the kid a hand. Once the boy was back on his feet, the two spoke. Soon, Rocco was leading the Comets player Charlie's way.

"This is Kyle," Rocco said, introducing the boy. Then he gave the kid an encouraging nudge. "Go ahead. Tell them what you just told me."

The boy glanced over his shoulder nervously at the coach from Orville Falls. From a distance, Charlie couldn't tell for sure, but he had more than a hunch it was Winston Lindsay.

"Come on," Rocco prompted. "You gotta trust us. We might be able to help."

The kid was practically trembling with terror. It took him a few moments, but finally he leaned in close and whispered, "Something's happening to my town."

"So it's not just the soccer team?" Charlie asked. "It's all of Orville Falls?"

"Yeah," Kyle told them. "Most of my friends are exactly like the guys on the team. My parents are too. That's them up there." He pointed to a couple in the bleachers. His mom's eyes had rolled back in her head, and his dad's tongue was hanging from his mouth. "They've been like that for a week now. It's like their brains have stopped working or something."

Paige's brow furrowed with confusion. "Your parents can't be brain-dead. I mean, they're *here*, aren't they?" she pointed out. "They're watching soccer and sitting in the stands. How did they get to Cypress Creek if their brains aren't functioning? How did they manage to *drive*?"

The boy shrugged helplessly. "Well, it wasn't very *good* driving," he admitted. "I mean, my dad sideswiped a tree and took out a whole row of mailboxes on the ride here. I kept my eyes closed most of the time."

"But he still *drove*," Paige said skeptically.

Kyle shrugged. "The Walkers do all sorts of things," he said. "I don't know how, but they do."

"The *Walkers*?" Rocco asked.

"That's what I call them," Kyle said. "Because it kinda looks like they're sleepwalking, except they're not asleep."

"Do you have any idea how they got this way?" Paige pressed.

Kyle's face lost a few shades of color. "Actually, I think I do."

"You do? How?" Charlie asked, his excitement growing.

"There's this drink that everyone's been trying." The boy leaned closer. He whispered softly as if he were worried that the conversation might be overheard. "They call it a tonic. People started drinking it because they weren't sleeping well."

"Were they having nightmares?" Rocco asked.

"Yeah," said Kyle. "But the nightmares aren't about monsters or anything. At least, mine aren't. In my dreams someone's watching me. And then I get this feeling—" He shivered. "It's like I've been left all alone and no one's ever going to help me."

"That sounds awful," Paige said.

"It is. My whole family was having the same bad dream, so my dad brought home some of that tonic a few days ago. Now my mom gives it to me every single night. She said if I drink it, my nightmares will go away. And if you drink a bottle every day for a month, you're supposed to feel like a million bucks."

"But you don't drink the stuff," Rocco guessed.

"Nope. I'd rather have bad dreams and feel like crud. I pour the stuff out the window as soon as she's not watching," the boy said. "But my brother drank some. And that's what happened to him." He pointed across the field to a boy who was about to walk face-first into a goalpost.

"Where did your dad get the stuff?" Charlie asked.

"He bought it." The kid seemed reluctant to say any more.

"We figured," Paige said. "*Where* did he buy it?"

The boy snuck another peek over his shoulder and gasped. Charlie saw Winston Lindsay shuffling toward them across the soccer field. The large wound on the coach's forehead made him terrifying to behold. "Look,

I really, *really* gotta go," the kid pleaded, almost squirming with discomfort. "The coach wouldn't want me talking about any of this. None of them would. It's not safe to say anything bad about the tonic."

Rocco grabbed the boy's arm before he could bolt. "But you've got to tell us where people are buying the stuff!"

"There's a shop in Orville Falls with clouds in the windows," the boy said. "Believe me, you can't miss it. But you've got to see it to believe it." And then he sprinted away.

Charlie's eyes passed over the crowd that was leaving the soccer stands. A lady Walker staggered toward the exit with her arms held out in front of her. When she reached the edge of the bleachers, she stepped right off—and into the air. Charlie winced when the woman landed in the grass on her rump, but she was up and moving before anyone had a chance to offer her help. "I think the kid was right," Charlie said. "That tonic is doing something terrible to people's brains."

"Are you sure it's a tonic that's doing it?" Paige asked. "Before we jump to conclusions, shouldn't we consider all the possibilities? What if they've contracted some kind of rare disease? Or what if there's something bad in the water up there?" She pulled out her phone.

"What are you doing?" Charlie asked.

"Solving the mystery," Paige replied. "My aunt Josephine lives in Orville Falls."

"You mean the aunt who comes to visit you some-times?" Rocco asked. It was a nice way of putting it, Charlie thought. Josephine often stayed with the Bretters when Paige's mother was too ill to take care of her.

"Yep, Aunt Josephine works for the Orville Falls news-paper. If anyone knows what's going on, it will be her."

Paige held the phone to her ear, her face darkening as the seconds ticked by.

"No answer?" Charlie asked. "Maybe she's at work."

Paige looked at her phone as if certain there had been some sort of mistake. "That's where I called her," she said. "Josephine always works on the weekends."

"Don't worry," Rocco assured Paige. "I'm sure your aunt's just busy."

"That's not it," Paige said. "I called the main line at the newspaper. It's supposed to be open every day of the week, but nobody picked up the phone."

❦ CHAPTER FIVE ❧

TRANQUILITY TONIGHT

The few times Charlie had visited Orville Falls, he'd always suspected it was too cute to be real. The village's center was filled with shops that sold stuff that no one really needed—like fancy tea towels and embroidered pillows. And the houses that ringed the town center were all revoltingly adorable. Even the people in Orville Falls seemed a little too smiley. The whole town had always struck Charlie as kind of creepy.

But when Charlie and Paige arrived at the bus stop in Orville Falls, the town looked deserted. No one was waiting on the benches out front of the bus station or loitering by the vending machine. The ticket booth stood empty, and there wasn't a single person strolling down the sidewalk outside.

"Never seen it like this before," the bus driver told Charlie. He was a burly man with a deep voice, but he sounded spooked. "Doesn't look like anyone's around. You kids sure you want to get off here? There won't be another bus back to Cypress Creek for a few hours."

Charlie wasn't so sure anymore. He stood in the bus door, craning his neck to search Orville Falls for some sign of life. The only movement was a crumpled brown paper bag being dragged down the street by the wind. The slogan on the side read *Don't Dream Your Life Away!*

"We're sure," Paige answered the bus driver. She squeezed past Charlie and hopped down onto the asphalt. "Don't worry, sir. I have family in town. And I always keep a bottle of hand sanitizer in my bag."

The trip to Orville Falls had been Paige's brilliant idea. Her mother hadn't been feeling well enough to make the drive, and her father had needed to stay home with her. So Paige and Charlie had hopped onto a bus right after Rocco's game. Back then, it had seemed like the only possible plan. Paige had spent the entire ride trying to come up with a simple explanation for the strange sickness that had overtaken the town. The flu, perhaps—or maybe an exotic parasite. Charlie noted that all of Paige's "explanations" were totally treatable. She didn't want to believe that any-thing truly terrible might have happened to Josephine.

Charlie locked eyes with the bus driver for a moment while Paige squirted a dollop of hand sanitizer onto her palm. The man raised an eyebrow, and Paige must have caught his bemused expression.

"Oh no, I'm not sanitizing my hands because of you!" she insisted. "It's the bus. It's just, public transportation can get germy and . . . it's important to stay—"

"I get it, I get it," the bus driver said mercifully. He looked at Charlie. "You gonna be okay, kid?"

Charlie swallowed the lump that had risen into his throat. Then he nodded and reluctantly stepped off the bus.

"Good luck," the driver said before he closed the door and drove off.

A perfect, eerie silence followed the bus's departure.

"What now?" Charlie asked.

"Now we find my aunt." Paige pointed up at a sign on the corner. FRANKLIN AVENUE, it read. "She lives on this street. I don't know the exact address, but this town isn't all that big, and I'll recognize her house the second I see it."

Paige took off down the sidewalk as if she didn't have a concern in the world. Charlie swallowed again and rushed to catch up with her. Orville Falls may have been the kind of town you'd see on a Christmas card, but it was the middle of summer and there was no one around.

"Aren't you even a *little* creeped out?" he asked.

"What do you mean?" Paige looked up at Charlie with a befuddled expression.

Charlie gestured to the storefronts and other buildings that lined both sides of the street. "For starters, all the lights are on, but there's no one inside." Then he stepped out into the street. "And when was the last time you saw a car drive by?"

Paige shrugged. "Maybe they're all at the hospital waiting to get flu shots or something."

Determined to prove his point, Charlie marched over to a jewelry store in the middle of the block. Gold and diamonds glittered in the sunlight that streamed through the shop's front window. Charlie threw open the door. The place was empty. "Hello!" he shouted at the top of his lungs. But there was only dead silence. "You guys mind if I help myself to a few of these things?" Charlie yelled even louder. And again, there was nothing. "See what I mean?" he told Paige. "Totally creepy."

Paige frowned as she looked around the store. Charlie could see that he'd finally made an impression. Then something out the window seemed to catch her eye. She hurried out of the shop, with Charlie right on her heels.

"Look!" Paige was pointing down the street. Charlie saw three teenage girls shuffling across the road two blocks away. Even from a distance, Charlie could tell that none of them had come in contact with a hairbrush for a while. Within seconds, they had disappeared from view. "They just went down Livingston Street," Paige noted. "Let's find out what's going on over there." She and Charlie took off running.

They rounded the corner onto Livingston Street and came to a sudden halt. They'd found the people of Orville Falls. Hundreds upon hundreds of townsfolk were standing single file along the sidewalk. The line stretched for as far as Charlie and Paige could see, across intersections and around fire hydrants. And right at the end of the line were the three teenage girls.

Charlie turned to Paige. The look in her eyes said she shared his suspicions. Something big was happening—and it definitely wasn't good.

Paige was the first to act. "What's everyone waiting for?" she asked one of the teenagers.

The girl slowly turned to face them. Paige took one look and gasped, stumbling backward into Charlie. He put a protective arm around his friend to steady her, though he was shaken too. The girl in front of them had probably been pretty once. Now her skin was blotchy and her face bloated. Dark purple bags hung beneath her bloodshot eyes, and the girl's tongue stuck out from between her lips, as if it were too large to stay inside her mouth. She blinked, wobbled a bit, and then returned to staring blankly at the back of the person standing ahead of her in the line.

"Oh, my . . . ," Paige sputtered. "They're all Walkers!"

"*Now* are you creeped out?" Charlie whispered.

"*Totally,*" Paige answered. "We should have listened to that bus driver."

Charlie rolled his eyes, but he didn't bother to point out that *he* had. "Well, I guess we can't go back to Cypress Creek at this point," he said with a sigh. "Now that we've seen *this,* we have to find out what's going on."

No one so much as glanced at Charlie and Paige as they followed the line to its source. The people all stood completely motionless, their eyes fixed on the back of the person in front of them, in total silence. There was no talking, or coughing or sneezing. The citizens of Orville Falls were as still and silent as statues. If Charlie hadn't known better, he'd have wondered if the people had been frozen in stone by a gorgon. The whole scene was like something right out of the Netherworld.

Charlie shivered and kept going. He and Paige walked five more blocks until they reached the start of the line. The very first person was standing outside the door of a humble little shop. The exterior of the store had been painted a peaceful pale blue, and puffy clouds of white cotton filled the window display. A sign hung above the door. Written on it were two simple words with fancy lettering.

Tranquility Tonight

"You've got to be kidding me. *This* is what they're all waiting for?" Paige scoffed. "I know that soccer kid told us to find a shop with clouds in the window, but I was expecting something a little more sinister. This place looks like a pillow store."

Before Charlie could answer, a bell chimed, and the store's door opened. A man came out with a small brown paper bag in his hand. The next person entered the shop, and everyone in line took a step forward in unison.

"I don't think that guy had a pillow in his bag," Charlie said. "It had to be the tonic."

"Let's have a peek," Paige said. She slipped between the first person in line and the door, and the man didn't even appear to notice. Paige waved Charlie over, and he squeezed in next to her. He had his hand on the knob, ready to turn it, when he noticed a small handwritten note taped to the door. *Please wait here*, it read. *We serve one customer at a time.*

"Wow, get a load of these letters," Paige marveled, running her finger across the elegant script. "Who writes in cursive anymore?"

Charlie opened his mouth to respond, but the bell over the door chimed again, and a woman emerged with a brown paper bag in her hand. This time, though, as the door swung open, Charlie got a glimpse inside the store. Shelves lined the walls, but they seemed to be stocked with nothing but little blue bottles. If that was the tonic, Charlie realized, it seemed to be the only thing in the shop for sale.

Behind the counter was a short man with a long pointy nose and a rather unfortunate toupee. For the briefest of moments, Charlie and the man caught each other's gaze. The man's eyes were black, beady, and unusually cold. There was something about them that made Charlie's skin break out in goose bumps. Then the door swung shut, and before Charlie could even reach out for the knob again, he heard the sound of a lock turning. And then just as quickly, a gnarled hand flipped the OPEN sign in the window to CLOSED.

"Did you see that?" Charlie marveled.

"Did we just get locked out?" Paige asked, astonished.

"Guess the guy didn't like the look of us," Charlie said, a chill trickling down his spine. The man in the shop was no good, and Charlie could feel it. "And from what I just saw, I don't think I liked the look of him either."

Charlie and Paige stepped out of line, but none of the Orville Falls people moved a muscle. "He closed up the shop," Paige told the guy at the front of the line. "Maybe you ought to come back later."

The man replied with a grunt and an exhausted blink, and then returned to staring at the door.

"This whole town is really screwed up," Paige said nervously. "I think we need to go find my aunt."

"Yeah," Charlie agreed. "Save our place, would you?" he jokingly asked the guy at the front of the line. But not even Charlie could find himself funny.

Charlie's spirits sank even further when they reached the house where Paige's aunt lived. The front lawn was in desperate need of a weed whacking. Foxtails that reached higher than Charlie's waist hid the path to the front door. The stalks shook as little creatures moved between them. A rat peeked out and didn't rush for cover at the sight of Charlie and Paige. Instead it glared at the two as if warning them not to invade its territory. Charlie would have preferred to stay on the sidewalk, but he followed Paige as she waded through the grass. Something with thorns snagged his jeans, and by the time they reached the porch, Charlie's shirt was covered with burrs.

"Looks like your aunt hasn't done much gardening in the past couple of weeks," Charlie said. A feeling of dread was creeping over him. He had a hunch that he didn't want to see what was inside the house.

"My aunt would never let her lawn get like this." Paige sounded as frightened as Charlie felt.

They rang the doorbell and waited for what felt like a very long time. Then Paige banged on the door. "Aunt Josephine!" she shouted. "It's me! Are you in there?"

Then she reached out and grabbed hold of the knob. And to Charlie's surprise, the door opened. Paige looked up at Charlie, and that was when he saw true terror in his friend's eyes.

CHAPTER SIX

DREAMLESS OBLIVION

Inside the house, it was as dark as night and as hot as an Easy Bake oven. "Holy mackerel," Charlie gasped, pulling his shirt up over his nose. The stench of garbage that wafted out through the front door was overpowering.

"Aunt Josephine?" Paige called out. The house was terrifyingly silent. Paige took a cautious step inside, and Charlie heard a soft thud and the tinkling of glass. Her foot had hit something. Charlie felt for the light switch on the other side of the door and flipped it, illuminating a long hallway littered with tiny sapphire-blue bottles. Paige knelt down and picked one up. The glittering silver label read:

Tranquility Tonic
Never have another nightmare.

"Can I see?" Charlie asked. Paige passed him the bottle, and he pulled out the cork stopper and peered inside. The bottle was empty, but the scent of the tonic could still be detected. To Charlie, it reeked of mold and dirt. "I've never had a dream bad enough to make me drink something that smells like this."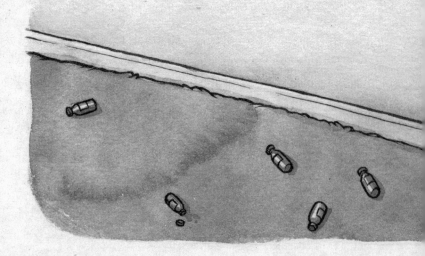

"You sure about that?" Paige replied skeptically, one eyebrow raised. Charlie knew she was right. Six months earlier, he would have guzzled a dozen bottles of Tranquility Tonic if he'd thought it would make his nightmares go away.

Then, from somewhere deep inside the house, they heard snoring. Paige rushed down the hall toward the sound, kicking aside piles of empty blue bottles. When they reached the living room, they found a creature in a filthy white nightgown stretched out on a couch. The pale skin of her legs, arms, and face was covered in blue bruises, and her light hair was so dirty that it was plastered to the sides

of her head. She looked nothing like the woman Charlie had met a half-dozen times.

"What happened to her?" Paige moaned. She dropped down to her knees beside her aunt. Then Charlie saw Paige squint and take a closer look at one of the bruises. She ran her index finger across the surface of Josephine's skin. "It's just paint!" she breathed out, relieved. She flashed a bright smile and held up her stained finger for Charlie to see.

But Charlie had a feeling it was no time for a celebration. Evidence of Josephine's painting was all around them. Everywhere Charlie looked, large paper signs had been left to dry. They were propped up against the walls and hanging from clotheslines that zigged and zagged across the room. On each sign, Josephine had painted a different slogan for Tranquility Tonic. Charlie watched Paige's face fall as her eyes passed from one sign to the next.

Sleep more soundly and wake refreshed!

Give your nightmares something to fear!

A deep dreamless sleep for all!

"It looks like advertising," said Charlie, stating the obvious. The only real art in the room was a painting of a girl in an old-fashioned dress. She was standing in front of what seemed to be a mirror, and her reflection stared out at Charlie. The girl's auburn hair was parted on the side, and her dark brown eyes had a glimmer in them that gave him the chills.

"My aunt must be working for that shop now," Paige said in a voice that was barely loud enough to hear. "But why would the shop need advertising? Seems like everyone in Orville Falls is already hooked on tonic."

"Good question," Charlie said. He looked around the room and noticed even more posters stacked up in the corners. All told, there had to be hundreds of them. If Josephine really was working for Tranquility Tonight, they had her slaving away night and day.

"Poor Aunt Josephine," Paige murmured. "What have they made you do?"

"Mrumph. *Mrrartist*," Aunt Josephine snorted in reply. Her body assumed countless shapes as she tried to find a comfortable position on the couch.

While her aunt tossed and turned, a smile lit Paige's face once more. "She just said *artist*, Charlie! She was talking! Do you think that could be a good sign? Do you think she'll be okay? Maybe she's just exhausted from working."

Paige looked so hopeful that Charlie didn't have the heart to argue. "Maybe," he said, trying to look like he believed it. But there was nothing okay with the woman on the sofa. Josephine's cheeks were hollow, and her limbs were as thin as saplings.

Paige must have seen the horror written on Charlie's face. Her smile disappeared. "You don't think so, do you?" she asked. She turned back to her aunt. "Josephine, wake up!" She shook the slumbering woman. "It's me, it's Paige. Can you please wake up?"

"Mrumph," replied Aunt Josephine.

Paige shook her even harder. "Aunt Josephine!" she shouted into the woman's ear.

Josephine's eyes suddenly opened. Their irises were just two blue circles in a sea of red. She stared at the ceiling, blinking lazily as a thin stream of drool trickled from the side of her mouth.

"Oh, thank goodness!" Paige gushed, hugging her aunt as the woman sat up. "I was so worried about you. I heard that the stuff you've been drinking eats people's—" Paige stopped short. Josephine had risen from the sofa without so much as a glance at her niece. "Aunt Josephine?" Paige asked, but the woman didn't seem to hear her.

Charlie and Paige watched helplessly as Josephine silently crossed the room and plopped down at a table in the corner. Her head flopped back and forth like a rag doll's as she pulled a large sheet of paper from a cardboard box and laid it flat on the surface of the table.

Then Josephine opened a can of sapphire-blue paint and began to work.

Following cautiously in the woman's footsteps, Charlie went to watch Josephine paint. Her eyes were empty as she stared at the page. Her right arm seemed to move on its own as she carefully crafted a series of words.

*Dreamless Oblivion Can Be Yours
When You Try
Tranquility Tonic*

"Dreamless oblivion. Dreamless oblivion," Charlie repeated to himself. There was something terrifying about those two words. Fear wrapped itself around Charlie and squeezed him tight. He felt like he could hardly breathe. "Uh-oh."

"What is it?" Paige asked frantically. "What does it mean? What do you know? Tell me, Charlie! *What's wrong with my aunt?*"

Charlie could barely bring himself to give voice to his suspicions. "I think I know how Tranquility Tonic turns people into Walkers," he said. "I think it keeps them from *dreaming.*"

"But I don't get it!" Paige cried. "As long as people *sleep* every night, what difference does it make if they skip a few *dreams*?"

For Charlie the answer was clear. He could feel it, but he couldn't find the words to explain it. "I don't know about everyone, but for me, dreaming makes all the difference," he said. "If I didn't dream . . ." He had to stop there. The very thought was too horrible to contemplate. That was when Charlie knew that he had no choice. He had to do something to save Orville Falls.

☙ CHAPTER SEVEN ❧

BRAIN CLEANER

She was right where he'd left her the last time he'd visited her in the Dream Realm, sitting on the front porch of his old house.

"Charlie!" she called out happily when she saw him.

"Hi, Mom," he said. She still looked exactly as she had nearly four years ago, before she'd gotten sick. Before she'd died.

When he took his regular seat beside her, she pulled him close with one arm and gave him a peck on the top of his head. "How are you?" she asked. "It's been longer than usual since you last came to see me."

"I had a few other people here that I needed to talk to," Charlie explained. "Well, not really *people*. I guess they used to be people. . . ."

His mom patted him on the knee. "It's okay," she told him. "You don't have to explain. You're growing up. I know I may not see you as much anymore."

"No, that's not it," Charlie argued. He couldn't even imagine a time when he might have better things to do. His visits to his mom were the most important thing he had. If those visits suddenly stopped . . . Charlie thought of Paige's Aunt Josephine and shuddered.

"What's wrong, Charlie?" his mom asked.

Charlie hung his head. "I was just thinking about how awful it would be if I couldn't dream anymore."

His mom laughed and gave him another squeeze. "That's not going to happen," she tried to assure him. "Every night, people either come to the Dream Realm or they visit the Netherworld. Sometimes they remember going, and sometimes they don't. But they always dream. Dreaming is just as important as eating or breathing. Human beings can't function without it."

"What do you mean?" Charlie asked.

His mom took a deep breath. "Let me see if I can explain this. I suppose you could say that nightmares and dreams help you clean out your brain. Every day you pack it full of thoughts and fears and hopes. At night, your dreams help you sort through the mess. Even when they don't seem to make any sense, dreams and nightmares are helping you figure things out. That's why the Waking World always seems so much brighter in the morning."

Charlie felt the dread building inside him. "And if somebody ever stopped dreaming, what do you think would happen to them?" he asked.

"Well, I imagine their minds would get clogged."

"Like a toilet?" Charlie offered, thinking of the time when Jack had tried to flush a teddy bear that he'd covered in Nutella.

"That's a rather disgusting example," his mom said with a grin. "But sure. It would be like a toilet that isn't able to empty. If a person wasn't able to clean out his head every night, after a while, there would be so much stuff crammed inside it that his brain wouldn't be able to function." She paused to give Charlie a playful peck on the top of his head. "But you don't have to worry about these things, Charlie. Like I said, nobody has ever stopped dreaming before."

"They have now," Charlie told her.

His mom's grin vanished. "Who?" she asked, a worried look on her face. "Not Jack or your dad? Or Charlotte?"

"No," Charlie assured her. "They're all fine. But I was just in Orville Falls. Almost everyone there has been drinking this stuff called Tranquility Tonic. It's made them stop dreaming, and now they're stumbling around like a bunch of sleepwalkers. And because the people of Orville Falls aren't dreaming, their part of the Dream Realm is fading."

"And you think a tonic is responsible?"

"Yeah. It comes in these little blue bottles. It says on the label that it's supposed to stop nightmares. But I think it stops dreams too."

"It comes in blue bottles?" The words seemed to have triggered something inside his mom's mind.

"Yes. Is that important?"

"Maybe, maybe not. Have you told Charlotte?" his mom asked.

"Not yet," Charlie said. "I will the next time I see her, though."

"Do," his mother urged him. "And when you talk to her, see if she thinks this might have something to do with ick and ink."

"Ick and ink?" Charlie repeated, but the Dream Realm was growing hazier, and he was suddenly overwhelmed by the scent of strawberries.

"What on earth are you talking about, Charlie?" someone asked.

Charlie tried to speak and got a mouthful of strawberry-scented hair. He'd fallen asleep with his head on Paige's shoulder. He opened his eyes and saw the lights of a town outside the bus window. The trip back to Cypress Creek had nearly reached its end. He could hear the empty bottles of Tranquility Tonic rattling in Paige's bag. He and Paige were lugging them back to Cypress Creek in the hope that Charlotte could come up with an antidote that would save Paige's aunt and the other people of Orville Falls.

"Sorry," Charlie told his friend. "Didn't mean to pass out on you."

"No worries," she replied. "You were talking in your sleep, though. Must have been quite a dream. You kept repeating the words *ick* and *ink*. Are they supposed to mean something?"

"I don't have a clue," Charlie said. "But I have a hunch that Charlotte does."

CHAPTER EIGHT

A BOTTOMLESS ABYSS

"Who knew fake meat could be so darn delicious?" Andrew Laird pushed his chair back from the dinner table, and a gigantic orange feline blob landed with a thud next to Charlotte's half-eaten Tofurky casserole. Before anyone could stop it, the beast stuck its entire head inside for a taste.

"Aggie!" Charlotte screeched, picking up the evil cat and depositing it on the floor.

"So much for leftovers," Charlie said. He took the casserole and scraped what was left of the family's dinner into the dog's bowl. Aggie was watching when he opened the back door. Rufus, the Laird family's dog, came running. "Good boy," Charlie said as the hungry dog devoured the casserole.

Aggie narrowed her yellow eyes and hissed. Charlie closed the door and responded with a snarl.

"So, what did you get up to today?" he heard Andrew Laird ask Jack. "Anything fun?"

"Yeah!" Jack exclaimed. "Me and Topher were hanging out at his pool, and his big brother, Frank, kept dunking us, so we got out of the pool and filled up all these balloons with shaving cream and pickle juice and other gunk. Then we got up on the roof and waited until it was time for him to go see his girlfriend. Then we dropped all the balloons on him and Frank was covered in all this nasty stuff, and he was shouting that he was going to kill us, but then their mom came home and told Frank he probably deserved it."

Charlie saw Andrew Laird stare at his youngest son for a moment as if he wasn't quite sure how to respond.

"Well, that certainly sounds exciting," he said at last. "And you, Charlie? What happened after you ran out to see to that 'emergency' this morning?"

"Nothing much," Charlie muttered as he began to clear the rest of the dishes off the table. "Just hung around with Paige."

"*Oooooooh.*" Jack waggled his eyebrows. "*Paige.*"

"Shut up," Charlie said a little too sharply. "Everybody knows Paige has been one of my best friends since kindergarten."

"Charlie and Paige, sittin' in a—" Jack started to sing.

"Okay, Jack, that's enough," Charlotte announced, hauling the little boy out of his chair by his arms and launching him toward the door. "You and your dad go to the living room and pick out a movie. I'll bring you guys some ice cream." She seemed to know that Charlie had something he was dying to tell her, something that would have to wait until they were alone.

Jack's eyes flicked back and forth between his brother and his stepmother. "Suuuure," he said. "Whatever you say." The kid was way too smart for his own good, Charlie thought. He always knew when trouble was brewing.

As soon as the others were gone and the ice cream had been delivered, Charlotte sat back down at the table and pointed to the chair across from her. "Take a load off," she told Charlie.

Sometimes it was hard to believe how much everything had changed, Charlie thought. Six months earlier, he would have done almost anything to avoid a heart-to-heart with Charlotte. Now the first place Charlie went with his secrets was Charlotte's favorite spot at the kitchen table.

"So what's up with you?" Charlotte asked once her

stepson was sitting. "You look like you have so many beans to spill that you're about to explode."

Charlie didn't need to be pressed. "Remember the guy I saw yesterday? The one who walked like a zombie? Well, I saw him again this morning at Rocco's soccer game." He filled Charlotte in on Winston Lindsay and the Comets and then started on the trip to Orville Falls.

Charlotte leaned across the table, her green eyes flashing. Two locks of her curly orange hair broke free from their bun and sprung out in coils on either side of her face. "Charlie Laird! You went to Orville Falls by yourself?" she whispered angrily.

"Of course not. I went with Paige," Charlie countered. "She has an aunt who lives there. Besides, I went to the Netherworld by myself, and you never bothered to give me a lecture."

"Like that makes any difference!" Charlotte scowled as if Charlie's response were ridiculous. "Do you know what your dad would do if he found out you and Paige left town together this morning?"

"There are a lot of things Dad doesn't need to know," Charlie pointed out. "Besides, we took hand sanitizer."

"Still!" Charlotte whispered. Then she shook her head and sighed. "Okay. That's enough parenting for one night. I'll let your own mother tell you what she thinks. Did you find anything out?"

"Yeah, we found this." Charlie reached into the pocket of his hoodie and produced one of the little blue bottles with the shimmering silver label.

Charlotte took it from Charlie and examined it closely, reading the fine print. "*Never have another nightmare*? Who do they think they're kidding?" She laughed nervously. "Nothing stops nightmares." Charlotte looked up at Charlie. "You and I know that better than anyone else."

But Charlie wasn't laughing. "I think this stuff can stop more than just nightmares. I think it stops *all* dreams."

The remains of Charlotte's smile were still on her face, but her eyes told a different story. "That's not possible," she insisted. "I've been working as an herbalist for more than fifteen years now, and I've never even heard of *anything* that could stop all dreams." Charlotte pulled the cork out of the tonic bottle and held the vessel's rim to her nose. Her head jerked back as she got a whiff of the remains of the substance that had once been inside.

"Whoa." She leaned in hesitantly and took a second sniff. "I've never come across anything like that before. It smells like . . ."

"Death," Charlie answered for her. He'd been trying for hours to label the odor. He could detect a note of stale cemetery dirt and a hint of mold, mixed with the pungent stench of rotting things.

"I smell far more sadness than death," Charlotte said. "But I can't place what's in it. I'm familiar with every plant, seed and fungus between here and Outer Mongolia. I don't think this stuff is from the Waking World."

"You're saying it's from—" It was such a scary idea that Charlie didn't even want to put his hunch into words.

Charlotte locked eyes with her stepson. "If it came from the Netherworld, we're in serious trouble. But we can't say anything for sure just yet. I'll need to run some tests before I draw any conclusions."

"Do you think it might have something to do with ick and ink?" He'd meant to slip the words into the conversation casually. But there was nothing casual about Charlotte's response. She dropped the tonic bottle like a hot potato, and Charlie had to dive to catch it before it rolled off the table.

"Did your mom tell you about ick and ink?" Charlotte demanded.

It took Charlie a few seconds to get back into his chair. "Not really," he admitted. "She told me to ask you if the tonic might have something to do with ick and ink. I don't even know what that means."

Charlotte looked at Charlie sternly for a moment before

she nodded. "And you don't need to. Not yet." She turned her gaze to the tonic in Charlie's hands. "I'll have to have a full bottle of this stuff if I'm going to study it. Do you think you could get your hands on one?"

"Maybe," Charlie said. The thought of the Tranquility Tonight store made him shiver. "But before I go back to Orville Falls, there's something we should do here at the mansion first." He turned his eyes upward, as if looking through the ceiling and into the tower high above.

"You want to open the portal, don't you?" Jack's voice came from behind Charlie.

Charlie spun around. "Have you been spying on us this whole time?" he growled. "You're such a sneaky little turd, Jack!"

Jack stuck out his lower lip and showed Charlie his empty ice cream bowl. "I just came in here to put my dish in the dishwasher," he said, trying his best to sound hurt.

Charlotte rolled her eyes and smiled. "Yeah, *sure* you did," she said, giving the kid a wink. "Never once have you ever put your dish in the dishwasher."

A wicked grin flickered across Jack's face. Then, in an instant, he returned to looking sincere. "If you guys are opening the portal, I'm coming too. I'm one of the guardians. I need to be there."

"Why do *you* need to be there?" Charlie snorted. "You're *eight*."

"I just turned *nine*," Jack reminded him. "And you're not even a teenager yet." His stubborn expression was the same one he wore whenever anyone told him to take off the Captain America costume he loved. Charlie knew Jack wasn't going to give in.

"Fine, fine, fine," Charlotte said with a huff. It was a well-known fact that nothing annoyed her more than hearing the Laird boys argue. "You can both be there if one of you can explain to me *why* the portal needs to be opened."

Charlie tapped the blue bottle with his finger. "The people who've been drinking this stuff have stopped dreaming, right?"

"That's your hypothesis," Charlotte said. "It hasn't been tested yet."

Charlie ignored the comment. "That means the people from Orville Falls haven't been visiting the Dream Realm. I've seen what's happening there. Parts of the Dream Realm are fading because nobody goes there anymore."

"So?" Jack asked.

"So if something like that is happening to the Dream Realm, there's no telling what's going on in the Netherworld," Charlie said. "I haven't had a nightmare in months. It's been a long time since I was on the other side. Have either of you gone to the Netherworld lately?" Charlotte shook her head, and Jack giggled, which Charlie chose to ignore. "See? That's why we have to open the portal. We need to find out what's happening on the other side."

Charlotte crossed her arms and leaned back against the kitchen island. She was silent for much longer than Charlie would have expected.

"Okay," she finally agreed. "But not until after your dad's asleep. We'll meet in the tower at midnight."

"Me too?" Jack asked as if he couldn't believe his ears.

"Yeah, him too?" Charlie asked, disappointed. The last thing he needed was Jack tagging along and causing trouble.

"*All of us,*" Charlotte confirmed. "We're a family. We're in this together."

It had been ages since Charlie had stayed up so late. The hour before twelve may have been the longest sixty minutes of his life. As soon as his alarm clock confirmed it was midnight, he was up and out of bed, tiptoeing through his bedroom door. He'd lived in the purple mansion for more than six months, but the second-floor hallway still felt as eerie as it had the day he'd moved in. Portraits of Charlotte's weird redheaded ancestors lined the walls. Some of the DeChants seemed to be glaring at the artists who had painted their pictures. Others appeared to be desperate to escape their framed prisons. And in the background behind them all was the purple mansion. These members of the DeChant clan had been its guardians. It was clear that not all of them had relished the job. But it hadn't mattered whether or not they'd loved their life's work. They had accepted the position because they hadn't been able to refuse.

Charlotte was the last of the portal-guarding DeChants. For almost two centuries, the DeChant family had watched over the entrance to the Netherworld. Now they had passed the torch to a new generation—and a new family. The mansion's latest guardians were Charlie and Jack Laird.

The boys were both still figuring out how to use their power. Even for Charlie, the portal wasn't always so easy to see. It was set in one of the eight walls of the octagonal tower, but it was well disguised. When the portal was closed and locked, there was nothing to suggest that the wall was anything but ordinary. When the portal was unlocked, Charlie could detect a faint shimmer that came through the cracks in the old plaster. And when the portal was open, the wall disappeared entirely, and Charlie's own worst nightmare lay on the other side.

Charlie was the last one up the tower stairs. At one time the little octagonal room at the top had terrified him. Now

Charlotte's office—with its cluttered shelves, messy desk, and secret portal—was the part of the mansion that Charlie loved most. It felt so safe and cozy that it was easy to forget just how dangerous the room could be.

When Charlie reached the chamber at the top of the stairs, he found Charlotte and Jack staring at the bare plaster wall that hid the Netherworld portal.

"It's still locked," Jack announced.

"Really?" Charlotte sounded frustrated. "How do you know?"

Jack shrugged. "I dunno. I can just tell."

"He's right," Charlie said. He felt a bit annoyed that they'd started without him.

Charlotte turned around. "Oh, hey, Charlie," she said. "I was just giving it one more go for old times' sake. But no dice." Ever since the boys had moved into the mansion, Charlotte had been having trouble seeing the portal. And her efforts to unlock it had apparently met with failure. The trick was to imagine the thing that frightened you most. Fear was the only force that could open the portal door. It took a very special person to summon a fear strong enough—and then manage to face it down.

"Maybe you weren't imagining something scary enough," Charlie offered. "What were you thinking about?"

"Nothing all that interesting," Charlotte said. But Charlie saw her eyes dart toward her desk and to a pile of official-looking papers that were stacked on top. "Do you want to give it a try?"

Charlie searched his brain for the last thing that had scared him. Paige's aunt Josephine popped into his mind. But it wasn't the woman herself who was terrifying. It was the thought of never dreaming again. For Charlie, never dreaming again would mean never seeing his mom. He shuddered at the thought. Then closed his eyes, set his jaw, and let the fear grow inside him. He dreaded what he might find when the portal appeared.

He opened his eyes when he heard Charlotte yelp. The wall had vanished, and in front of them a steep road cut through a forest. The only light came from the moon. It lit up the trees with a haunting glow that was bright enough to make it clear that they'd left civilization behind.

Charlie immediately knew it wasn't his nightmare. His worst dreams had once taken place in the woods, but he'd conquered those fears months before. Someone else had just opened the portal. There was only one other person who could have done it, and he'd done it faster than Charlie had ever managed. "Jack?" he marveled.

"Was that *you*?" Charlotte asked, looking down at the kid in awe.

"Charlie was taking too long," the little boy complained. "I gotta get to sleep soon. I have chores to do in the morning."

"Oh really? When was the last time you did any *chores*?" Charlie scoffed. "And how did you get the portal open so fast on your first try?"

Jack's face was a portrait of puppy dog innocence. With his floppy brown hair and freckles, it was a look he wore well. "I dunno. Luck?" Jack shrugged.

That was all Charlie needed to realize the truth. "You've opened it before, haven't you?"

"Who, me?" Jack asked, looking around the room as if Charlie couldn't possibly be talking to him.

"You have!" Charlie turned to their stepmother. He was furious. The Netherworld was dangerous. It was no place for a nine-year-old kid. But more important, though Charlie wouldn't have said so, the Netherworld was supposed to be *his*. "Charlotte, Jack's opened the portal before!"

Charlotte looked worried. "Jack, have you been visiting the Netherworld by yourself? Tell us the truth."

Jack studied his shoelaces while he struggled to hide the smile that was spreading across his face. "Okay, maybe I've been there a few times, I guess."

"A *few* times?" Charlie demanded. "How many is that?"

"Ten?" Jack said when he looked back up. "Twelve at the most."

That was far more trips through the portal than Charlie had taken. "What have you been doing . . . ," Charlie started to ask, but he stopped as he caught sight of something hovering in the Netherworld sky just on the other side of the portal. It was a silver spaceship with multi-colored lights. A long, blinding beam shot straight from the hull of the craft to the ground.

"What the heck is that?" Charlie heard Charlotte mutter behind him.

"I think it's a UFO," Charlie said. He looked down at Jack. "Is this your worst nightmare? You're afraid of aliens?"

"Not really," Jack said. "I guess I'm just good at pretending. I imagined that aliens had landed in the forest between Cypress Creek and Orville Falls and that I was really, really scared."

"But you're *not* really scared?"

"Nope. Why would aliens travel all the way to Earth just to hurt us? They have better things to do with their time." Jack stepped through the portal and called for the others to follow. "Come on. This is gonna be a blast. Let's go say hi."

Charlie gaped at the boy on the other side of the portal. He had been scared senseless on his first trip to the Netherworld. But his brother acted as if the land of nightmares were his second home.

"Interesting," he heard Charlotte murmur to herself.

"The kid's always been nuts," Charlie grumbled.

The temperature dropped the moment he stepped

through the portal, and Charlie shivered in his shorts and T-shirt. It was cold in Jack's nightmare. Why hadn't Jack imagined a summertime alien invasion? "Hold on," Charlie ordered his brother, who was already making a beeline for the spaceship. "We gotta wait for Charlotte."

But his stepmother was still stuck in the Waking World. An invisible barrier seemed to be keeping her out of the Netherworld. "I can't get through!" Charlotte called out to Charlie. "Something's blocking the way. You and Jack need to come back. We have to postpone the trip until I can figure out what's wrong."

Charlie groaned and turned to tell Jack, but his brother was too far ahead to hear. Charlie saw the boy step into the column of light beneath the spaceship. A second later, his brother had been beamed aboard.

"Jack!" he shouted.

"Oh no!" Charlotte cried. She'd clearly been watching as well.

"Don't worry," Charlie tried to assure her, hoping this would be the last time he was forced to take his little brother on a mission to the Netherworld. "I'll go get him."

It wasn't a very large spaceship, Charlie thought. In fact, it was barely bigger than a standard RV. And the beam of light that hit the ground was only just wide enough to sur-round him. As he stepped into it, Charlie felt a strange tin-gling sensation, and when he glanced down at his body, he could see right through it, as though his molecules had come unglued. Thankfully, he didn't even have time to scream. Before he knew it, he was aboard the ship, hanging suspended in the air, and then, *thunk,* on the ground.

"Ouch!"

Charlie scrambled to his feet, rubbing his bruised butt as he took in the interior of the spacecraft. The circular room was decorated in standard UFO décor—stainless steel walls, neon green glowing screens, and an examina-tion table in the center of the space. Jack hadn't wasted too much imagination on the design, Charlie thought bitterly as six small gray creatures with giant black eyes formed a circle around him. The alien with the largest eyes spoke. "Prepare the probes. We must examine the earthling." Its voice was high-pitched and robotic.

"Don't bother," a voice called out. "That's my big brother, and he's not scared of you either." Jack was twirl-ing around in a weird chair shaped like a sideways cup in what appeared to be the command center of the craft.

"Are you kidding me?" the head alien dropped his probe to the floor and angrily threw his arms up in frustration. "Do you know how hard it was to get all this stuff together?

The uniforms and the ship and these guys?" He pressed a button on the cuff of his space suit, and the five smaller aliens deflated like balloons.

"Sorry," Jack told him. "I had to dream up somebody who could give us a ride."

"A ride?" the alien snorted angrily. "Do I look like a taxi service to you?"

Charlie stepped forward and offered the alien his hand to shake. "I apologize for my brother. He's new to all this."

The alien reluctantly reached for Charlie's hand. "Could have fooled me," he grumbled. Then his eyes narrowed and he sniffed the air through the two holes that appeared to function as his nose. "You stink," he observed.

"I do?" Charlie replied. He was pretty sure he'd had a shower that morning.

"Your kind shouldn't smell like anything." The alien eyed him suspiciously. "Unless—"

Then he reached out and poked Charlie with a long gray finger. His eyes widened and he stumbled backward in terror. "You're here in the flesh. I've heard rumors about little humans who've been causing trouble in the Netherworld. Who are you? What are you doing here?"

Charlie knew it was critical to stay cool and calm. Though visiting the Netherworld in your sleep was scary, it wasn't actually dangerous. But being there in the flesh meant that Charlie and Jack could be injured—or worse. "My name is Charlie Laird. That's my brother, Jack." Charlie pointed to Jack, who was still spinning around in the captain's chair. "We're sorry to have bothered you. We're going to leave now. Will you please beam us back to the ground?"

"Beam *him* down if you want," Jack yelled. "I'm not going anywhere!" He stopped spinning, folded his arms across his chest, and sat back in a huff.

"Yes. You. Are," Charlie snarled through gritted teeth. If he had to drag Jack's butt out of the chair himself, he would. In fact, the idea was beginning to appeal to him. "Charlotte couldn't get through. We need to go back."

"But we're already inside the UFO!" Jack cried. Then he turned to the alien. "This thing flies, doesn't it?"

The extraterrestrial bristled at the question. "Of course it flies," he snapped. "It's not called a UO, is it?"

"That's right! It flies!" Jack told Charlie. "So he can take us to see it."

"See *what*?" Charlie demanded. The hijacked alien might have been annoyed, but Charlie was on the verge of completely losing his temper.

"Orville Falls!" Jack shouted. "We can fly right over it!"

For a moment, no one spoke. Jack was right, Charlie suddenly realized. The UFO wasn't just some crazy stunt. The kid had actually dreamed up the perfect way to survey the Netherworld. It was certainly the fastest and safest way to see what kind of problems the Tranquility Tonic had caused.

The alien was the first to break the silence. "What do you humans know about Orville Falls?" he asked in a strange, steady voice.

"We come from the Waking World," Charlie confessed. "Our town is close to Orville Falls, and something terrible is happening there. People have been drinking a tonic that prevents them from dreaming. It's done bad things to their brains, and now the whole town acts like it's sleepwalking. And because no one in Orville Falls is dreaming, the Dream Realm is suffering. Parts of it are already vanishing. But the tonic doesn't just stop good dreams. It stops nightmares too. Which means it must be harming your world as well. So we came here to the Netherworld to check out the damage."

"You're here to help?" the alien asked skeptically. "Why would two humans want to help Nightmares?"

Jack leaped out of his chair with the answer before Charlie had a chance to respond. "Because humans need Nightmares! You show us how to face our fears!"

The alien's thin gray lips appeared to form a smile. There seemed to be no one that Jack couldn't win over. "You're familiar with our leader's teachings?" the creature asked warmly.

"Teachings?" Jack looked confused, and Charlie was pleased.

"*I'm* familiar with Medusa's teachings," he announced. "In fact, you could say your president is an old friend of mine. I was here in the Netherworld the day she turned your last leader to stone. And I heard her tell the crowds that a Nightmare's true job is to help humans."

The alien sighed like a love-struck schoolboy. "Ah yes, it was a glorious day. Medusa freed our land from that tyrant and his goblin armies. And there's no doubt in my mind that she'll solve our latest problem as well—even though there are many here in the Netherworld who say she's to blame."

"To blame?" Charlie felt his stomach drop. "For what?"

The alien shook his head with such sadness that Charlie was almost sorry he'd asked. "There are no words to describe what is happening here. It will be better if I show you." The little gray Nightmare took his rightful place in the captain's chair. From his perch he pointed to a long strip of glass. "You may stand by the windows."

Jack and Charlie stood side by side as the spaceship soundlessly rose higher into the air. The Netherworld forest lay just below them. Overhead there was nothing—no stars in the sky and no moon. Just darkness designed to look like night.

The UFO traveled smoothly above the treetops until suddenly they reached the edge of the woods.

Charlie pressed his forehead to the glass for a better look.

"What is that?" Jack whispered, his voice filled with awe.

Beyond the trees lay a hole bigger and wider than any that Charlie had ever seen. Gunshots rang out, and Charlie almost ducked for cover. Then he realized they weren't gunshots at all but the sound of tree roots snapping. As he watched, a giant oak toppled into the abyss. Charlie waited, but he never heard it hit bottom. He suspected the chasm didn't have one. And it was growing.

"If you travel around the Netherworld, you'll see that most bad dreams aren't set in exotic locations," the alien explained. "People's nightmares usually take place in their own hometowns. That's why almost every town in your world has a double over here."

The alien rose from the captain's chair and joined Charlie and Jack at the window. Charlie watched the creature as he stared down at the hole.

"And?" Jack asked impatiently.

The alien looked up at the two boys, his expression grim. "And below us is all that's left of the Netherworld's Orville Falls."

Charlie felt his knees go weak. The damage was worse than he had ever imagined. "You mean it's all gone?" he asked. "Where did it go?"

"No one knows for sure," the alien explained. "A couple of weeks ago, humans stopped showing up at night. The buildings started to crumble, and then a few days ago, the whole place started to sink. We don't know how deep the hole is. But every night, it gets wider. It won't be long before the entire forest is gone."

Another tree plunged into the abyss, its roots sending a dark spray of dirt into the air.

"You two live in Cypress Creek?" the alien asked.

"Yeah," Charlie confirmed.

The alien pointed to a cluster of lights on the other side of the forest. "That's Cypress Creek," he said. "Unless someone stops this, you guys are going to be next."

CHAPTER NINE

THE LIGHTHOUSE

The UFO beamed Charlie and Jack down next to a crumbling copy of the Colosseum at the edge of the nightmare version of Cypress Creek. Charlie led the way, annoyed that Jack seemed more familiar with the lay of the land. Twice, Charlie would have taken a wrong turn if his little brother hadn't stepped forward to guide them. When at last they reached the Netherworld Cypress Creek courthouse, they found it surrounded by angry Nightmares. There were giant spiders and oozing blobs, slithering millipedes with human heads, and ghosts without any heads at all. The hideous crowd was chanting. "FILL THE HOLE! FILL THE HOLE!"

Charlie pressed down his growing anxiety. The monsters assembled at the Netherworld courthouse would have made anyone tremble, but Charlie wanted to show his brother which Laird family member was bravest.

"Isn't this awesome?" Jack marveled, grinning wildly. "It's like something out of a comic book."

"Wait. You're *still* not scared?" Charlie asked, more disappointed than shocked.

"Of what?" Jack responded. "These guys?" He gave a little wave to a hulking, one-eyed Cyclops across the square. To Charlie's utter surprise, the creature waved back.

"Do you know that thing?" Charlie whispered to his brother.

"Bruno? Not well" was the reply. "We played chess a few times, but he wasn't very good." Jack leaned toward Charlie and whispered conspiratorially, *"No depth perception."*

Charlie's heart sank, and he slowed down until he came to a stop. He watched his little brother continue along, forging his way through the crowd and chattering as if Charlie were still by his side. Charlie felt sick. For as long as he could remember, Jack had always been the cute Laird brother. The charming one. The boy no one could find the heart to punish. The boy no one ever said no to. And Charlie had always been utterly *normal*.

He'd thought his adventure in the Netherworld had changed all of that. For a little while, *he'd* been the special one. Charlie should have known that it was never going to last. He tried to tell himself not to be so selfish, but he just couldn't help it. The Netherworld was supposed to be his, and he didn't want to share it.

Charlie snapped himself out of it and rushed to catch up with his brother. The boy had made it as far as the courthouse entrance, where he'd been stopped by a rather officious-looking ogre. Only a few feet away stood the statue of Medusa's heroic son, the gorgon Basil Meduso, who had retired from the Netherworld by turning himself into stone.

"No one goes inside the courthouse. Orders of the president," the ogre was announcing as Charlie walked up.

Jack answered with a winning smile. "Hey, are you one of the—" he began to ask.

"We're here to see Medusa," Charlie interrupted before his brother could get them both into trouble. "It's a matter of life and death."

The ogre tightened his grip on his club as though he were itching to use it. His skin was the mottled green of an algae-covered pond, and two yellow tusks protruded from his lower lip. "No one goes in," the ogre repeated. Then he bent over and sniffed at them, his nostrils only inches from their chests. "Especially not stinky humans."

It wasn't much of an insult, coming from someone whose breath reeked of rotting meat. "But—" Charlie started to protest, and Jack tugged on the back of his shirt.

"Let me try," he begged.

Charlie threw up his hands. "Be my guest," he said, and stepped aside.

"You know, you look really familiar." Jack smiled up at the monster. "Are you one of the Nightmares who live under the Allen Street Bridge?"

The ogre glowered down at the strange little scamp. "So what if I am?"

"I'm friends with Orog," Jack said. "How's he doing these days? Still feeling okay?"

The ogre's eyes narrowed. "You are the tiny human he speaks of?" he demanded. When Jack nodded, the ogre threw his club to the side and snatched the boy off the ground. Charlie figured his brother was done for—until he realized that the Nightmare creature was squeezing Jack in a hug.

Charlie watched the scene in horror and awe. "Who is Orog?" he asked weakly.

"My brother," the ogre said, choking back tears. "For years, no one was frightened of him. They would just laugh and say he looked like someone named Shrek. It was so bad that Orog gave up and planned to retire. And then this human helped him remember how to be scary." He held Jack out at arm's length. "What can I do to repay you? You can have anything. Anything!" he declared.

"Can you please put me down?" Jack wheezed, struggling to breathe.

"So sorry!" the ogre cried, gently lowering the little boy to the ground.

Jack sucked in a deep breath, and his blue face returned to a healthy pink. "Thanks! Maybe now you can tell us where to find Medusa."

"Yes! I can do that!" The ogre sounded thrilled to oblige. "She's just inside the building. Climb the stairs to the second floor and look for a room with two big doors. You'll find her there. Do you need an escort? Would you like me to carry you?"

"Nope. We're all good," Jack said. He'd already dusted himself off and was starting for the courthouse. "Thanks for the help," he called back at the ogre. "And tell your brother I said hi!"

Charlie waited until they were safely inside and out of earshot before he asked the question that had been bouncing around in his mind.

"How many times have you been to the Netherworld, Jack? And tell me the truth this time."

"A dozen?" Jack replied.

Charlie couldn't believe it. "Really?"

"Okay, maybe two?" Jack admitted.

"Two dozen times?" Charlie croaked, barely able to get the words out.

"I dunno. Maybe three?" Jack said.

Charlie decided right then not to ask any more questions.

The last time Charlie had visited the courthouse, it had been filled to the rafters with giant grubs, talking cockroaches, and bloodsucking vampires. Now the place was practically empty. The only creature he and Jack passed on their way up the cracked marble stairs was an addled-looking gremlin who was so intent on getting to the exit that he barely glanced at the boys as he rushed by. Charlie and Jack looked at each other, shrugged, and kept on climbing.

The staircase ended at a set of double doors just like the ogre had described. Charlie stopped, but Jack didn't hesitate. He walked right up to the doors and threw them open, revealing a once grand room that was now in shambles. The velvet drapes hanging from the windows were shredded from top to bottom, as if something with very long claws had ripped through them. Black beetles scuttled across the wood-paneled walls, and the dust floating in the air was so thick that Charlie could barely breathe.

The room was enormous and the table in the center seemed a long way off, but Charlie still managed to spot Medusa at the end, surrounded by her advisors. There was a lady with the face of a pig, a man with two heads, a giant toad—and a particularly terrifying human-shaped creature who wore thick white face paint and a round rubber nose. Medusa was dressed in a somber black suit from the waist up. Her long tail was coiled beneath the table.

"Stop!" The order came the second Charlie and Jack stepped through the door. Guards appeared on either side of the brothers.

Medusa looked up and the snakes that sprang from her head writhed and hissed when they spotted the two boys.

"I said no interruptions!" the gorgon cried, one elegant hand reaching for the sunglasses that shielded her deadly eyes. "Remove the intruders at once!" she ordered the guards.

The clown by her side began to giggle maniacally. "Wait just a moment, Madam President." He rose from his seat. "Is that Charlie?"

"Charlie?" Medusa repeated as if trying to place the name. Then her face broke into a magnificent smile that showcased two sharp fangs. "Charlie!" She rose quickly, knocking over her chair, and slithered toward the two boys. When she reached Charlie, she pulled him into a heartfelt hug. "Oh, I've missed you!"

"Welcome back!" Dabney cried, grabbing Charlie as soon as Medusa had set him free.

"I've missed you guys too," Charlie said. And once he'd been released from the clown's embrace, he pointed to the boy beside him. "I'd like you to meet my little brother."

Medusa bent down and examined Jack from head to toe, but she didn't seem satisfied. "Close your eyes, boy," she ordered. "I want to have a better look at you. Don't sneak a peek or you'll be turned to stone."

Jack squeezed his eyes shut as Medusa removed her glasses.

"Yes, I thought I recognized you," Medusa said. She replaced her glasses. "This little troublemaker has been spotted all over the Netherworld. He's starred in countless hours of security footage, all of which I've reviewed myself. And I can't tell you how many calls I've received from terrified Nightmares who claim to have seen or smelled a human child. We've been trying to catch him for months."

Dabney squatted down and stuck his face close to Jack's. "You've had us all quite worried, you know. Humans aren't meant to run loose on this side."

Charlie shot his brother a furious look, and Jack grinned mischievously. Then Medusa smiled and Dabney broke into giggles. A hot wave of jealousy rushed over Charlie. It seemed unbelievable, but Jack's charms were just as effective on Medusa as they were on everyone else.

Yet Medusa's smile didn't last long. "As much as I would love to spend time with you humans, I'm afraid you'll have to go," she said.

"We're experiencing a bit of an emergency here," Dabney began to explain, "and—"

"We know what's happening. We saw the hole," Jack interrupted the clown. "And we think we know what caused it."

"You do?" Medusa asked, clearly surprised. She looked to Charlie for confirmation. "Is this true, Charlie?"

He could have kissed the gorgon for asking *him* and not his brother. "We do," Charlie solemnly confirmed. "That's why we're here."

"Then, please." Medusa gestured to two empty chairs at the end of the table. "Have a seat."

Medusa and Dabney returned to their places, and Charlie told the president and her council everything he knew about the Tranquility Tonic and the Walkers in Orville Falls. For the first time all night, Jack stayed quiet. Charlie's audience listened with rapt attention. And every word seemed to make Medusa more upset.

"Your stepmother was correct," she said once Charlie had finished. "The tonic is not from the Waking World. Nothing on your side is powerful enough to stop dreams or nightmares. The tonic could have come from only one place—the Netherworld." The gorgon sounded almost proud. "Someone must have smuggled it into the Waking World."

"But that's just not possible! We've been guarding the portal the whole time!" Charlie insisted. "No one could have brought it through!"

The large, wart-covered toad hopped up onto the table

and cleared his throat. "Madam President," he croaked. "Perhaps we should consider the prophecy?"

"Absolutely not!" Medusa snapped. "Everyone knows that the prophecy is nothing but nonsense! *All* prophecies are! Have you forgotten all those nightmares humans kept having about Y2K? And then the end of the Mayan calendar? Every ten years, the humans are convinced it's the end of the world, and we're no better. And remember that prophecy that said goblins would take over the Netherworld this year? You know who started it? *Goblins!* And there's no more truth in this one. It's just a bunch of lies cooked up by bigots to make Nightmares hate humans."

"What's the prophecy?" Jack asked innocently. Charlie had been thinking the very same thing.

The two-headed man answered, both of his mouths speaking at once. The voices were deep, and when they spoke as one, the tone was ominous. "It has long been said that there will one day be a human child with the power to destroy the Netherworld."

"Oh," Jack replied quietly, sounding as if he wished he hadn't asked. Charlie couldn't have agreed more. A prophecy about an evil human child was the last thing either of them needed.

"Yes, but the prophecy also says that there will be another little human with the power to save us," the pig lady added in a prissy voice.

"Nonsense again," Medusa said with a dismissive wave of her manicured hand. "Humans don't have the power to either help us or harm us. The only creatures they're likely to destroy are themselves. No offense," she told Charlie. "Now let's get back on track here. If these boys are right, there's a tonic with the power to stop dreams. The tonic must have come from the Netherworld. Charlie, are you sure that no Nightmares have slipped through the portal?"

"Absolutely positive," Charlie told her.

"And *you*." Medusa faced Jack, and her snakes slithered down to look the boy in the eye. "Have you taken any souvenirs home from your many visits to the Netherworld?"

"Nope," Jack said with a vigorous shake of his head. "That's one of the rules in my stepmom's book—don't bring anything back to the Waking World."

"Like you ever follow rules," Charlie muttered under his breath.

Jack looked a little wounded by Charlie's jab, but the rest of the crowd hadn't heard.

"Well then," Medusa replied. "If the tonic didn't pass through the purple mansion's portal, it must have reached the Waking World some other way."

Charlie frowned. As far as he knew, there was only one passage between the two worlds. "But how?" he asked.

"I believe there may be a second portal between our

land and the humans'," Medusa reluctantly announced to the group.

Charlie was stunned. For more than a century and a half, his stepmother's family had been dutifully protecting the purple mansion—and yet there could have been another portal the whole time? It was like they'd been standing guard at the Waking World's front door while the back door had been left wide open.

"No!" the pig lady squealed. She'd started to sweat, and she dabbed at her forehead with a lace-trimmed hanky. "That can't be true!" Apparently the idea of a second portal was just as upsetting to her.

"Where is the second portal?" asked Dabney. The giggle that followed couldn't hide the fact that he was not only surprised but also a little hurt that Medusa hadn't shared her suspicions.

Medusa didn't seem to notice. A change had come over the gorgon, Charlie thought. She looked as though she'd seen a ghost, and when she spoke, she sounded far away. "There's a lighthouse that stands at the border between the Netherworld and the land of goblins," she stated.

Jack jumped out of his seat. "I've heard about a place like that!" Charlie shot him a look that shouted "SIT DOWN!" and Jack dropped back into his chair.

"It's unlikely you've heard about this one," Medusa said. "It's so remote that I wouldn't be surprised if no one else knows it exists. But I've seen the lighthouse with my own two eyes, and I believe there may be a portal to the Waking World inside it."

"So you're not *completely* certain, then," said the pig lady with a sigh of relief.

"You've never been able to confirm it?" Dabney asked.

"No," Medusa confessed. "I can't prove that the portal exists, because the lighthouse cannot be entered."

Charlie and Dabney exchanged glances. Medusa's statement didn't make any sense. In the Netherworld, every building had a purpose. Each was built to house a human's worst fears. As soon as the fear was conquered, the building was either knocked down or reused. From what Medusa was saying, the lighthouse sounded empty. But that was impossible. No Netherworld building ever sat vacant. Nothing there went to waste.

"How long has the lighthouse been here in the Netherworld?" the pig lady inquired.

"I've known about it for almost eighty human years," Medusa replied.

"And it's been empty all this time?" Dabney asked.

Medusa regarded the clown with a somber expression. "I said that the lighthouse couldn't be entered. I never said that the building was *empty*."

CHAPTER TEN

THE WEIRDEST TRIO ON EARTH

Charlie was thankful that the ride to the lighthouse was taking so long. Making their way through the angry crowd outside the courthouse had been an ordeal, and he needed some time to recover. The Nightmare creatures had mobbed Dabney, Charlie, Jack, and Medusa as the group had made its way to the presidential limousine waiting at the curb. The Nightmares had shouted, jostled, and thrown rotten fruit. Charlie had seen the fear in their eyes, and he'd understood their anger. The creatures' lives and their land were in terrible danger, and their leader had been unable to help.

As Dabney drove in silence, Charlie thought about all he'd heard. It felt like there was a puzzle that he needed to put together, but several of the most important pieces seemed to be missing.

Jack, on the other hand, didn't appear to be troubled at all. For the first part of the trip, he sat with his forehead pressed to one of the limo's windows, happily watching the Netherworld pass by. But the farther the limo drove, the less there was to see. Eventually the vehicle was enveloped in darkness. The headlights barely cut through the black that washed against the windows. It was as if they were driving through an ocean of ink. By the time the limo finally rolled to a stop, Jack was sound asleep.

Charlie reached over to wake him up. "No," Medusa said, touching Charlie's arm gently. "Let him rest."

Charlie knew his brother would want to see the lighthouse. Jack would be angry if Charlie let him sleep through an adventure. But with Jack around, Charlie felt ordinary. He couldn't resist the desire to feel special just a little while longer. He could deal with Jack later.

Medusa slid out of the car, and Charlie followed, careful not to slam the door behind him. Dabney joined them from the driver's seat. In the wasteland outside, the limo's headlights illuminated a remarkable scene. A massive pillar of white bricks rose up before them and reached into the starless night. At its base was a rusty red door made of solid metal. The structure was topped with an enormous lantern that remained unlit. It was the sort of lighthouse that's usually pictured with frothy white waves crashing around it. But there was no ocean here. There was nothing at all.

Charlie could see two tiny windows carved out of the round brick walls. White lace curtains hung behind the glass, and both of the windows were dark. Beyond the lighthouse lay sheer emptiness. They were at the edge of the Netherworld. In the darkness on the other side was where the goblins lived. The goblins were terrible creatures that delighted in tormenting human beings. They'd been banished from the Netherworld several times in the past,

but they never really went away. From what Charlie had been told, the goblins lived in underground caverns—and they never stopped plotting their return to the surface.

"How did you know that the lighthouse was here?" Charlie heard Dabney ask Medusa. "I've never even been this close to the border."

"On my mountain I can see most of the Netherworld from my living room windows," she said. Charlie remembered the elegant, well-appointed cave Medusa called home. "I use a telescope to monitor the parts I can't view with my own two eyes. It was ages ago when I first spotted the lighthouse. I thought nothing of it at the time. Strange buildings come and go here in the Netherworld. But this one never disappeared. As I said earlier, it's been standing on this very same spot for at least eighty years."

"Wait. Does that mean that someone's had the same nightmare for that long?" Charlie asked. The idea was almost too horrible to bear.

"I believe that may be the case," said Medusa.

"Poor soul." Dabney giggled.

"That's precisely what I thought," Medusa told him. "So one night about forty years ago, I drove out here to help. No human being should stay frightened forever. Terrible things can happen if they lose all hope. But when I got here and tried to go inside, I discovered I couldn't."

"The door was locked?" Dabney asked.

"I don't know if it was locked or not," Medusa said. "I never made it as far as the door. I can't explain what stopped me except to say that the closer I got to the light-house, the more it felt like the life was being drained from me. I knew if I entered that building, I would never make it out again. I would be stuck in there—alone and aban-doned. The humans inside that lighthouse were more powerful than me."

"*Humans?*" Charlie asked. "And there was more than one of them inside?"

"Yes," said Medusa. "A few days after my first visit, I brought a friend here, a friend with wings. He couldn't get close to the windows without being overcome by the same feeling of dread that I'd felt, but he flew around to the other side of the lighthouse and saw shadows inside. He said the silhouettes belonged to human-shaped beings. He was convinced there were two of them. And he said he could smell them."

"Smell them?" Dabney asked as if he couldn't believe it. "You mean—"

Medusa nodded. "He believed they were here in the flesh."

"If the humans had come to the Netherworld in the flesh, they must have passed through a portal," Charlie said.

"That was my conclusion as well, and I've never been able to find another explanation," Medusa told him. "Nor have I managed to investigate any further. I've returned to this lighthouse many times over the years, but I've never been able to go inside."

"Maybe I should give it a try," Charlie said, half hoping that someone would stop him.

When no one did, Charlie marched across the wasteland until he reached the sturdy metal door at the base of the lighthouse. It was a dark, rusted red with a wheel where a knob would be. Charlie reached out for the wheel, but before his hands could make contact, he yanked them back. His fingers felt frozen, and no matter how hard he rubbed them, the cold continued to spread. A feeling of hopelessness began to take hold of him. For a moment, the world seemed dark and lonely. He jumped back, and the horrible feeling faded a bit. The more distance he put between himself and the lighthouse, the better it got.

Charlie hurried across the field of nothing, rubbing warmth back into his hands. "That was the worst thing I've ever felt," he said when he got back to his friends. As soon as he'd said it, he realized it wasn't true. The darkness he'd felt after his mother's death had been worse.

"Yes, it's truly terrible," Medusa agreed. "I'm quite sensitive to such things, and I could feel it as we drove here. It's getting stronger. The beings inside are growing more powerful."

"You're sure they're still in there?" Charlie asked. "If

the lighthouse has been here for eighty years, the people who built it must be ancient by now."

"Yes, the humans are still there," Medusa said. She pointed up at the lighthouse. Charlie turned around and stumbled backward in surprise. Lights had appeared in the two little windows. Someone—or something—was inside.

The light in the window flickered, as if it came from a candle. Charlie stared at the window and imagined what it might be like to live in the lighthouse. *Cold, lonely, and miserable,* he thought. Whoever was in there, it made sense that there were two of them. No one could survive in that place on their own.

"You think that the humans in the lighthouse are smuggling Tranquility Tonic out of the Netherworld?" Charlie asked.

"As far as I know, there are two ways the tonic may have reached the Waking World," Medusa said. "One is through the portal that may exist in this lighthouse."

"And the other way?" Charlie asked.

"We don't want to consider the other way," Dabney said. "But there will be those who do if word gets out."

Charlie saw Dabney the clown glance back at the limo, where Jack was sleeping, and the truth hit Charlie right in the gut. The only other way to smuggle something into the Waking World was through the portal in the purple mansion—the portal his brother had passed through dozens of times. If Charlie couldn't prove that the creatures in the lighthouse were the smugglers, his little brother would be suspect number one. Jack had been spotted all over the Netherworld, and the "evil child" prophecy might seal his fate.

"What do we need to do?" Charlie asked.

"We must stop whoever is in there from smuggling out any more of the tonic," Medusa said. "We need to get inside that lighthouse."

"But how?" asked Dabney with a giggle. "None of us can bear to go near it."

"The lighthouse here in the Netherworld may be impenetrable," said Medusa. "But if this lighthouse has a portal, the building will have a double in the Waking World. It's possible we can gain access on the other side. Someone will have to find the Waking World lighthouse."

Jack was furious that Charlie had let him sleep through the excitement. He'd opened his eyes just after the group had arrived at Medusa's opulent cave, and for an hour afterward, he'd stomped around with his arms crossed, muttering to himself. Every so often, he'd look over at Charlie and say something like "I would have woken *you* up!" Or "Who made you boss?" Or "I really wanted to tell Indy that I'd finally seen a lighthouse!"

Charlie sat silently while Jack got his frustrations out. He would have been angry too. But Charlie was too busy thinking about other things—important things—to waste time calming his brother down. They had to find a way to stop the smugglers. Otherwise, Jack might have a lot more to worry about than sleeping through a trip to a lighthouse.

Charlie had wanted to set out in search of answers, but Medusa refused to allow such a thing. She was a mother as well as a Nightmare, and she wasn't about to send a twelve-year-old human to find the lighthouse's Waking World double. Instead, a team of three of the Netherworld's finest Nightmare creatures was quickly assembled to deal with the crisis. The Nightmares the gorgon chose all possessed three traits. They were loyal. They were brave. And most important, they could (almost) pass for human. The team was prepped inside Medusa's enormous wardrobe. As owner and operator of the Netherworld's most popular theater, she had racks upon racks of nightmarish costumes—everything from rabid poodles and monstrous bats to grade-school bullies and science teachers.

Dabney the clown was the first to take a seat in the makeup chair in front of a brightly lit mirror. He watched, giggling maniacally, as his face was spackled with a thick layer of flesh-colored foundation. Slowly but surely, the natural chalkiness of his skin was covered up and the red diamonds around his eyes disappeared. A bit of black dye took care of his three little tufts of orange hair. When his makeup was finished, Dabney was handed a pair of gray slacks and a white button-down shirt. He was unrecognizable when he emerged from the changing room. The only sign left of the clown Charlie had known were the feet that looked at least ten inches too long—and the crooked yellow teeth that seemed a little too pointy.

"What do you think?" he asked, twirling around to show Charlie and Jack. "Will I be able to pass for a human?"

"Actually, yeah . . . ," Charlie started to say, when the clown burst into a fit of giggles. The sound was half hyena, half donkey. And coming from a man who looked like a tax accountant, it seemed 100 percent insane.

"That laugh's gonna be a problem," Charlie heard Jack say under his breath, and Charlie had to agree.

"When you're in the real world, try not to think of anything funny," Charlie advised.

"I'll give it my best shot," Dabney promised. "But it won't be easy. You humans are all so hilarious! The things you worry about are a hoot!"

Ava, a creature known as a Harpy, was the next to undergo the transformation. She and Medusa had been friends since the olden days, and they chattered away as Medusa worked on the costume. Ava's top half was perfectly pleasant and human. Disguising the rest of Ava's body was the challenge. Her legs were those of a fierce bird of prey, with two giant claws and razor-sharp talons. And two powerful wings sprang from her shoulders. Medusa had managed to conceal these features with a shawl and an ankle-sweeping dress. But human clothing couldn't hide Ava's penchant for pouncing on the furry little creatures that often ran across the floor—and tossing them into her mouth. Charlie watched with growing anxiety as Ava chomped on a Netherworld mouse.

"You know, real people don't usually eat things like that," Jack offered helpfully.

"Sure they do!" Ava said, a tail popping out of her mouth as she spoke. "I've heard you humans just grind it up, fry it, and call it fast food."

Charlie didn't have a chance to think about what Ava had said. Bruce, the third team member, had stepped forward to be costumed, and Charlie's anxiety turned to outright panic. Bruce was tiny. He stood no higher than Charlie's knee. Thankfully, Bruce had two human arms and two human legs, but his face bore a snub nose, and a tooth poked out from either side of his mouth, making him look a bit like a bulldog.

"What are you?" Jack asked.

"A changeling," Bruce answered

matter-of-factly. His voice was deep and raspy, like a gruff, elderly man with a fondness for cheap cigars. "I usually get called in after a baby is born. Parents are always scared they've given birth to a monster. I get to be the monster."

"Cool," Jack said.

"Yeah," Bruce agreed. "But it's getting a little old playing human infants all the time." He groaned as Medusa approached with an outfit decorated with little yellow duckies. "It's cruel what your kind make the little ones wear. No style whatsoever. It's humiliating, actually. And you wouldn't *believe* the chafing you can get from a onesie."

Charlie sat for hours, watching the Nightmares transform into humans and listening to Medusa issue detailed orders to her troops. Ava, with her wings, would be sent in search of the lighthouse. Dabney and Bruce would investigate Orville Falls.

When Medusa's work was done, the three Nightmares gathered around the mirror. Dabney cradled Bruce in his arms. Ava smiled so sweetly that no one would ever have guessed what she was chewing. Jack grinned, and Charlie gulped.

Medusa stood back to appraise her work. "I've never been to the Waking World," she admitted. "And you boys are the only humans I've ever met in the flesh. Do you think these costumes will be convincing?"

"They're awesome!" Jack exclaimed.

Charlie stared at the reflection in the mirror, taking the Nightmares in. He wasn't as confident as his brother, but he had to admit that without the giggling and the mouse eating, they might actually succeed in passing for human. There was no getting around one thing, though: together, the three of them would be the weirdest trio on earth.

"Got any tips for us?" Bruce asked, scratching at his stubble.

Charlie honestly didn't even know where to begin.

"Well, if you're going to be a baby, you should probably think about shaving," Jack offered wisely.

CHAPTER ELEVEN

ICK & INK

"You're back!" a relieved Charlotte enveloped Charlie and Jack in an enormous hug the second they stepped through the portal and into the octagonal room at the top of the purple mansion's tower. The sun was rising, and the tower room glowed with a magical golden light. "I nearly had a heart attack when you two got beamed up by that spaceship! Jack, you really shouldn't have—" The lecture came to a halt when Charlotte realized that the boys were not alone. She gaped over Charlie's shoulder as, one by one, the Nightmares stepped out of the portal and entered the Waking World.

Before Charlie could open his mouth to explain, Charlotte had burst into action. "No, no, no!" she cried, straining with all her might to push Dabney back through the opening. "Nightmares aren't allowed here! It's against every rule!"

Dabney's good nature prevented him from fighting back—and his giant feet kept him firmly rooted in place. "Lottie, is that *you*?" he asked.

Charlotte stopped shoving and stood back to get a better look at the bland-looking man. "No one's called me by that name in twenty-five years."

Dabney broke into a fit of giggles. "Lottie, it's me!"

"Dabney?" Charlotte blinked several times as if she couldn't quite believe her eyes. Then she threw her arms around the clown and hugged him. "What happened to you? You look so *different*."

"It's just a disguise," Dabney assured her. He held his old friend by the shoulders and shook his head. "But look at you! Last time I saw you, you were eleven years old. Now you're a full-grown lady."

Listening from the sidelines, Charlie felt a little stab of sadness. His own mother, Veronica, had been responsible for introducing Charlotte to Dabney. When the two girls had been Charlie's age, they had traveled together to the Netherworld. Dabney had been Veronica's Nightmare—and after she'd faced her fears, he'd become her friend.

"It's funny. I don't feel like I grew up," Charlotte said, and then she laughed and gave the clown another hug. "But I guess it happens to the best of us."

"Hey, lady, enough with all the affection! You trying to smother me or something?" complained Bruce, who was hanging from a baby carrier that was strapped to Dabney's chest.

"Oh, I'm sorry!" Charlotte said. "I didn't even see you!" She bent down to offer an apology to the counterfeit baby. Her head jerked back when she got a good look at the creature. "Why, aren't you just the . . . creepiest . . . little thing."

"You ain't so bad yourself, toots," Bruce said, waggling his eyebrows. Apparently Charlotte's revulsion had been a compliment.

"That's Bruce," Charlie told his stepmother. "He's a changeling. And the other Nightmare is Ava." Charlie gestured to the Harpy in disguise.

Charlotte offered the Nightmare her hand. As Ava shook it, one of her wings popped out from beneath her shawl. Jack laughed, and Charlie saw Charlotte struggle to hide her surprise.

"So what's going on, Dabney?" Charlotte asked. "Why are the three of you here?"

When a fit of giggles prevented the clown from answering, Charlie stepped forward.

"It's like I thought, Charlotte. The Netherworld is in serious trouble, just like the Dream Realm. Jack and I saw the evidence. There's nothing but a giant hole where Orville Falls used to be. The hole swallowed the entire Netherworld town, and it's growing wider every night. Pretty soon it's going to reach Cypress Creek."

"No!" Charlotte clapped a hand over her mouth in horror.

"Yep." Jack had appeared at Charlie's side, and he looked eager to join the conversation.

"The Tranquility Tonic must be responsible. It's the only explanation," Charlie added quickly before his little brother could steal the show. "And you were right, Charlotte. The stuff couldn't come from the Waking World. Medusa thinks someone's smuggling it here from the Netherworld. Then they give it to the man in the shop to sell."

"But who could be smuggling it, and how do they get it here?" Charlotte asked in confusion. "The only passage between the two worlds is the portal in this room. And as far as I know, you and Jack are the only people who've been through the portal in the last twenty-five years."

Charlie watched as his stepmother's eyes briefly landed on Jack.

"Why does everyone keep looking at me?" the boy cried. "I've never smuggled anything. I swear!"

"Then how—" Charlotte started to ask.

"Medusa thinks there may be a second portal between

the Netherworld and the Waking World," Charlie explained. "It's inside a lighthouse near the goblin territory. We had a look at the place tonight."

Charlotte blanched. She pulled the chair out from behind her desk and collapsed onto it. "You're joking. A lighthouse?" she asked weakly. "Did you go inside?"

"We couldn't," Charlie said, watching his stepmother closely. Her face was as white as a sheet, and her hands were trembling. "But if the lighthouse has a portal, then the whole building will have a double somewhere in the Waking World. That's why Ava is here." Charlie gestured to the Nightmares. "She's going to take to the skies to search for it while Dabney and Bruce check out Orville Falls."

Ava shook the shawl off her wings. "I would love to stay here and make human talk with you, but I must begin my journey. Charlie has told me that the Waking World is a very big place. I hope I can find the lighthouse before that terrible hole swallows your town too."

"The lighthouse you're looking for is in Maine," Charlotte said.

"What?" For a moment, Charlie couldn't think of anything else to say. It seemed none of the others could either. A stunned silence filled the room.

"How do you . . . ," Jack started to ask.

"It's hard to explain how I know," Charlie's stepmother replied. She rose from her seat and pulled a battered old book from the shelf above her head. On its spine was written *Lighthouses of New England*. Charlotte thumbed through the brittle, yellowing pages until she found the picture she was looking for. Then she turned the book around so that the rest of them could see.

There on the page was a lighthouse that was identical in every way to the one Charlie had seen in the Netherworld, except this one seemed to grow out of the sea.  A sliver of wave-battered rock linked it to the mainland. It was hard to imagine anyone using it as a bridge—without getting washed away. The caption below the photo read *The Kessog Rock Lighthouse. In Private Hands.*

Charlotte handed the book to Dabney. "I found the lighthouse book at a yard sale a couple of years ago. I started flipping through the pictures, and when I came across the one I just showed you, I nearly fainted."

"Why?" Jack asked.

"Because up until then, I'd only ever seen the Kessog Rock Lighthouse in my nightmares," Charlotte told him.

Charlie felt a chill, and he wrapped his arms around

himself for warmth. He'd just returned from the Nether-world, and he was standing beside three accomplished Nightmares, and yet the quaver in his stepmother's voice scared him far more than anything else he'd seen or heard that night. Charlotte wasn't easy to frighten, which meant whatever had gotten to her had to be pretty darn bad.

Charlie almost hated to ask. But he did. "You used to have nightmares about the lighthouse?"

"We both had them." Charlotte held Charlie's eyes for a few beats when she said it. That was how Charlie knew—it wasn't just Charlotte. His very own mother had dreamed about the lighthouse too. "It was a couple of years after our adventure in the Netherworld. Your mom and I must have been fourteen or fifteen at the time. I'd already moved away from Cypress Creek by then, but Veronica and I still spoke on the phone every day. She was the one who got the first note."

"Note?" Jack pressed when Charlotte couldn't seem to find her voice again.

Charlotte nodded. "Veronica told me she'd been having a nightmare about school. I can't remember much about the dream except that it was typical teenage stuff. Some-thing about bullies or boys or geometry quizzes. Anyway, in her nightmare, she was sitting at a desk in a classroom, and at some point she glanced up at the blackboard, and there was a note written there, one that didn't have anything to do with her nightmare. It said, *We're lonely. Come over and see us.* And it was signed *ICK and INK.*"

"Ick and Ink?" Charlie asked. When his mom had mentioned them, he'd assumed the words were some kind of code. "Those are names?"

"Yes," Charlotte said. "But the words were always written in capital letters. I think they may have been initials."

"*Whose* initials?" Jack inquired.

Charlotte shrugged. "We never found out, and I'm almost glad we didn't. When I got the second note, it scared me half to death. I was having a nightmare about a dog in my neighborhood that always chased me down the street. I remember running for my life past a house with a message spray painted on the side. *We know you've been here. ICK and INK.* Whoever had painted the message knew about the portal—and knew I was able to visit the Netherworld in the flesh."

"But how?" Charlie asked.

"Beats me. Veronica and I never told a soul about our trips to the Netherworld," Charlotte said. "We each got a few more notes, and then we both began having the same dream. We'd fall asleep and find ourselves standing together outside a lighthouse. There was always a note, written in sand or spelled out in seaweed, even though there was no ocean nearby. The messages would say *We've been waiting for you. ICK and INK.* Or *We want to be friends.*

ICK and INK. And one time we found a basket with a little blue bottle inside. There was a tag around the top that said *We want you to feel better.*"

Charlie shuddered. *The tonic.* His mother and Charlotte could have been ICK and INK's first victims.

"Did you drink the stuff in the bottle?" Jack asked.

"No," Charlotte said. "And we never went inside the lighthouse either. We couldn't have, even if we'd wanted to. The closer we got to that place, the worse we felt. It seemed like the whole building was surrounded by a cloud of darkness. Whatever was in there wasn't good. We suspected the notes were some sort of trap. And as it turned out, we were right."

"How do you know?" Charlie asked. "What happened?"

Charlotte shook her head. "That's a story for another time," she said sadly. "After a few months, your mom and I stopped getting notes from ICK and INK. I'd almost forgotten all about them until I found this book. That was when I realized that the lighthouse was a real place. It's in Maine, on a treacherous stretch of coastland where ships often wreck."

"Did you ever see it in person?" Jack asked.

"I was planning to go. But then my grandmother died, and I was called here to take charge of the mansion. I never had a chance."

Charlie jumped at the sound of Dabney's giggle. The

Nightmares had been so quiet that he'd almost forgotten they were there. "Ava will go to Maine," the clown announced. Then he paused. "Where is Maine?"

"It's north of here," Jack said. "I think."

"It is," Charlotte confirmed.

"Where is north?" Ava asked.

Charlie sighed. The Nightmares knew nothing about the Waking World. The mission seemed doomed from the very beginning.

"It's going to be a long trip," Charlotte told Ava. "Before you go, I'll need to find you a map."

"What about money?" Jack said. "You know, for snacks and stuff?"

"If she gets money, I want money too!" Bruce demanded, though Charlie was pretty sure the changeling had no idea what he was talking about.

Charlie saw Charlotte's eyes dart down to a pile of papers that were stacked on her desk. Before she answered, she opened a drawer and swept them all inside. "I wish I could give you all the money you want," she said. "But the truth is, I don't have much to give right now."

"That's okay," Jack said without a second's hesitation. "I'll go get my piggy bank."

Charlie shook his head. Sometimes it was easy to forget just how young Jack was. "A bunch of change isn't going to help anyone," he said miserably.

"It's mostly bills," Jack replied innocently. "I've been saving up for a while. You think they'll need more than five hundred dollars?"

"Where did you *get* five—" Charlie started to say. Then he remembered it was Jack he was talking to, his magic little brother who always seemed to have an ace up his sleeve. "Never mind," he grumbled. "Go get your piggy bank."

THE SECOND STORE

"It's the big day!" Andrew Laird announced as he came down the stairs. "Where's America's next bestselling author? You ready for the trip?"

Charlie watched nervously as his enormous father lumbered toward the breakfast table, his chunky glasses tucked into the pocket of his pajama shirt. Andrew Laird yawned, ran his hand over his beard, and scratched his butt. He was just about to claim a chair at the table, when he realized that all the seats were taken. Charlie gulped. The glasses were on his dad's face in an instant, along with a bewildered expression.

Charlotte jumped up to greet her husband. "Andy, I'd like you to meet my friend Dabney and his little boy, Bruce," she trilled unconvincingly. "They came by to wish me luck on my trip to New York."

Charlie saw his dad's puzzlement grow as he checked the watch on his wrist. It was eight-thirty in the morning. Jack was fast asleep, and Charlie would have been dozing too, but he had dragged himself out of bed early to do some snooping while the house was quiet. He'd wanted a look at the papers Charlotte had swept into her desk drawer the night before. He'd had a hunch that they were important, and he was right. What Charlie had discovered on those pages had frightened him far more than ICK, INK, or the Netherworld abyss.

"It's a pleasure, Mr. Laird," Dabney offered. "We've heard so much about you."

"Yeah!" Bruce added, and Dabney shoved a pacifier into the changeling's mouth.

"Welcome to our home," Andrew Laird said with a sideways glance at the unusually talkative infant. "Sorry to greet you in my pajamas. Charlotte didn't tell me we'd be having guests this morning."

"Oh, no worries." Dabney shoved a heaping forkful of kale pancakes into his mouth. "We've seen everyone in Cypress Creek in their pajamas."

Charlie didn't give his father any time to ponder the

strangeness of that statement. "Here, Dad," he said, hopping out of his seat and taking his plate to the sink. "Have my chair. I'm done."

Andrew took Charlie up on his offer. Sitting down, he was able to get a better look at the pair across the table.

"Your baby is so . . ." He couldn't seem to find the right word.

"He's a little *angel,* that's what he is," Dabney cooed. He bent down and nuzzled the changeling's snub nose with the tip of his own.

Bruce issued a low warning growl and bit the end off his Binky.

"You feeling okay this morning, hon?" Charlotte asked her husband. She'd arrived at the table just in time with a plate of pancakes. "You look a little out of sorts."

Andrew Laird seemed grateful for a chance to focus his attention on someone other than the scrawny man and his ferocious child. "I didn't sleep very well," he admitted. "I guess I've been under a lot of stress. I spent the whole night tossing and turning. Maybe I'll pick up some of that new Tranquility Tonic."

He didn't seem to notice the effect his words had on everyone in the room. Charlotte went completely pale, and Dabney was doing his best to stifle a giggle.

"Tranquility Tonic?" Charlie asked weakly.

"Yeah," Andrew Laird said between bites of pancake.

"Don't know what it is exactly, but I saw a man putting up a big sign for it on my way home last night. Says it helps you sleep more soundly."

"You saw a sign for Tranquility Tonic in Cypress Creek?" Charlotte asked.

"Yep, down by the gas station," said Andrew. "Guess there's a store opening up on Main Street in a few days. But I heard there's already one in Orville Falls. I was thinking of driving up there—"

"Don't drink it!" Charlie blurted out. He couldn't help himself. The thought of his dad turning into a Walker was too much to bear. "It does terrible things to people! It stops their dreams and clogs their brains."

The outburst got Andrew Laird's attention. He froze, staring at his older son. His mouth was hanging open wide enough for Charlie to see the half-chewed pancake inside.

"Plus that shop's sort of our competition, you know," Charlie added quickly, trying to cover his strange reaction. "If you need something for sleep, let Charlotte make it. You don't need that tranquility stuff."

"I've heard that the tonic makes your breath smell like kitty litter," Dabney offered casually. He took a bite of pancake to muffle the giggle that followed.

"Really?" Andrew said. He grimaced and resumed chewing. "Then I think I'll just stick with valerian root. Thanks for letting me know."

The doorbell rang, and Charlie leaped at the opportunity to flee the odd little gathering. He found Paige standing outside on the front porch beside a milk thistle plant. Charlie had been neglecting his plant-tending duties, and the thistle was looking quite sickly. But Paige seemed like she could have used a little help herself. She was panting as if she'd run all the way across Cypress Creek. There was a five-dollar bill clenched in her fist and a look of sheer horror on her face.

"Has Charlotte made the antidote yet?" The words spilled out of Paige's mouth so rapidly that Charlie guessed she'd been holding them in for blocks.

Charlie shook his head gravely, and Paige groaned. "There wasn't enough tonic left in the bottles we brought back last night," he explained. "She needs a full bottle of the stuff so she can try to figure out what's in it. Why? What's going on?"

"I went out to buy orange juice this morning, and . . ." Paige stopped and struggled to catch her breath. "My aunt Josephine's ads—they're all over town. And there's a Tranquility Tonight store opening on Main Street."

Why did everything have to happen all at once? Charlie was working on zero sleep, and things were rapidly getting out of control. "My dad was just talking about it," Charlie said. "Sounds like we've only got a few days to keep the store from opening."

"No." Paige shook her head. "We don't have a few days. The signs say the shop's opening *tomorrow*. We have to do something *now*. Rocco's away at a soccer match, but I called Alfie and told him we'd pick him up on our way downtown."

Charlie's heart skipped a beat. Paige was right. Something had to be done immediately. "Stay here," he told her. "I'll get my stuff."

Charlie ran back into the mansion to grab his backpack and found his stepmother making awkward conversation in the kitchen. Her husband couldn't understand why he'd never met her good friend Dabney before. Charlie took Charlotte's arm and pulled her into the drawing room. A fat orange blob darted out from beneath a purple chair and disappeared down the hall, hissing at Charlie along the way. Aggie had taken one look at Bruce and gone into hiding that morning. If having a changeling in the house was what it took to keep Charlotte's evil cat out of everyone's hair, Charlie might have been tempted to ask Bruce to stay.

"Charlie!" Charlotte whispered frantically. "I can't talk right now. It's really not a good idea to leave those Nightmares alone in the kitchen with your father!"

"Paige is outside." Charlie struggled to keep his voice down. "She says there are ads for Tranquility Tonic all over town. The Cypress Creek store is opening *tomorrow*."

"Tomorrow?" Charlotte repeated, as if the word made no sense to her. "But I'm supposed to be flying to New York in four hours! I won't be back until tomorrow evening!" Then she drew in a long, deep breath. "That's it," Charlotte said as she exhaled. "I'll just have to cancel my trip. If the publishers really want my book, they'll be willing to wait."

Charlie had expected her to say exactly that. "You can't cancel your trip, Charlotte," he said firmly.

"I have to!" Charlotte almost barked in frustration. Then she cast an anxious eye at the kitchen door and lowered her voice. "There are Nightmares sitting at my breakfast table, someone's smuggling harmful substances into the Waking World—and now my husband is talking about trying a tonic that would turn him into one of those Walkers. Now is *not* a good time to go to New York, Charlie."

Charlie stared at his stepmother without saying a word.

"What?" Charlotte demanded.

Charlie took another few seconds to consider his answer. He was about to confess to a serious crime. Charlotte did not approve of snooping. "I read the letters, the ones you have hidden in your desk drawer upstairs."

"That's impossible," Charlotte replied. "I always keep that drawer locked."

Charlie reached into his back pocket and fished out a bobby pin. Charlotte's hair shed dozens of them every day. They could be found all over the house—wedged between floorboards, tucked under sofa cushions, even trapped in the bathtub drain. "I found a Martha Stewart lock-picking tutorial on the Internet," Charlie told her. "I opened your drawer with one of these."

Charlotte's hands were suddenly on her hips. "You went through my personal files?" she demanded.

"We're a family now! They're my personal files too!" Charlie cried. He was surprised to realize how angry he was getting. "Hazel's Herbarium is losing money every month, and the bank is threatening to take the mansion! How is that even possible? I thought it was built by your great-great-grandfather!"

"I had to mortgage the mansion to open the shop—" Charlotte began.

"Why didn't you tell me?" Charlie demanded.

Charlotte's head dropped, and she rubbed at her eyes wearily. "You're just a kid, Charlie. I didn't want to worry you."

Of all the people in the world, Charlotte was the last one Charlie would have expected to use that tired old excuse. "Yeah, you're right. I'm just a kid," he said. "I'm a kid who's supposed to be protecting the portal upstairs.

And if our family loses the mansion, I won't be able to do that. So you have to go to New York, Charlotte. And you have to convince someone to buy your book. We need the money. There's no other way."

"But the situation here is getting really bad—" Charlotte started.

"It doesn't matter how bad things look right now," Charlie butted in. "We both know they could get a million times worse if the portal isn't protected."

"I can't leave you alone to deal with this." Charlotte sounded like she was on the verge of tears.

"I'm not alone!" Charlie argued. "I've got Dabney and Bruce and all of my friends."

"And Jack," Charlotte added. She said it as if Jack were the one who'd make all the difference.

Charlie stayed silent.

"And *Jack*," his stepmother added once more, wiping a stray tear away. "You've seen what he can do, Charlie. You're going to need his help."

"Yeah," Charlie grumbled. "And I've got Jack too."

Charlie and Paige spotted four on their way to pick up Alfie. And they counted twelve on Main Street alone. The ads were everywhere.

Spend your nights without nightmares!
Get more out of life when you sleep like the dead!
The only sure way to cure snoring!

Four doors down from Hazel's Herbarium, workers were renovating a *shoppe* that had once sold candies and scented candles. The walls of the store had already been repainted a blissful blue. It was the same color paint that Winston Lindsay had purchased at the Cypress Creek hardware store. And there he was, the original Walker, hanging puffy white cotton clouds in the front windows, behind an enormous sign that read OPENING SOON!

"I walked by this place yesterday, and it was a mess. Somehow the Orville Falls Walkers managed to fix it up in a single night," Paige said. She sounded impressed.

"Well, now we know why Winston Lindsay was buying all that paint," Alfie remarked as a construction worker stumbled by, carrying an intimidating piece of machinery. "How are they doing this stuff without hurting themselves?" he whispered. "Look, that guy's about to use a nail gun, and he's barely able to walk straight."

A loud pop came from the nail gun, and a long piece of metal was suddenly sticking out of the Walker's work boot. He didn't seem to realize he'd just shot himself in the foot.

"There's your answer," Paige said. "They *do* get hurt."

"Oh, *man*." Alfie winced. "I really hope that nail went between his toes."

Charlie was about to point out a man with a chain saw, when someone tapped him on the shoulder. He spun around to find a pretty woman wearing a pale blue dress and an enormous blond wig. Her large, unblinking eyes were ringed with blue eye liner that perfectly matched her dress. The woman's wide red smile reminded Charlie of a comic book villain, but she looked and smelled far better than her fellow Walkers. Swinging from the woman's arm was a basket filled with blue brochures. She held one out to Charlie, smiling and nodding robotically until he took it. As soon as he did, she shuffled away. On the front of the pamphlet was a photo of a child sitting at a classroom desk, his hand held high. Posted on the bulletin board at the front of the room was a sinister message.

Give your children the advantage of a good night's sleep!
Give them Tranquility Tonic and say goodbye to:
Bad Behavior
Moaning and Groaning
Back Talking
Free Thinking
Nose Picking

"Wow," Charlie heard Paige say. His friends had been peeking over his shoulder as he'd read. "What kind of person would give this stuff to a kid?"

"Hey, Charlie!" Someone was calling out to him.

Charlie looked up to see Ollie Tobias on the opposite side of the street, waving a perfectly rash-free arm. His mother was nearby, chatting with one of her croquet-playing friends. The instant she spied Charlie, she snatched her son's hand and dragged him away. Tucked into Mrs. Tobias's handbag was a brochure for Tranquility Tonic. Paige's question had been answered.

"Oh no," Charlie muttered.

"Don't drink the tonic, Ollie!" someone shouted. Charlie didn't need to see the boy's face. He knew the voice all too well.

"Hey, Jack," said Paige.

Charlie turned to see his brother coming toward them.

"Where's your Captain America costume?" Alfie asked the small boy as he approached. "You know, Cypress Creek could really use a superhero right now."

"I'm going incognito today," Jack informed him. "Nobody ever expects a *nine-year-old* to save the world. The element of surprise is on my side."

Charlie rolled his eyes. "What are you doing here, Jack?" he asked. Charlie's patience was wearing thin, and tolerating his brother was getting harder and harder. "You know you're not allowed to wander around town by yourself."

"I'm not wandering and I'm not by myself," Jack replied defiantly. "Dabney and Bruce are with me. And Charlotte's mad that you snuck out of the house with Paige and left the rest of us behind."

Technically, Charlie had only promised to keep Jack involved *after* Charlotte left for New York. And slipping out without the two Nightmares in tow had seemed like a wise decision. The clown and the changeling were far too conspicuous for a daytime reconnaissance mission. Charlie had worried they'd draw attention. Now they were standing a few yards down the sidewalk, watching the Orville Falls Walkers assemble the latest Tranquility Tonight shop. Luckily, no one who passed gave either of the Nightmares a second look.

"Wait a minute. Is that Dabney from the Netherworld?" Alfie asked, squinting in the clown's direction. "Charlie? You let a Nightmare creature come through the portal? Isn't that against every rule in the book? The book your own stepmother wrote?"

"And what's that thing he's carrying?" Paige asked. "It's dressed like a baby, but it looks more like a warthog."

"That's Bruce," Charlie said, sighing.

"Bruce?" Alfie asked with a raised eyebrow.

Charlie realized that he had a lot of explaining to do. He'd only just begun, when a battered white van drove up and pulled to a stop outside the shop. The engine puttered out, and a man slid from the driver's seat, stumbled to the back of the vehicle, and opened the doors. Workers gathered to unload the van's contents. They carried stacks of giant blue signs into the store. Charlie recognized Josephine's work.

"Are those more ads?" Alfie marveled. "They're going to have everyone in Cypress Creek hooked on the tonic in no time."

Suddenly the van's motor sprang to life. A long, thin arm with an abnormally large hand at its end emerged from the driver's-side window and gestured to Charlie and his friends.

Only Paige seemed to understand what was going on. "Genius," she said.

There was no time for Charlie to stop Paige from climbing into the back of the van. He was suddenly faced with a terrible choice—join Paige or let her go it alone. Charlie hastily checked to make sure that no Walkers were watching, and then he scrambled inside, yanking Alfie in after him.

"I'm not sure this is the best idea you've ever had, Paige," Alfie whispered after he'd pulled the doors closed.

"We need to find out who's behind all of this, right?"

Paige asked. "Well, Dabney just got us a ride to Orville Falls."

"That was Dabney at the wheel?" Alfie asked. "I thought this was his first time in the Waking World. How does he know how to get to Orville Falls?"

Charlie looked around. He groaned when he realized there was one face missing. "Because Jack is up in the front with him," he replied. His brother was taking over.

CHAPTER THIRTEEN

THE TROLL IN THE WARDROBE

Charlie was relieved when the van finally pulled to a stop. He, Alfie, and Paige had bounced around like kernels in a popcorn maker for half an hour, and Charlie had come dangerously close to painting the van's walls with his breakfast. The van's back doors were yanked open, and Charlie blinked as bright summer sunshine poured in. The sky was a brilliant blue, and a flock of birds was flying overhead. It looked like a perfectly ordinary day. Then a tiny creature in red overalls hopped inside.

Paige's eyes went wide, and Alfie squealed.

"Hiya. I'm Bruce," the changeling announced.

Fortunately, Paige recovered quickly. "Hi, Bruce. I'm Paige." Always polite, she held out her hand. Ignoring it, Bruce reached into his overalls, pulled out the diaper he'd been wearing, and flung it into a corner.

"Wooh!" Bruce sighed with relief. "Now that it's just us and the Walkers, I don't guess there's a need for *that* part of the costume. *Man,* those things are uncomfortable! I mean, I see the appeal, but it's just not worth it!"

Paige quickly pulled her hand away, and Alfie didn't offer his own when he told the changeling, "Nice to meet you. I'm Alfie."

"Alfie. Paige. You dudes ready to rock 'n' roll?" Bruce asked.

"I taught him that," Jack said, appearing at the van's back doors with Dabney at his side. "Get out and take a look around," he urged them. "You guys are not going to believe this place."

"Paige and I saw it *way* before you did," Charlie said as he slid out of the van. It annoyed him to hear Jack acting like he'd personally discovered the town. "Both of us were here yesterday."

Alfie was the next one out of the van. He stood next to Charlie, taking in their surroundings. "Are you guys sure this is Orville Falls?" he asked, confused.

"Where else would we be?" Paige said. She pointed at an enormous banner that was stretched across the empty street where they'd parked.

Be a Doer, Not a Dreamer!

"What's that supposed to mean?" Alfie asked.

Charlie looked around. In the few short hours since he and Paige had last visited, Orville Falls had changed even more. The shops along the street looked empty—and not just of people, of *everything*. Doors hung open, windows yawned wide, and the storefronts had been picked clean. Charlie peeked inside one of the stores and saw that everything of value was gone.

"Maybe we should ask *them* what the sign means." Jack was pointing to a family that had just emerged from one of the buildings on the street. The parents carried stuffed garbage bags slung over their shoulders, and each of the kids was struggling to schlep a pillowcase crammed with bulky objects.

The family passed by Charlie and his friends as if they were completely invisible. The family was crossing the street, when the father's bag burst. The man kept on walking as silverware, tin cans, and potatoes tumbled out.

"Where are they taking that junk?" Bruce asked.

"Let's follow them and find out," Jack suggested. "Come on!"

Charlie refused to let a nine-year-old lead the way. "*Let's*," Charlie said brusquely, stepping out in front of his brother and nodding for his friends to follow.

At the edge of Orville Falls, where mountains rose above the dense forest, Charlie and his friends came to a tall wall built of rock. It was already close to thirty feet high, but it was still under construction. Burly Walkers with drool dripping from the sides of their mouths were stacking rocks and cementing them in place. The wall seemed to stretch for miles, and it appeared to have a single gate. Charlie saw the Walker family pass through, lugging their pillowcases behind them. Then they disappeared into the forest on the other side of the wall. Charlie wasn't sure where they'd gone, until he spotted a narrow road that cut through the trees. The sound of hammers in the distance guided his eyes up to an enormous old house that had been built directly into the mountainside. It was constructed out

of moss-covered stone, and it looked like something out of a terrible fairy tale. Crumbling turrets erupted from its front two corners, and tiny dark windows randomly dotted its face.

"Whoa," said Bruce. "That's quite a crib. It looks like something you'd see back at home."

"When I was at summer camp in Orville Falls, the kids used to talk about this place," Alfie said. "They call it the castle. Some crazy rich guy built it about a hundred years ago. It's been abandoned since he died."

Charlie had heard those rumors too. People said the man who had lived in the castle had been a hermit who'd left his family and locked himself away. It sounded to Charlie like he'd had a lot in common with Silas DeChant, the man who'd built the purple mansion—and the man whose fear had opened the Netherworld portal. The castle's owner had died all alone, and Silas DeChant might have met the same fate, if not for the woman who had refused to let him.

"Well, it looks like the castle won't be empty much longer," Charlie heard Paige remark.

The building was at least twice the size of the purple mansion, and was growing larger every minute. Walkers crawled across the structure like ants, working to expand the already enormous structure. The town of Orville Falls might have been empty, but the house on the mountain was bustling with activity. Everyone seemed to have gathered at the spot.

"Who's moving in?" Jack wondered out loud.

The answer was obvious, Charlie thought. The mansion was a classic villains' lair. It was the perfect home for the people responsible for Tranquility Tonic, villains so evil that they'd turned a whole town into Walkers and forced them to work as slaves. Charlie had never seen ICK or INK, but he remembered his brief glance of the man inside Tranquility Tonight, and he shuddered at the thought of meeting him face to face that very afternoon. But Charlie knew he had no choice. So he started down the path through the trees toward the strange building, gesturing for his miniature army of seventh graders, Nightmare creatures, and Jack to follow him. Charlie tried to look like he had a plan. He hoped he could come up with one before they reached the castle.

As Charlie and his friends made their way up the hill, the Walkers never paused in their work. Charlie could see that most were in terrible shape. Their clothes were filthy and hung from their limbs. The people looked like they hadn't been eating, and the stench that surrounded them made it clear that they hadn't been washing up either.

Hastily built storage sheds lined the road to the house. The men, women, and children of Orville Falls were loading each of the buildings with goods they'd sorted into unusual categories. There was a shed filled floor to ceiling with boxes of potatoes and bags of dry cat food. The one beside it was devoted to disposable batteries in all shapes and sizes. They even passed a shed that was overflowing with lightbulbs. The stuff must have come from Orville Falls's shops and houses.

"New owners sure are pack rats, aren't they?" Alfie joked halfheartedly.

That was one explanation. But there were others as well—and one was so frightening that Charlie could barely ponder it. From the looks of things, Charlie was pretty sure that the castle's owners were stocking up on food and supplies. The house on the hill was going to be the head-quarters of a big operation.

When Charlie and his friends reached the front door, they were surprised to find no one guarding it. After a moment's hesitation, they entered a cavernous foyer one by one. Just a few steps inside, and Charlie would never have guessed it was a sunny morning in July. The only light in the entry-way came from two blazing torches. Charlie squinted, his eyes adjusting to the dim room. Gradually he was able to see what the torch flames illuminated. Lining the walls were heaping piles of precious objects. There was a mound of gold jewelry, a small hill of silver utensils, and a pyramid composed only of chocolate coins.

"Those torches look like a fire hazard," Paige said nervously.

"Then it's a good thing the fire department is here." Alfie pointed, and for the first time, Charlie noticed the three big men in flameproof pants who were painting something on the far side of the room. "What are those guys doing to the windows?"

Charlie took a few quiet steps toward the men for a closer look. They were covering the glass in the windows with thick black paint.

"That's what happens when you let Walkers do your interior decorating," Paige said. "They probably can't tell the difference between the walls and the windows."

"No." Charlie shook his head. "It's not an accident. I think the owners are having them paint over the glass because they don't want anyone to be able to see inside."

"Or maybe the gentlemen just prefer the dark?" Dabney offered hopefully.

"Yeah." Bruce nodded. "The guys are probably vampires."

Paige held back a smile. "We don't have many vampires here in the Waking World," she informed the changeling.

"That's what *you* think, little miss smarty-pants," Bruce replied matter-of-factly.

"Well, I say we find the owners and *ask* them why they want to live in a cave," Jack announced. Two halls led toward different parts of the house. Jack chose one and set off without even missing a beat.

"Get back here!" Charlie ordered, but Jack ignored him and charged ahead into the dark unknown. Charlie could have shouted, he was so irritated with his brother. Now someone had to go after him.

"Paige, please help me find Jack," Charlie said. "The rest of you check out the other side of the house. Let's all report back here in exactly fifteen minutes."

Charlie and Paige didn't have to go far to locate Jack. The little boy had made it only a few yards down the hallway before he'd stopped in front of an open door.

Jack excitedly waved his brother closer. The kid's eyes zipped left and right as they explored the room. "This is some crazy stuff!"

Charlie reluctantly peered in over his brother's shoulder and gasped at what he saw. The room was set up like a medieval banquet hall. At the far end was a fireplace with an enormous fire burning in its hearth. The structure was large enough to roast at least five full-grown pigs.

Even from the doorway across the room, Charlie could feel the heat of the flames licking either side of the opening. Between the fire and the door, in the center of the room, stretched an enormous rustic wooden table set with dozens of hammered metal plates and knives.

"Where do you go to you buy stuff like this?" Paige asked. "Transylvania IKEA?"

"More like Crate and Barely Human," Charlie replied as he counted place settings. There was room at the table for at least forty people. Whoever owned the place seemed to be expecting a lot of company.

Before Charlie could stop him, Jack set off across the banquet hall, and then stopped beneath a mural that filled one of the walls.

"What do you think you're doing?" Charlie hurried over to retrieve his brother. "We can't just walk around this place like it's some kind of museum!"

But when he looked up at the painting Jack was staring at, Charlie found himself mesmerized. The mural showed hundreds of figures in black hoods walking up the winding road to the house they were standing in. In the painting, the house's door stood wide open as if waiting for the guests to arrive, and high above, hidden in the shadows, two people were watching the scene from one of the building's turrets. All Charlie could make out was a swatch of reddish-brown hair and three brown eyes.

"That almost looks like a girl I know," Jack said. "She—"

A female's shriek echoed off the stone walls. Paige pushed past Charlie and rushed up to the wall. She stopped with her nose almost pressed to one corner of the mural. With her index finger, she traced a shape that Charlie hadn't spotted. Only when he drew closer could he see it was a sloppy letter *J*. In an instant, he knew that the artist responsible for the bizarre painting must have been Paige's aunt Josephine.

Paige held her finger up to Charlie. The tip was covered in black paint. "It's still wet," she said. "My aunt might be somewhere in the building!"

She grabbed Charlie's hand and dragged him out of the banquet hall. Jack hurried after them, and Charlie saw him smirk at the sight of his brother holding hands with Paige. Charlie glowered back at Jack, hoping his expression would serve as a warning. The last thing he needed was someone making embarrassing "Charlie and Paige sittin' in a tree" jokes. Not that Paige would have noticed. She was too busy searching each room they passed for signs of her aunt.

The three of them raced from doorway to doorway down the hall. Paige was squeezing Charlie's hand so tightly that he worried she might cut off his circulation. But he wasn't about to complain. Unfortunately, Josephine was nowhere to be found. From time to time, they ran past a Walker who was putting the final touches on a bit of décor, or adding an extra coat of black paint to the windows. Otherwise, their wing of the house was empty. Empty, and yet it didn't feel deserted. Fires were lit in every room. It was as if the house were waiting for its inhabitants to return. Charlie couldn't help but think of Snow White stumbling upon the empty cabin in the middle of the woods. Whoever lived in the mansion would soon be back, but they weren't likely to be Sleepy and Dopey. The people who had chosen this castle for a home were definitely *Grumpies*. Charlie had never been all that picky when it came to interior decorating, but even he could see that the rooms they passed were filled with the most hideous furniture ever crafted. Most of it seemed better suited for a dungeon. And Charlie knew a thing or two about dungeons.

They finally slowed to catch their breath at the very last room in their wing of the house. It seemed to be the same as the rest—dark, dreary, and empty.

"Let's find Alfie and Dabney," Paige urged, turning to go. "Maybe they saw my aunt on the other side of the castle."

Charlie nodded, but just as he went to leave, something small and fast darted out of a shadow and into a wardrobe. Charlie grabbed Paige's arm to stop her and called Jack back with a soft "Psssst!" He held a finger to his lips and pointed at the wardrobe in the corner of the room. The three of them tiptoed to the large wooden cabinet. Charlie grabbed both knobs, and on the silent count of three, he threw the doors open.

The creature inside flinched. Then it went limp, and its head flopped to one side. Charlie was almost positive that the thing was a little girl, but it was so filthy that it was hard to tell.

Jack stepped closer to get a better look and screwed up his face. "You're not a Walker," he announced. "Stop trying to pretend."

The kid huffed and wiped the slobber off her face with her shirtsleeve. "Walker—is that what you call them?" she asked. "How'd you figure out I'm not one of them?"

Jack leaned in and sniffed. "You smell good. Like toothpaste," he told her.

The girl held a hand to her mouth. "Who knew oral hygiene would end up being my downfall," she muttered. She looked miserable.

"Your downfall?" Paige asked. "Who exactly do you think we are?"

The girl eyed them suspiciously. "I figured anyone who could still speak proper English at this point had to be one of the bad guys."

"We're not bad guys," Jack said. He sounded appalled

at the thought. "We're from Cypress Creek. I'm Jack. That's my big brother, Charlie, and his friend Paige."

"I'm Poppy," said the girl. "Are all of the people in Cypress Creek still normal? Don't you have the tonic?" Charlie could see hope beginning to sparkle in her hazel eyes.

"Not yet," Paige told her. "But there's a Tranquility Tonight store opening up in our town tomorrow."

Poppy lurched out of the wardrobe and grabbed Charlie and Paige by their T-shirts. "Don't drink the tonic!" she cried, her eyes wild. "It eats people's brains!"

Up close, Charlie could see that the girl's hair was probably red and quite possibly curly. And she was definitely older than she had first looked—and stronger too. Charlie put his hand on Poppy's, and her grip on his T-shirt relaxed. "We know what it does," he told her in his calmest voice. "But why are you the only person in Orville Falls who figured it out?"

"I'm not," said Poppy. "Other people tried to avoid it too. But you don't have a choice anymore—they keep a record. Everyone has to drink a bottle a day for a month. But after a while, they don't need to be forced. Once people start drinking, they just want more."

"What happens after a month?" Jack asked.

Poppy shrugged. "I'm not sure. I've heard that after thirty days, you'll never have a bad dream again. But I've been drinking the stuff for at least two weeks, and it doesn't do anything at all to me. I just pretend I'm a Walker and try to do my best to blend in."

Paige suddenly gasped. "You must be immune to the tonic!" she said. "Is there anyone else like you in Orville Falls?"

Poppy's face fell. Charlie could sense her exhaustion and sadness. "No. I've been searching for days. I haven't given up yet, but it's starting to look like I'm the only one," she said.

Jack stepped forward and gave the girl a hug. Taken by surprise, Poppy resisted for moment, and then gave in. "We'll get you out of here," Jack said. "I'm sure our dad and stepmom will let you stay at our house until things are safe in Orville Falls."

"Yeah," Paige agreed. "You're too little to stay here by yourself."

"Too little? I'm twelve!" the girl told them. "How old are you? Look, I wish I could go with you guys, but I can't. My parents are here. So are all of my friends. They aren't a whole lot of fun anymore, but I'm not gonna leave them. I need to make sure they eat, and I change their clothes once a day. You wouldn't believe how bad some of the people here smell."

"Have you ever considered helping your parents and

friends escape?" Charlie asked her. "Maybe if we took them back to Cypress Creek, we could find a cure for their—"

The kid shook her head violently, stopping Charlie before he could finish. "He wouldn't like that. Not at all. He'd send someone to find us."

"Who would?" Paige asked, shooting Charlie a wary glance.

Poppy looked around hesitantly and then whispered two words. "The Shopkeeper."

"You mean the guy who sells the tonic?" Jack whispered back.

Poppy nodded sadly. "This is his house. They make me work here."

Charlie and his brother locked eyes. "What do you know about this guy?" Charlie asked. "What's his real name?"

"I've never heard his name," the girl admitted. "Everyone just calls him the Shopkeeper."

"What's he like?" Jack asked.

"Short," Poppy told them. "He's not that much taller than us. He has a big nose, and I think he wears a wig. His hair doesn't fit right on his head. And his fingers are super-long."

It wasn't the most vivid description that Charlie had ever heard, but it sounded like the guy he'd seen in the shop. "What else can you tell us?"

"He doesn't like to have people around," Poppy said. "The only time I see him is when I pick up my tonic. And when I'm in the shop, I try my best not to look at him. I don't know what would happen to me if he found out about my condition."

"What could he do to you?" Jack asked lightly. "He's just a short little man."

"He's not alone," the girl told them. "I've never seen the people he works for, but I know they're real. They kidnap people. Anyone who refuses to drink the tonic disappears. Then they show up a day later acting just like the rest of the town." Poppy paused for a moment, and her brow wrinkled. Charlie could see she'd remembered something. "I've listened to him talking to his bosses too. Yesterday I heard him tell somebody that the job was almost over. Then he asked when they'd be ready to open the door."

He'd been talking to ICK and INK! Charlie thought, his heart thumping inside his chest. "What else did you hear?"

Poppy shook her head. "That was it."

Just then there were footsteps in the hallway outside the room.

"Get in here," the girl whispered. She looked terrified as she pulled Charlie and his brother into the wardrobe. Paige squeezed in beside them.

"What is it?" Charlie whispered back.

"That's got to be one of the bad guys!" the girl said. "Whoever's out there is walking like a normal person."

Charlie tried to peek, but Poppy pushed him back.

"No!" The girl reached out and gently pulled the door shut, but not before Charlie got a glimpse of the shadow cast upon the stone wall. It looked like a man with one unusually long finger shoved halfway up his giant nose.

THE HEIST

"It's him!" Poppy whispered. She was clutching Charlie's sleeve and shaking with such terror that she nearly pulled him over. "It's the Shopkeeper!"

Charlie glanced down at the glow-in-the-dark numbers on Paige's Swiss Army watch. It was half past ten in the morning. Shouldn't a shopkeeper be at work in his shop? An idea had just sprung into Charlie's head, when Jack announced, "I've got an idea!"

Charlie rolled his eyes.

"Shhhh!" Poppy begged, though the sound of the

Shopkeeper's footsteps was fading as he disappeared into the far reaches of the mansion.

Jack lowered his voice. "If the Shopkeeper's here, that means no one's watching his shop! We can steal a whole bunch of the tonic and take it back to Charlotte."

"Good thinking, kiddo," Paige said brightly, grinning at Jack as she mussed his hair.

Charlie gritted his teeth. That was exactly what he'd been thinking, but Jack—as always—had rushed in first and gotten the credit.

"Are you sure you want to stay here?" Charlie asked Poppy. "Come to Cypress Creek with us. When my step-mother makes the antidote, you can bring it back to your parents and friends."

"I told you before. I can't leave them," Poppy said firmly. "I'm their only hope."

"But . . ." When Jack started to argue, Paige stopped him.

"I understand," she told Poppy. "They depend on you. And you can depend on us. We'll find you when we have the antidote. Right, Charlie?"

"Absolutely," Charlie said. "But if you change your mind or need any help, just come to Cypress Creek and look for the purple mansion. You won't be able to miss it, and that's where we'll be."

Charlie let Paige lead the way back through the dark, dreary castle. His mind was still on Poppy. He couldn't imagine how much courage it must have taken for a twelve-year-old kid to live all alone in a town filled with Walkers. The only person he knew with that kind of guts was Paige.

"You look like you've got something on your mind," Paige told Charlie as the three kids waited for a group of Walkers to pass by.

"I was just thinking that Poppy's pretty amazing," Charlie replied honestly.

"Charlie and Poppy, sittin' in—" Jack started to sing.

"Shut up!" Charlie snarled at Jack so suddenly and ferociously that the little boy obeyed an order for once.

"Old grump," Jack muttered under his breath.

"Little brat," Charlie responded in kind.

He was so embarrassed that he couldn't bring himself to look over at Paige. They walked the rest of the way back to the strange castle's entrance in silence. Charlie was so deep in his own thoughts that he didn't notice Alfie until his friend spoke.

"Wow, what happened to you guys?" Alfie said, stepping out of the shadows. "You all look really pale."

"Did you run into one of those vampires you think don't

exist?" Bruce asked. Dabney giggled nervously, but Bruce was the only one who seemed amused.

"No, we just had a chat with the only non-Walker in Orville Falls," Paige said. "Her name is Poppy and she's twelve. She's been drinking the tonic for over a week, but it doesn't do anything to her."

Alfie's eyes nearly popped out of his head. He hopped up and down like he always did when he got really excited. "You found someone who may be immune to the tonic? Where is she? Why didn't you bring her? She could be the key to making the antidote!"

"She has to stay here and take care of her parents," Charlie said. "What do you mean, she might be the key?"

"Something is protecting Poppy from the tonic," Alfie said. "It could be lots of different things. It could be a gene in her body. Or something she puts in her body—like a food or a medicine. Or something in her environment. Or—"

"It doesn't make any difference right now," Charlie said, getting more frustrated by the second. "We can't study her, because she won't come with us. And we don't have time to talk about this anymore because we need to get out of this place."

"The Shopkeeper is here in the house," Jack blurted out.

"And that means he can't stop us from paying a little visit to his shop," Charlie added.

The line that led to the front door of Tranquility Tonight still stretched through most of Orville Falls. Hundreds of bedraggled citizens waited their turn to enter the shop. Charlie and Paige had seen it before, but the sight brought the rest of the team to a standstill.

"Remarkable," Dabney gasped.

"What are they doing here?" Jack asked. "The shop's not even open!"

"So the Shopkeeper just comes and goes as he wants, and everyone stays lined up and waits for him?" Alfie wondered out loud.

"Guess so," Charlie said. Then a familiar face caught his eye, and his heart sank. Kyle, the boy who played for the Comets, was standing in the line, wedged between his parents. They'd finally found a way to make him drink the tonic, Charlie thought miserably.

The jingle of a bell made Charlie look up just as an Orville Falls Walker exited the store. Before the door closed again, another Walker entered, and the entire line took a step forward in unison.

"Hey, what's going on?" Paige asked. "Does that mean the shop's open?"

There was only one way to find out. Charlie gestured for his friends to follow. Then he navigated his way around the Walkers, right up to the store's front door. Just like before, the door was shut tight, but this time a sliver of light was shining through a crack in the store window's curtains. Paige locked eyes with Charlie, and when they both rushed to peek in, their cheeks brushed against each other.

"Sorry," Charlie said, nervously rubbing his face as he peered into the shop. There behind the counter was the Shopkeeper.

Paige's head bumped into Charlie's again as she craned her neck to see, but she didn't seem to mind. "He's in there! How is that possible?" she marveled.

"No idea." Charlie was baffled. "Either he got back to town even faster than we did, or . . ."

"Or there's more than one of him," Paige finished the sentence.

"I guess that means we can't break into the store and steal the stuff," Jack said. "So why don't we just go in and *buy* some?"

"We tried the last time we were here," Charlie explained. "I don't know how the Shopkeeper figured out that we don't belong in Orville Falls, but he did. He locked the door in our faces."

"So if we can't buy the tonic and we can't steal it, what do you suggest we do?" Dabney asked. He clapped a hand to his mouth to stifle the giggle that followed.

"I suggest you let *me* take care of this," Bruce said. He freed himself from the sling that was strapped to the clown's chest and hopped down to the sidewalk.

The person at the front of the line was a woman with a baby carriage. She didn't even notice as Bruce hoisted himself over the side of the pram and pushed the lady's dozing baby to one side.

"I can get in with no fuss, but I doubt I'll be able to leave without one," Bruce warned them. "So you all be ready to run for the hills. And don't forget to take me with you when you do. Got it?" He didn't even wait for an answer before he pulled the top of the pram down, shielding its precious contents from view.

Alfie looked reluctant. "Are we sure about this?" he asked. "It feels wrong to let a baby do our dirty work."

Charlie shrugged. "You got a better idea?"

The door of the shop opened. Paige's aunt Josephine came out. The line took another step forward in unison, and the woman with the pram disappeared into the shop.

"Aunt Josephine!" Paige cried.

Charlie was too shocked to try to quiet Paige down. Every inch of Josephine's skin was covered with paint. She blinked a few times at the sound of her name. Then she cracked open the blue bottle that she held in her hands and chugged the contents right there on the spot. She tossed the bottle into the street and shuffled down the sidewalk.

Charlie felt a tug on his sleeve. It was Paige. He'd seen
the calm, determined look on her face before. She was
about to do something courageous.

"Charlie," she said. "I have to go with Josephine. I'm
going to stay with her till she's better."

"Here? Are you crazy? You can't!" he cried. The idea of
staying in Orville Falls with the Walkers made Charlie's
skin crawl.

Paige pointed at her aunt, who was so thin that a strong
breeze could have carried her away. "Look at her! She
hasn't been eating. Charlie, I'm worried something terrible is going to happen to her. You guys understood when
Poppy said she had to stay with her family. Well, now I
need to stay with mine."

Charlie was thinking of all the terrible things that might
happen to Paige, when the sound of shattering glass came
from inside the shop, followed by a voice screeching in an
unfamiliar language. A bottle of tonic crashed through the
glass of one of the store's front windows and exploded on
the street. None of the Walkers budged an inch.

Charlie could see that big trouble was going to burst
out of the shop at any moment. Paige would be safer at
Josephine's house. "Go," Charlie told her, suddenly eager
to send Paige away. "Now," he added urgently.

Paige lingered for a moment, as if she were hoping there
was something else he would say.

"I'll keep you company, Paige!" Jack chimed in. It was clear the kid wasn't afraid. And from the smile on Paige's face, that was exactly what she'd been hoping Charlie would say.

Paige took Jack's hand, and together they ran after Josephine. Charlie watched them go. He could feel something terrible surging inside him. Something rotten and green. He knew exactly what it was. He was jealous of his little brother.

The shop door flew open, and a tiny creature bolted out, clutching two bottles of Tranquility Tonic in its hands. "I've got the goods!" Bruce shouted. "Let's hit the road."

Charlie didn't need to be told twice. He started off after Bruce. Then one of Dabney's terrible giggles brought Charlie to a halt. He turned to see Alfie standing motionless in front of the shop, staring at a man with a beaked nose and hunched back. As the man panted, he reached up with his long fingers and fixed the toupee that had slid to one side of his perfectly bald head.

"I think I've seen you somewhere before," Charlie heard Alfie say just as Dabney scooped the boy up and tossed him over his shoulder.

The man in the doorway smiled, revealing a mouthful of pointy black teeth.

He raised his hand and pointed an oddly long finger

right at Charlie and his friends. Then he yelled, "Get them!"

The hundreds of Walkers waiting in line perked up at the sound of his voice. Their heads swiveled in Charlie's direction. They started to shuffle toward him. Then they picked up speed. And then they started to run.

CHAPTER FIFTEEN

THE GIRL IN THE LIGHTHOUSE

Charlie and Alfie spent most of the afternoon hidden in a Dumpster behind a Piggly Wiggly supermarket. Charlie knew how lucky they were that the weather was good. They would never have made it through one of Orville Falls's bitter winter nights. And had it been August, they might have fried in the heat. But even though Charlie and his friend weren't in danger of frostbite or heatstroke, that didn't mean they were safe. If they were ever going to make it home, the boys would have to find a way past the Walkers outside.

Charlie could still hear the unruly mob. They grunted

and shuffled around the supermarket parking lot, banging on car windows, searching for the children and Nightmare creatures that had given them the slip. Charlie had never expected the droolers to turn dangerous. Even after they'd begun to chase after him, Charlie hadn't really been scared. Then he'd watched three of the Walkers tackle a plastic trash can, thinking one of the kids might be hiding inside. They'd ripped apart the heavy plastic so easily that you'd have thought it was a paper cup.

Charlie and Alfie held their breath a few times while the Walkers tried their best to pry open the Dumpster. Fortunately, it was chained shut, and only Dabney had the keys to the lock. The clown had hidden the boys when it had looked as though they might be captured by a group of speedy teenage Walkers in tracksuits. Once the boys were safe, Dabney and Bruce had made a run for it. Dabney was fast, and Bruce was small enough to carry.

"We'll be back," the clown had promised. And if there was one creature Charlie trusted, it was Dabney. The Nightmare had saved his behind before. But according to the clock on Alfie's cell phone, it had been more than six hours since they'd climbed into the Dumpster. The boys had passed the first hour whispering about the Shopkeeper. Alfie swore that they'd all met the man before, but he couldn't remember where. Charlie agreed the guy looked familiar, but he couldn't quite place the face either.

The conversation came to a halt when they heard crickets chirping. It was Alfie's cell phone ring. He silenced the ringer and stared at the phone's lit-up screen, his thumb hovering over the *Answer* button.

"It's your mom," Charlie said.

"Yeah," Alfie replied. He and Charlie had known all along that rescue was just a phone call away. But none of them wanted their loved ones anywhere near the danger in Orville Falls.

Alfie hit *Ignore*. A few minutes later, the phone lit up again. After the third call, he turned his phone off.

With nothing else to do in the dark, the boys decided to take turns catching some sleep. Charlie drew the first watch. Crouched between his slumbering friend and a moldy ham, he thought of Jack and Paige and hoped with every ounce of his being that his best friend and his brother were safe.

Charlie had always admired Paige's courage. She was the sort of kid who always did the right thing, no matter how hard it might be. Staying in Walker territory to help her aunt was just Paige's style. It was Jack who had taken Charlie by surprise. His brother had volunteered to keep Paige company without a second thought. Charlie was the one who had hesitated. He'd wasted time worrying, when he should have been the one to grab Paige's hand. If only he'd been as brave as his brother, he could have been at

Josephine's house right now, smelling Paige's strawberry shampoo—instead of rotten meat and garbage. But Paige was with Jack, and Charlie couldn't stand it.

Sometimes it seemed like his nine-year-old brother had never known any fear. Jack took solo trips to the Netherworld for fun. He hung around with Nightmares and helped ogres remember how to be scary. There was something special about Jack—something Charlie didn't have. Even when Charlie wasn't scared, he was usually a bit on edge. It was like he expected to encounter danger around every corner. Charlie hated to admit it, but he could never have set off on his own through the Shopkeeper's castle the way his little brother had. He simply didn't have Jack's courage.

Alfie's watch beeped, and Charlie shook his friend awake. "It's your turn to be lookout," he said.

"What am I supposed to look at? It's pitch-black in here," he heard Alfie gripe, but Charlie was already drifting off.

After the horrifying events of the day, Charlie expected to find himself in the Netherworld. Instead, he opened his eyes to a hazy white light. He knew it was probably the Dream Realm, but there was nothing around him to see. Charlie recalled the thick fogs that often settled over the mountains outside Cypress Creek in the morning. Once, during a camping trip with his dad, he'd woken up in a fog. Unzipping the tent, he'd discovered the world had been swallowed by white. When he'd stuck his arm out in front of him, he'd watched in terror as everything up to his elbow had disappeared in the mist.

But this was worse. It wasn't fog. It was *Nothing*. It seemed to press against him and fill his ears and mouth. Charlie felt panic beginning to build inside him.

"Hello?" he called. But the Nothingness absorbed his voice like a cotton ball sucking up a drop of water. He started to walk blindly, his arms stretched out in front of him. There was nothing there. He could wander forever, Charlie realized, with no hope of escape.

All of a sudden, a long forked tongue shot out of the fog and slid up the side of Charlie's face. He let loose a shrill screech that he instantly regretted.

"Found him!" someone called out.

"Are you certain it's him?" replied a smooth, deep voice. "That sounded more like the squeal of a wounded piglet than the cry of a twelve-year-old boy."

"Yeah. No doubt about it. It'sss him," the first voice confirmed. Its owner spoke with a nasally New York accent. "Kid alwaysss tastesss just like chicken. *Rotten* chicken."

"Larry?" Charlie asked in astonishment. "Is that you?"

A brown snake's head poked through the Nothingness and appeared right in front of Charlie's eyes. "Long time, no sssee," he said. "Though I think I coulda gone a little bit longer."

If Larry was there, he couldn't be alone. "Meduso?" Charlie called out, relief rushing through his body with such force that he felt weak in the knees. "You're really here?"

"Of course I am! Who else would wade through something like this just to save someone like you?" A hand reached through the mist and grabbed hold of Charlie's shirt. It tugged him along for several minutes until they broke through into the Dream Realm sunshine.

The last time Charlie had seen Basil Meduso was the day the gorgon had retired from the Netherworld by turning himself to stone. Before that, Meduso had worn nothing but well-tailored suits. Now, as a retired Nightmare in the Dream Realm, he appeared to favor tacky Hawaiian shirts, board shorts, and flip-flops. But Charlie was pleased to see that Meduso hadn't gotten rid of his old fedora. Three snakes emerged from beneath the brim. Like his famous mother, Medusa, Meduso was a gorgon with snakes for hair. But while his mother's snakes numbered in the dozens, Meduso had only three—Larry, Barry, and Fernando. Barry was a biter. Larry was a talker. And the Spanish snake named Fernando was Charlie's good friend.

"Sssso good to ssssee you," said Fernando, brushing against Charlie's shoulder. "It'ssss been far too long."

"Yeah, you'd think he'd have paid usss a visssit after everything we did for him," Larry complained.

The lovely emerald-green snake named Barry slithered down, stroked the side of Charlie's cheek, and then bared his fangs and disappeared back under the hat.

"Well, aren't you going to thank usss?" Larry demanded sourly. He never seemed to be in a good mood.

"Thank you, Larry," Charlie said sincerely. "And I'm glad to see you too, Fernando. Where was I just now?" He looked back at what appeared to be a solid white wall. "What is *that*?"

Meduso frowned. "That, my boy, is all that is left of the Dream Realm's Orville Falls," he told him.

Charlie shivered. "It's horrible."

"It's utter emptiness," Meduso replied. "And I spent half the afternoon inside it, looking for you. You can thank my snakes, by the way. I was as blind as a bat in there. It was their sense of smell that led the way."

Charlie smiled up at Larry, Barry, and Fernando. "But how did you guys know where to look for me in the first place?" he asked.

"Your stepmother, of course," Meduso said with a snort. "Charlotte showed up this afternoon while I was surfing the most divine wave. She said you went to Orville

Falls this morning, and she was worried you might get stuck. She asked me to help you if you visited the Dream Realm. I'm not sure why I keep doing her favors. . . ."

"Maybe because you like her?" Charlie said.

"Yes, well," Meduso admitted with a theatrical sigh. "I suppose everyone has a weakness."

For some reason, Meduso's words made Charlie think of Jack, and the thought left a sour taste in his mouth. If his brother had a weakness, Charlie sure hadn't found it yet.

"So," Meduso said, dragging Charlie back to the conversation. "I imagine you're eager to get started as soon as possible. My snakes and I won't take up any more of your time."

"Get started on what?" Charlie asked, confused.

"Fixing this little problem." Meduso gestured to the white wall. It stretched from the ground up to as far as Charlie could see, and it seemed to loom over them.

"I'm not sure I'm the one who can fix it," Charlie told him. The only way to stop the creeping Nothingness and fix the hole in the Netherworld was to find an antidote for the tonic. And there wasn't much Charlie could do while his body was locked in a Dumpster that was sitting in a parking lot filled with Walkers.

"I don't think you have much of a choice," Meduso replied solemnly. "Come with me."

"Where are we going?" Charlie asked.

Meduso sighed again. "I see you still ask stupid questions," he answered. "If you haven't figured out where we're going, why don't you wait a moment and see for yourself?"

Charlie followed the gorgon through a thicket of trees. On the other side lay a narrow street. Charlie recognized it at once. The road marked the western edge of Cypress Creek, and the Nothingness was no more than a few yards away. It had already reached the town limits.

"By the way, how's my dear mother?" Charlie heard Meduso ask. "Have you seen much of her lately?"

"Who?" Charlie had to force himself to look away from the Nothingness and focus on his companion.

"My mother—*Medusa*? I imagine she must have her hands full right now. Is the Netherworld suffering as badly as we are?"

"A giant hole swallowed a big part of it," Charlie reported. "I'd say your mom's pretty busy."

Meduso stopped in his tracks and spun around to face Charlie. "A giant hole?"

Charlie didn't have time for the whole story. "Yeah. There's a tonic that stops dreams and nightmares. We think it's being smuggled into the Waking World by these two weird people who live in a lighthouse and call themselves—"

"ICK and INK," Meduso finished.

Charlie studied the gorgon's face. Basil Meduso looked spooked. "Charlotte told you about ICK and INK?" Charlie asked.

"Years ago," Meduso said. "At the time, she and your mother were receiving strange notes. They asked me to go to the lighthouse and have a word with whoever—or whatever—had written them."

"And?" Charlie asked after a pause that felt like it went on forever. "What happened?"

Meduso crossed his arms and started walking again. "I'd rather not talk about it," he said.

"Yeah, bessst not sssay any more," Larry urged.

"It'ssss too ssssad." Even Fernando agreed, his head drooping as if a terrible memory were weighing it down.

Charlie hurried to catch up with the gorgon. "You have to tell me what happened! Whoever is inside that lighthouse could be responsible for the tonic that's destroying the Dream Realm and the Netherworld."

Meduso whirled around and grabbed Charlie by both shoulders.

"Have you been to the lighthouse?" he demanded.

"Yes," Charlie said. Meduso's fingers were pressing into his flesh, and Charlie squirmed. "You're hurting me."

Meduso relaxed his grip. "Whatever you do, don't go inside! Promise me, Charlie! Promise me right now!"

But Charlie knew he couldn't make that promise. If ICK and INK were going to be stopped, someone would have to find a way to get into the lighthouse. Charlie hoped it wouldn't be him, but something told him it might be.

"Basil Meduso, is that you?" someone called.

Meduso let go of Charlie's shoulders and straightened his Hawaiian shirt. "My apologies, Veronica. I was just having a stern word with your son. About the lighthouse."

Charlie suddenly realized that he and Meduso were standing in front of their destination, the lawn of the Dream Realm house where Charlie visited his mother whenever he dreamed. As always, she was there in her jeans and clogs, tending the flower gardens that her boys had helped plant when they were both little. She was walking toward Meduso now, and Charlie met her halfway with a hug.

"He's been there," Meduso said while Charlie still had his arms wrapped around his mother.

Charlie felt his mom freeze for a moment. "Did you see anybody?" she asked her son, her lips close to his ear.

"No," Charlie assured her. "And I didn't go inside."

Veronica Laird released Charlie from the hug but kept one hand on his shoulder. "Thank you as always for your help, Basil. Do you mind if I take it from here?" she asked.

"Absolutely not," Meduso said. "I believe I have a wave to catch. Charlie, I hope to see you soon."

"Vissssit ussss more often," Fernando said.

"If you manage to ssstay alive," Larry called back as Meduso began to walk away.

"Nicccce mannersssss," Charlie heard Fernando scold his fellow snake.

"What?" Larry answered. "If the kid can't handle the truth, how'sss he gonna sssave us all from that big cloud of Nothing?"

Charlie looked up at his mother. "Why do they think *I'm* the one who's supposed to save the Dream Realm? Have things really gotten that bad?" he asked. He didn't need a response. He could see the Nothingness behind her. It couldn't be more than half a mile away. How long would it take for it to reach his mom's house? Charlie wondered. A few hours? A day?

"Let's sit down and talk," his mom said. Suddenly they were seated on the steps of the front porch, in the same spot they'd always chosen while Charlie's mom had been alive. "Why did you go to the lighthouse?" she asked.

Charlie told his mother about everything, from the smugglers who were sneaking the tonic into the Waking World, to Medusa's theory that there was a portal located inside the lighthouse.

"Another portal?" The thought appeared to have taken his mom by surprise. She seemed to be turning the idea over and over in her mind. "That might explain what Basil saw."

"What did he see?" Charlie wasn't sure he wanted to know, and Veronica Laird didn't look like she relished telling the story.

"Charlotte told Basil about ICK and INK, and he went to investigate. When he got to the lighthouse, he said he saw a child standing at one of the windows—a little girl. He told Charlotte he'd never seen anyone look so utterly hopeless."

It took a moment for Charlie to find his voice. "Who was she?"

"Basil never found out," his mother told him. "She must have fallen into ICK and INK's trap, the same one they set for Charlotte and me. Basil tried everything he could think of to rescue her, but every time he got close to the lighthouse, he was overcome by a terrible feeling."

"I know what it's like," Charlie said. "When I was at the lighthouse, I felt it too."

"So did I," his mom said. "The day Basil saw the girl, it must have been particularly powerful. He couldn't get inside to save her."

Charlie recalled Meduso's mother telling him about her son's fondness for humans. He didn't mind scaring them, but he didn't like it when they got hurt. Charlie had a feeling he knew what was coming next.

"What happened to the little girl?"

"We don't know. She disappeared. Basil never saw her

again," Charlie's mom continued. "We assumed the worst. Basil was crushed. I think he's haunted by that girl to this day. But if there's a portal in the lighthouse, perhaps she didn't perish after all. Maybe she escaped to the other side."

"So ICK and INK kidnap children?" Charlie asked. No wonder Meduso hadn't wanted him anywhere near the lighthouse.

"I don't know," his mother admitted. "I'm sorry, Charlie. Charlotte and I should have tried to stop them decades ago. Now the burden has fallen on you. If ICK and INK are responsible for the tonic, you have to deal with them before the Nothingness reaches Cypress Creek."

Charlie followed his mother's gaze up to the white wall that was threatening the town. He could have sworn that it was a little bit closer than the last time he'd looked. Once again, he was in danger of losing the one thing that mattered most to him. The fear he'd worked so hard to conquer was back again.

"I don't think I'm the one who can do it," he admitted to his mom.

"Charlie—" she started to disagree.

"Stop!" Charlie interrupted a little too loudly. He corrected himself quickly. "*Please* stop, Mom. We both know Jack's the special one. He's the only one who has a chance of beating ICK and INK. He's not scared of anything."

Charlie's mom chuckled. "Yes, he's always been that way," she said. "I remember one time when Jack was about five, he saw a frog hop into a sewer drain outside our house, and he decided to go in after it. It was pitch-black at the bottom, but that didn't bother Jack at all. When the fire department pulled him out, he was laughing the whole way back up. And then there was the time he decided it would be a good idea to climb into the bear enclosure at the zoo. . . ."

"So you agree with me," Charlie muttered. "Jack is the one."

Charlie's mom wrapped an arm around her son and squeezed. "I agree with you that Jack is special. But being fearless isn't the same thing as being brave. In fact, I believe that in order to be brave, you *have* to be afraid."

Charlie put his head in his hands. His mother's attempt to make him feel better really wasn't helping. "That doesn't make any sense."

"Doesn't it?" his mom asked. "In order to be truly brave, you have to be able to see things clearly. Brave people analyze every side of a situation. They know exactly where the dangers lie, and they know what's at stake. They're terrified of all the things that might go wrong. So they don't act impulsively or foolishly. But when it's necessary, they do what they have to do. Being brave doesn't mean you're not scared. Being brave means you *are* scared, but you do the right thing anyway."

Charlie looked up at his mom. He could see from her expression that she wasn't just trying to make him feel better.

"Don't you see?" his mom asked him. "Jack is the fearless one, Charlie. But you're the one who's brave."

☙ CHAPTER SIXTEEN ❧

VERY BAD NEWS

"Hey!" whispered Alfie. "Wake up, Charlie. I think some-one's outside!"

The Dumpster lid popped open, and the golden light of the setting sun washed over Charlie. When his eyes adjusted, he could see the cadaver-white face of a deranged clown hovering over them. Its leering smile stretched from ear to ear, and red diamonds framed its crazed eyes. Charlie managed to clap a hand over Alfie's mouth before the kid could scream.

"Get your hand off my mouth!" Alfie ordered in a muffled voice. "I know it's just Dabney!"

"Sorry, boys!" the clown said softly. "I didn't intend to scare anyone. You two can get out now. The Walkers have disappeared. The Shopkeeper must have called off the search."

Charlie and Alfie cautiously climbed out of the Dumpster. The Piggly Wiggly parking lot was eerily deserted.

"What happened to your costume?" Charlie asked. "Weren't you supposed to stay disguised as a human?" He couldn't pull his eyes away from Dabney's clown suit. He had never been able to figure out why anyone would ever be amused by the sight of a grown man in a white jumpsuit with pom-pom buttons.

"I figured the Walkers would be looking for a man, not a clown," Dabney explained. "So I took off my disguise before I came back to Orville Falls."

Charlie followed the logic, but he wasn't sure it was the best idea. Getting Dabney back into Cypress Creek was going to be tricky. "And where's Bruce?"

"In the Netherworld," Dabney said. "He took one of the bottles of Tranquility Tonic to Medusa. He left the other bottle in the purple mansion for Charlotte."

"Bruce went back to the Netherworld?"

"Yes," Dabney confirmed. "I took him to the mansion, and then I came back here to get you."

"But how did Bruce get through the portal?" Charlie asked. Neither he nor Jack had been there to open it.

Dabney shrugged. "Is there meant to be a trick to it? Bruce just walked right through. I saw the whole thing."

Charlie couldn't believe it. There were only two possible explanations. Either he'd left the portal open by accident, or Jack had left Paige alone and returned to Cypress Creek.

"You better take Alfie home before his mom sends out a SWAT team to search for him," Charlie told Dabney. "I'm going to check up on Paige."

"By yourself?" Dabney asked.

"Are you nuts?" Alfie asked.

"I don't think so," Charlie told them. But if he'd been perfectly honest, he would have admitted that he wasn't quite so sure anymore.

The sun set quickly, and once it disappeared behind the mountains, Orville Falls was strangely dark. The street-lights were out, and the windows in the buildings that lined the main road remained unlit. It seemed every lightbulb in town had been removed and piled into one of the storage shacks outside the Shopkeeper's castle. In the gloom, Charlie could see the dark silhouettes of rats scampering from building to building, feasting on whatever goodies the owners had left behind. Passing a pastry shop, he heard a commotion inside and paused to peek through the window. Charlie immediately knew that the moonlit scene he witnessed would be etched in his memory for the rest of his life. Inside the shop, thousands of rats were gorging on doughnuts, cupcakes, and éclairs. Charlie nearly screamed when a giant black specimen popped out of the cake in front of him, globs of pink icing clinging to its fur and a white rosette stuck to the top of its head.

Charlie was scared—and he was glad for it. When he didn't try to fight it, the fear sharpened his senses. His ears could detect the faintest sound. His eyes busily scanned his surroundings, picking up any sign of movement. But more often than not, it was Charlie's sense of smell that saved him. The second he detected the scent of BO on the wind, he would duck into the nearest alley or crouch in the shadow of the closest trash can. Soon after, a group of marauding Walkers would thunder by, torches in hand. Charlie knew that if he hadn't been so wary, he might not have smelled them. And if he hadn't smelled them, he might not have made it to safety in time.

When Charlie arrived at Josephine's house, however, the fear reached an unbearable level. The little cottage's windows were as dark as those in the rest of the town. It didn't look like Paige and Jack had made it there. The house was deserted—or so it seemed, until Charlie waded through the weeds in the front yard. That was when he realized that the windows weren't just dark—they were completely black. Someone very smart had painted them.

Charlie rapped at the front door, using the emergency knock he and Paige had invented in fifth grade. It was two loud raps with the knuckles followed by three softer beats and an open-handed slap. If Paige was inside, she would know it was Charlie and let him in. Charlie waited nervously, and a few heartbeats later, the door flew open and he was pulled into a dark room and greeted with a hug. Charlie could smell strawberries in the air. Then the front door closed and the lights were flipped on.

Charlie gasped at the sight before him. The last time he'd been to Josephine's, the place had been a disaster— paint everywhere, food on the floor. Now it not only looked fit for habitation, it even felt . . . homey.

"You did all of this in one day?" Charlie marveled.

Paige gave him an exhausted smile. "I had some help," she said, pointing to a little body that was curled up asleep on the couch. It was Jack.

"He's been here the entire time?" Charlie asked, confused. It didn't make sense. If Jack hadn't opened the portal in the purple mansion for Bruce, then Charlie must have left it open by accident the previous night. Never before had he been so careless.

"Well, he went out for a little while to gather food," Paige said. There was a tall stack of cans on the counter that separated the kitchen from the living room. "He said he couldn't find anything fresh that hadn't been nibbled by rats."

"But you're both all right?" Charlie asked. He looked around the living room. Josephine's paints had been tidied up, and the latest batch of ads were neatly stacked in a corner. But something was missing, and Charlie couldn't put a finger on what it might be.

"So far, so good," Paige said. "You should take Jack home. It was sweet of him to come, but I think I'm going to be okay here."

A long silence followed while Charlie searched for the right thing to say. More than anything, he wanted to apologize. He wanted to tell Paige that it should have been him who had stayed by her side. Instead he asked, "How's your aunt doing?"

The question seemed to jog Paige's memory. "I can't believe I almost forgot! Come see." She led Charlie into the bedroom at the back of the house. Charlie found himself stuck in the doorway the moment he caught sight of Paige's aunt sitting up in her bed. She was clean and wearing a fresh white nightgown, though she stared at the wall in front of her with unblinking eyes. She was clearly still in a stupor. But Charlie suddenly saw what he'd never noticed before. Paige was the spitting image of her aunt.

"Crazy, isn't it?" Paige asked with an embarrassed grin. "It's weird knowing what you'll look like when you're all grown-up."

Charlie figured most girls would have been thrilled. But Paige had never been like most girls.

"I got her to eat a little bit," Paige said. "She really likes canned mushroom soup. And look at this."

Paige unscrewed the top on a small glass container. Inside was a thick yellow gel. Paige passed the stuff under her aunt's nose, and Josephine's eyes darted back and forth as if she'd been startled out of a bad dream. Then she blinked twice and fell back into the stupor.

"Did you see that?" Paige asked, excited. "It's like she wakes up for a few seconds!"

"What is that gunk?" Charlie held out his hand, and Paige passed him the container. A label on the lid simply said LIP BALM.

"I found it under one of the chair cushions when I cleaned. Josephine's lips were chapped, so I put a little bit of that stuff on her. Look on the bottom of the container."

Charlie turned the lip balm over and found another label, one he knew well. "She bought this stuff at Hazel's Herbarium!"

"I know!" Paige was practically bursting at the seams with excitement. "Do you think there might be something in there that could help Charlotte make an antidote?"

Charlie had watched Charlotte make plenty of lip balms. She didn't use any fancy ingredients as far as he could remember—just stuff like beeswax and shea butter. "Maybe," he said. "Is it okay if I take this back to Cypress Creek to show her? She's in New York right now, but she'll be back tomorrow evening. Can you hold out here for another twenty-four hours?"

"You make it sound like I have a choice," Paige joked, but her face was serious.

"What about your parents?" Charlie asked. "Won't they be worried?"

"I called them. They know where I am," Paige said. Then she sighed. "My mom hasn't been feeling well lately—and my dad doesn't have time to worry about me. Aunt Josephine usually watches out for me when my mom is sick. But I don't think Josephine's able to worry about anyone right now."

Charlie wanted to hug her. "Then I'll worry about you," he promised.

Paige smiled. "And I'll worry about you too," she told him. "I guess that's what friends are for."

On his way into Josephine's house, Charlie had noticed bike handles sticking out of the weeds in the front yard. When it was time to head home, he wheeled the bike out of the overgrown flora. He was somewhat dismayed when he realized the bike was painted bubble-gum pink, but he wasted no time in pushing it to the curb, where Jack was waiting, looking half-asleep.

"Hop on," Charlie told Jack, and he helped his brother climb onto the rack above the rear wheel.

"You sure this is safe?" Jack asked with a wide yawn.

"Nope," Charlie replied.

"Awesome," Jack said.

Charlie got up on the seat and felt Jack's arms wrap around his waist. He started to pedal and hoped he remembered the way out of town. The dark provided some cover as they rode through the streets of Orville Falls. Twice, bands of Walkers spotted them and gave chase, but they were no match for a terrified twelve-year-old on a hot-pink bike. As soon as he and Jack reached the Orville Falls town limits, Charlie barely needed to pedal.

The road was downhill to Cypress Creek. They sped through the woods that Charlie had once dreaded, but the forest no longer scared him at all. He had far bigger fears to face.

A light rain met Charlie and Jack on Cypress Creek's Main Street. As eager as he was to get home and dry off, something made Charlie stop the bike for a moment as they rode past Ollie Tobias's house. He searched for signs of life through the windows.

"Why are we spying on Ollie Tobias?" Jack wanted to know.

"Just making sure he's okay," Charlie replied.

"You guys are friends?" Jack asked in amazement.

Charlie shrugged. "I guess," he said. He'd never really thought about it that way.

The housekeeper appeared in Ollie's living room window. As she tidied up, a smaller figure in ninja attire stalked her across the room. Every time the housekeeper glanced over her shoulder, the little ninja would disappear behind the drapes or the sofa.

"That's so cool," Jack said, laughing. "Ollie's my hero."

"I bet," Charlie said. "You two have a lot in common." And for the first time in what seemed like days, Charlie felt himself smile.

By the time the boys arrived at the purple mansion, the clouds had broken open and rain was pouring down. As Charlie rode into the driveway, he noticed a tall figure hiding behind one of the trees in the yard.

"Boys!" it called out, so softly that Charlie barely heard it over the rain. The whisper was followed by a much louder giggle.

"Dabney?" Charlie asked, and the clown stepped into view. He was sopping wet.

"Why are you out in the yard?" Jack asked.

"Your father was home when I got here, and I couldn't let him see me like this!" Dabney told him.

"Why?" Jack asked. "I thought everybody loved clowns."

Dabney looked horrified. Charlie knew that if that had been true, his friend would have been out of a job. "Come on," he said before Dabney had a chance to take offense. "Let's get you back home to the Netherworld."

Charlie had planned to create a diversion so that Dabney could sneak up the stairs to the tower. But when he opened the front door, he realized it wouldn't be necessary. They could hear Andrew Laird on the phone in the kitchen.

"It's after dark, and he doesn't know we're home," Jack whispered. "He's probably calling the cops."

It wouldn't have been the first time the police had been

asked to search for Charlie. But Charlie had promised his dad there would not be a second time.

"Take Dabney up to the portal," he told Jack. "I'll talk to Dad and be with you in a minute."

"If you're still alive when he's done with you," Jack said merrily.

But Andrew Laird didn't even notice when Charlie showed up in the kitchen. Charlie's father was sitting at the kitchen table with his head resting on one hand. Whoever was on the other end of the phone had not called with good news.

Charlie cleared his throat, and his father jumped.

"The boys are back," he told the person. It had to be Charlotte, Charlie thought. He saw his dad check his watch. "Yes, I suppose it is pretty late. I should probably go and get dinner started." Andrew Laird listened for a moment and then handed the phone to Charlie. "She wants to talk to you."

"Hi, Charlotte," Charlie said.

The voice that answered barely sounded like his stepmother's. "So what's the latest?" Charlotte asked wearily.

Charlie stepped out of the kitchen so his father couldn't hear and made his way to the parlor. "Bruce stole two bottles of tonic from the Tranquility Tonight shop in Orville Falls," he told her. Avoiding the purple-upholstered antique furniture that Charlotte had inherited along with the house, he chose a seat on the sill of a window that looked out over the lawn. "He took one of the bottles to Medusa. The other one should be waiting here for you."

"Great." Charlie could hear the relief in Charlotte's voice. But there was something else in it as well. "So nobody got hurt? Everyone is okay? I asked Meduso to look out for you in case something went wrong."

"And he found me," Charlie told her. "I'm fine. I just—" A flash of movement outside on the lawn caught his eye, and he stopped. Holding the phone between his ear and shoulder, Charlie pressed his forehead against the glass and cupped his hands around his eyes. The rain was still pouring down. Charlie searched the sodden lawn but saw nothing. "Never mind about me. How are you?"

"Great," Charlotte said with fake cheer. Then she gave up trying. "No, that's not true. I've been better."

Charlie turned away from the window, the phone once again clutched in his hand. He could feel his heart sinking. "How did your meeting with the first publisher go?"

"He said he'd buy the book—as long as I make the Nightmare creatures look a little more cuddly."

"What!" Charlie exclaimed. "But they look exactly how they're supposed to look! That's the whole point of the book!"

Charlotte didn't need to be convinced. She and Charlie

had both come face to face with the creatures that Charlotte had drawn. "I know, I know. But he thinks the book as I wrote it is way too creepy for kids."

"Most people my age would choose creepy over cuddly any day of the week!" Charlie said. "Has the guy ever *met* any kids?"

Charlotte chuckled. "That's a really good question. But try not to get too bent out of shape," she told Charlie. "I'm not going to let some silly man in Manhattan tell me my book is no good. I'm meeting with another publisher in the morning. Then I'll be back in the evening and we'll find an antidote for the tonic."

Charlie was relieved. Charlotte still seemed to think making an antidote was possible. "Okay," he said. "We're going to need it fast. I think I found something today that will help, but it's getting pretty bad in Orville Falls. Almost everyone in town has been turned into a Walker. Paige's aunt is one of them, and she's not doing very well. Paige won't leave her side until we come up with a cure."

"Paige is still in Orville Falls?" Charlotte asked, sounding concerned.

"She refuses to come back," Charlie told his stepmom.

"I can't even imagine how terrified she must be," Charlotte said. "Let's try to get her home as soon as possible. But if we're going to find an antidote tomorrow, I'm going to need you to do something for me tonight."

Charlie had been looking forward to a nice dinner and a good sleep. He should have known better. "Sure. What is it?" he asked.

"You and Jack need to cross over to the Netherworld and talk to Medusa. Now that she has a bottle of the tonic, see if she can tell us what's in it."

"Okay," he agreed over a giant yawn. It was going to be another long night.

Charlie turned back to the window, just in time to see a figure dart behind a tree a few feet from the house. For a moment, he wondered why on earth Dabney had gone outside. Then he realized that Dabney was probably back in the Netherworld already. Also, the figure outside wasn't dressed in a white costume, and it was more kid-sized than Dabney-sized. Whoever it was had been spying on him through the window. The hairs on Charlie's arms stood up, and a feeling of dread began to creep through his body. The figure had moved much too swiftly for a Walker. It was something else, and it was up to no good.

As Charlotte chattered away, Charlie stood up from the windowsill, trying to look as casual as possible. "Charlotte, I really gotta go," he said, calmly interrupting his stepmother.

"Excuse me?" She seemed a bit surprised by his sudden rudeness. Then she figured it out. "Is something going on over there?" she asked.

"I just need to talk to Dad for a minute," Charlie said. "I'll call you back a little later."

Charlie clicked off the phone and walked to the kitchen, where his father was reading a piece of paper and absent-mindedly stirring a pot of spaghetti sauce. As a protector of the purple mansion, Charlie knew he should deal with the intruder himself, but the night seemed darker than usual, and its shadows felt sinister. Charlie had explored every last inch of the mansion's yard, and yet it suddenly felt unfamiliar and dangerous. He had a bad feeling about the figure he'd spotted, and he couldn't bring himself to go outside.

"Hey, Dad?" Charlie said.

"Hmmm?" Andrew Laird responded. He wasn't really listening.

"There's somebody hiding behind a tree in our yard."

The news got his attention. "What?"

"It's someone really short. I think it's been watching us through the windows."

"You're kidding." But Andrew Laird knew Charlie wasn't. He dropped his spoon and slapped the sheet of paper down onto the counter beside the stove. Without bothering to grab an umbrella or even put on shoes, he charged outside, pausing briefly at the back door to whistle for Rufus. The dog came running, barking wildly.

Charlie flipped the light switch by the back door and

headed for the parlor. He could see his father and Rufus patrolling the lawn, but the mysterious figure was long gone.

The pasta sauce was popping loudly as it began to boil on the stove. Charlie rushed back to the kitchen to turn down the heat. That was when he got a glimpse of the paper that Andrew Laird had left on the counter. Charlie didn't even need to snoop. A single glance was all he needed to see that it was a letter from the bank. The Lairds had until the end of the month to pay the mortgage—or they'd lose the purple mansion.

CHAPTER SEVENTEEN

THE PROPHECY

Charlie didn't say much at dinner. At first, Jack wouldn't stop pestering him with questions about the stranger who'd been lurking in the yard. Charlie responded with as few words as possible, even grunting whenever he could get away with it. Eventually Jack got the hint and focused on twirling as much pasta as possible onto his fork. Only when the glob of noodles was as big as a tennis ball would he take a bite.

Andrew Laird was just as quiet as

his sons. Charlie guessed his dad was worried about the same thing he was. *Parents like to think they're able to protect kids from bad news,* Charlie thought miserably, *but the kids always know when something's wrong.* In this case, even the *cat* knew. The mood at the table was so dark that Aggie was careful to keep her distance.

After dinner, Charlie and Jack cleaned up the dishes and said their goodnights to their dad. Then they headed upstairs to the tower. Usually Charlie would have waited until their father was asleep before he tried to open the portal. But tonight he had a pretty good feeling that Andrew Laird wouldn't be in the mood to check up on his sons. And Charlie didn't blame him.

It wasn't until Charlie and Jack were inside the tower that Charlie remembered what had been nagging at him earlier that day.

"Dabney said Bruce went through the portal this afternoon, but neither of us was here to open it."

Jack looked up at his brother in surprise. "Yeah, I forgot to tell you. It was still open when I came up here with Dabney."

"Do you think we might have left it open last night?" Charlie asked.

"Nope," Jack replied with a vigorous shake of his head. "You'd never forget to close it."

Charlie stared at the wall in front of them. It looked perfectly ordinary, which meant that the portal was shut.

"Do you think it could have opened on its own?" Jack asked. "Or maybe one of us opened it by accident, like when you went to the Netherworld the first time?"

Charlie was about to say no, when the wall suddenly disappeared. The Netherworld was right where it should be—only, Charlie was certain that his brother hadn't opened the portal.

"That wasn't me!" Jack yelped, answering Charlie's thoughts. "I swear!"

"I know," Charlie said. He could see a bit of what was in store for them. The nightmare on the other side was very real, and it was his. Charlie stepped over the threshold and into the Cypress Creek bank.

His father and Charlotte were sitting in front of a desk inside a glass-walled office. They looked more like mannequins than real human beings, which told Charlie that they were nothing but figments—products of his own imagination. But the creature behind the desk was no figment. It was an enormous wolf dressed in a dapper blue suit. The way the wolf kept licking its lips, there was no doubt in Charlie's mind that the beast planned to devour his parents. He'd been waiting for Charlie to show up and watch.

"I'm terribly sorry, but there's absolutely nothing we can do," the wolf was saying in a manner that indicated he wasn't sorry at all. "You couldn't pay your bills, so the old DeChant property belongs to the Amalgamated Bank of Cypress Creek now. If you haven't vacated the premises by the end of the month, we will be forced to send in a team of movers to assist you. At your expense, of course. Incidentally, if you'd like to open a credit card to pay for that, just let me know and I'll fetch you a form."

Charlie could hear his heart pounding in his ears. He'd conjured his very worst nightmare. His parents had lost their house—and the bank was about to eat his family alive. It was the first time in ages that Charlie's real fears had been strong enough to open the portal.

"What's going on?" whispered Jack. "Charlie, is this your nightmare? Why are you dreaming about Charlotte and Dad? And why are you so scared of the bank?"

Charlie looked at his little brother. What would happen if they lost their home? Would they have to move to some terrible house? Even worse—would he and Jack end up sharing a room? And how would they manage to protect the portal?

The wolf caught sight of them watching from the bank's lobby. He seemed particularly interested in Jack, whose back was turned to him. Charlie watched the Nightmare lift his snout and sniff at the air. Whatever he smelled seemed to make his mouth water. That was when Charlie realized that the wolf could tell the boys were there in the flesh.

"We need to get out of here now," Charlie told his

brother. He grabbed Jack by the arm and practically dragged him from the bank.

"But what about your nightmare?" Jack asked once they were outside on a street of the Netherworld's Cypress Creek. "You can't run away from it!"

"I know," Charlie told him. "Don't worry. I'll come back later and face it." He wasn't scared for himself anymore. There was something about the way that wolf had looked at Jack that made Charlie cringe.

They headed for the Netherworld courthouse. When they got there, they found it deserted. There were no longer any protestors shouting and waving signs. Even the guards seemed to have abandoned it.

"Where is everyone?" Jack asked. Charlie knew the answer, but he didn't say it out loud. The Nightmare creatures had all hit the road. The hole was growing, and it was only a matter of time before it managed to swallow the entire town. Before they'd fled, though, one of the Nightmares had taken the time to leave a message on the courthouse wall. In large red letters it said, *BEWARE THE PROPHECY. FIND THE SMALL HUMAN.* Charlie looked down at his brother. He'd almost forgotten about the Netherworld prophecy—that one day a child would come, a child with the strength to destroy all Nightmares.

"Hey, fellas!" someone called, and Charlie nearly jumped out of his skin. "What are you waiting for, you big lug? Take me over to see my friends, or I'm gonna start screaming my head off again."

Charlie spotted a miserable-looking couple heading his way. The woman had purple bags beneath her eyes and patches of something nasty all over her sweater. Her empty stare was that of a figment. The man by her side was the dreamer. His eyeglasses were cracked, and his hair hadn't been washed in days. He was toting a small creature dressed in bright red overalls with an embroidered Cookie Monster on the front.

"Say hello to my new parents," Bruce said with a nasty chuckle. "Suckers don't know what hit 'em."

Apparently Bruce was already back to work as a changeling. The man he was with must have just had a baby. The dad was afraid the kid might be a monster, and Bruce got to play the part.

"Hi," Charlie said, and the man flinched.

"You gonna be rude to my friends?" Bruce asked his temporary father. "Just for that, I'm gonna leave you a little something *special* in my diaper."

"That's okay," Charlie assured the changeling. "We weren't offended. Hey, listen, Bruce. There's something I need to ask you. Dabney said that when you got to the mansion this afternoon, the portal was open." It was bugging him more and more.

"Yep," Bruce confirmed.

"Did you see anyone who might have opened it?"

"Nope," said Bruce. "I just came right through and got back to work."

"Wow, that fast?" Jack asked.

Bruce scratched at his five o'clock shadow. "Yeah, well, after I delivered the tonic to Medusa, the call went out for a changeling in Cypress Creek. No one else is taking jobs here anymore, but I s'pose this place has grown on me. I figured I oughta spend a little more time in town before it all goes down the hole."

"What hole?" asked the man.

Bruce reached up and gave the dream dad's chin a playful pinch. "You don't need to worry about it, sweet cheeks," Bruce answered. "In fact, way things are heading, you ain't gonna have to be worried about anything at all pretty soon."

"How long do you think we have before the hole destroys the town?" Charlie asked.

"Saw it this afternoon when I got here." Bruce whistled. "Unless Medusa figures something out pretty fast, I figure this place's got a day left—two at the most."

"Where *is* Medusa?" Jack asked, looking around at the empty streets.

"Up at that cave of hers," Bruce said. "Not sure she's gonna be able to do much with the tonic I dropped off, though. She was pretty busy when I got there. Had one eye glued to that telescope the whole time."

"Telescope?" Charlie asked.

"Yeah. She's watching that lighthouse. It's a real tourist destination these days. Seems to be pretty popular with the goblin crowd. They've been coming over the border by the hundreds. They ain't done nothing yet, but *something's* got them crawling out of the muck."

Charlie shot his little brother a grave look. "We need to go see Medusa."

"Be careful and stay outta sight," Bruce warned them. "Everyone around here is hunting for some little human. They think he's the one who's been smuggling stuff to the other side."

Charlie glanced at his brother again.

"They think it's me, don't they?" Jack asked. He actually looked worried.

"Of course not," Charlie told him, hiding the truth with a forced smile.

Near the top of Medusa's mountain, the trees thinned out, and there was a perfect view of the giant abyss below. Charlie kept his eye on the hole as they climbed, and he could see that it was still expanding in every direction. As tired as the sight made him, Charlie picked up his pace. Jack stayed right by his side.

When they knocked on Medusa's door, she answered immediately. Her snakes were a writhing mass on her head, and her normally long blood-red nails had been chewed down to the quick.

"Boys!" she exclaimed as she ushered them inside. "You must leave the Netherworld immediately—and this time you cannot return. It's not safe here for humans. It's not safe for anyone anymore."

Charlie spied the bottle of tonic sitting on a small table beside the front door. He had a hunch that was right where Bruce had left it.

"You haven't opened the tonic," he said.

"Of course I have!" Medusa snapped. "But it's not going to give us the answer we need. And now there are new problems to face. Take a look through the telescope and see for yourself."

Charlie went to the telescope as he was told and pulled it down to his eyes. In the distance he could see the lighthouse. The enormous lantern at the very top of the structure was brightly lit. It cast a bold white beam across the border and into goblin territory. It was acting as a beacon, Charlie realized. And crowded around the base of the lighthouse were thousands of goblins.

"What are they doing?" he asked.

"They appear to be waiting for something," Medusa said. "I've sent all my best troops out there, and I pray they'll be able to reach the lighthouse in time. If the door opens and those goblins find their way inside and through the portal, the results could be catastrophic."

Charlie thought of the Harpy who'd been sent to investigate the lighthouse. "Ava's still in Maine." *And in terrible danger,* he realized.

"Have you had any word from her?" Medusa asked.

Charlie shook his head. He could see his own fears reflected in Medusa's face. If the goblins were able to cross through to the Waking World, their friend Ava—and the entire state of Maine—might soon have some very unwelcome visitors.

"Goblins or no goblins, we still need an antidote to the tonic," he told Medusa. "If Charlotte can find out what it's made of, she might be able to come up with an antidote and stop the hole from swallowing the Netherworld."

Medusa shook her head. "I told you, the answer we need isn't in the tonic. The substances that were used to make it don't have the power to keep humans from dreaming."

"But I've seen what it does!" Charlie argued.

"The tonic's power doesn't come from an herb or a mushroom," Medusa said. "The tonic's power comes from the hand that made it. Its secret ingredient is *despair*."

CHAPTER EIGHTEEN

OPEN FOR BUSINESS

Medusa's discovery was a serious setback. It had kept Charlie awake long after he'd returned from the Netherworld. Before he'd finally fallen asleep, he'd set his alarm for eight, hoping to make it downtown for the eight-thirty grand opening of the Cypress Creek branch of Tranquility Tonight. Unfortunately, he'd hit the snooze button a few too many times. Now it was ten minutes past nine, and there were already four people waiting in line outside the tonic shop. One of them was Ollie Tobias's mother.

To Charlie's surprise, Rocco Marquez was there too, clutching a stack of papers and handing one out to each person who passed. Few people bothered to glance down at the paper, though. Most wadded it up into a ball and threw it away without looking. Charlie could see that the trash can at the end of the block was already filled with them.

"Don't drink the tonic!" Rocco was shouting at a man who was swinging a leather briefcase. The man took a flyer and offered Rocco the stink eye in return.

"Tranquility Tonic will eat your brain!" Rocco told a woman on her way to work at the ice cream parlor.

"Excuse me?" It was Mrs. Tobias, calling out to Rocco from her place at the front of the Tranquility Tonight line. "Excuse me, young man. Are you a doctor?"

"No," Rocco told her. "But I've seen firsthand what the tonic can do."

Mrs. Tobias gave the next person in line a satisfied smirk and then turned back to Rocco. "So you're *not* a doctor," she sniffed.

"Of course not," Rocco replied. He was clearly getting frustrated. "I'm *twelve*."

Mrs. Tobias looked down her nose and cocked her head. She was putting on a show for everyone watching. "Then you should leave the medical advice to professionals. My child has been suffering from terrible nightmares, and I have it on good authority that the tonic will cure him. Perhaps a twelve-year-old like you should be at home playing with his toys instead of preventing people from getting the help they need."

"Playing with my *toys*?" Rocco repeated as Charlie drew near. That was when Charlie decided it was best to step in.

"What's going on?" Charlie asked his friend.

"Charlie!" Rocco cried in surprise. He sounded desperate. "What does it look like? I'm doing my best to save Cypress Creek! I tried to find you and Alfie and Paige after I got home from my game yesterday, but you were all missing! Then I heard that the tonic store was opening today, and I figured I had to take matters into my own hands. But no one is listening to me, Charlie! I feel like that kid Geppetto in that story with the naked emperor and the three dwarves where the sky was falling—"

Charlie grabbed Rocco by the shoulders. "It's okay," he said as calmly as he could. "I'm here."

"Well, well, well!" Mrs. Tobias's shrill voice broke Charlie's focus, and his arms dropped to his sides. "Look who it is. If it isn't Charlotte Laird's extremely *observant* stepson. By the way, Mr. Laird, I'm observant too, and I noticed that Hazel's Herbarium is closed today. And from what I hear, it's going to stay that way."

The woman had found Charlie's weak spot, and he felt his fists clenching. "You heard wrong," Charlie said. He turned to face the woman at the front of the line. "My stepmom is just in New York visiting publishers. She's going to be a bestselling author."

In the brief moment before Mrs. Tobias could answer, the sound of a key turning in a lock filled the silence. It was the shop's front door. Mrs. Tobias snickered, then, in a saccharine-sweet voice said, "Of *course* she is. Now if you children will excuse me, I have a purchase to make."

Ollie's mother opened the shop's door, and Charlie rushed forward to get a quick peek inside. He made it in time to get an eyeful, but the Shopkeeper was nowhere to be seen. Behind the counter stood a well-groomed Walker wearing an enormous blond wig. Charlie was certain it was the same woman who'd been handing out pamphlets in front of the shop the day before. When Mrs. Tobias turned and slammed the door in his face, Charlie returned to where Rocco was standing and nudged the boy with his elbow. "Come on," he said.

"I can't!" Rocco's eyes were wild. "I need to stay here and warn everyone!"

"They're not going to listen," Charlie answered. "But I know someone who will."

They rang the doorbell three times before the housekeeper opened the door at the Tobiases' house. She'd obviously just woken up from a nap. Someone had drawn a purple Magic Marker mustache above her lip.

"May I help you?" she asked wearily.

"We'd like to see Ollie," Charlie told her.

"Are you sure?" the housekeeper asked.

"Of course," Rocco answered, sounding a bit confused.

"Oliver!" the woman shouted.

There was a sound that could have been a herd of elephants pounding down the stairs, and Ollie appeared at the front door.

"You've got company," the housekeeper told him.

"Thank you, Mrs. Hawthorne," Ollie said kindly. "By the way, have I told you how lovely you look today?"

Charlie had to force himself not to laugh as the housekeeper narrowed her eyes and turned to look in the mirror by the door. "Oliver!" she screeched. Then she turned to Charlie and Rocco. "Can you keep him busy for five minutes while I wash this mustache off?"

"Certainly," Charlie told her, trying his best to sound reliable.

The housekeeper stalked off, and Ollie greeted his friends as if nothing were out of the ordinary. "Hey, Charlie. Hey, Rocco," he said. "What's up?"

"We just saw your mother in town," Charlie said. "She was standing in line at the new Tranquility Tonight store. We're here to tell you that whatever you do, you shouldn't drink the tonic."

"I have to," Ollie said. Charlie had never heard him sound quite so serious.

"No, you don't," Rocco insisted. "When she gives it to you, throw it out the window or flush it down the toilet. Come on—you're Ollie Tobias. You'll think of some way to get out of it!"

Ollie shook his head. "You don't understand. I've been having terrible nightmares. I can barely get to sleep at night."

Now that he mentioned it, Ollie did look tired, Charlie thought.

"But the tonic won't just get rid of your nightmares," Charlie explained. "It will keep you from dreaming and eat your brain."

Ollie shrugged. "I don't care," he said.

Charlie cast a look at Rocco, who was already eyeing him. It wasn't the response either of them had anticipated. Whatever Ollie saw in his dreams had to be pretty bad.

"What are your nightmares about?" Rocco asked.

"A little girl," Ollie said. Charlie noticed that the kid was trembling slightly as he spoke. And his usually ruddy face had gone pale. "She follows me around every night. I've only seen her a couple of times, but she's always watching me. I feel awful whenever she's around. I think she's going to do something terrible."

"Nightmares can't hurt you, Ollie. But you can't run from them either," Charlie counseled. "You have to figure out what really scares you and face it. Otherwise you'll just keep having the same nightmare every night."

"I know what scares me," Ollie said, suddenly annoyed instead of scared. "It's the little girl. And she's not just a regular old Nightmare. I think I saw her in town today."

"You *saw* her?" Charlie asked.

"Just what do you think you're doing!" a woman shouted up from the sidewalk. "Get off my porch, you grade-school hoodlums!"

Charlie grimaced at the sound of Mrs. Tobias's voice, but he didn't turn around. "You have to trust me," Charlie told Ollie. "Don't drink the tonic. There are other ways to conquer your nightmares. There's a book I could show you—"

"I'm calling the police!" Mrs. Tobias was charging up the stairs, a brown paper bag clutched in one hand.

"She's not joking. She calls them all the time," Ollie said. "She has them on speed dial. Thanks for dropping by, guys, but you'd better go."

Charlie and Rocco walked back toward town, discouraged.

"What the heck is *speed dial*?" Rocco asked.

All Charlie could offer was a miserable shrug.

"Nobody believes us," Rocco muttered. "Not even the town's best-known juvenile delinquent."

"Yeah, and how can a little girl be all that scary, anyway?" Charlie groused. "It's not like Ollie's dreaming about a witch who wants to eat him. Or an evil principal who wants to make him repeat the seventh grade."

"Don't knock little girls," Rocco said, bumping Charlie with his shoulder. "Little girls can be totally scary. Aren't you best friends with Paige? She's the scariest person in town when she wants to be. And who knows, maybe the girl in Ollie's nightmare is a cannibal or something."

"Maybe," Charlie admitted. "But I've spent plenty of time in the Netherworld, and I haven't seen too many Nightmare creatures disguised as little girls. Giant grubs, yes. Talking cockroaches, sure. Little girls, no."

But even as he said it, Charlie realized that Ollie wasn't the only one who'd encountered a little girl in the Netherworld. Meduso had seen one too—trapped inside ICK and INK's lighthouse. It seemed like a weird coincidence.

"So what are we going to do now?" Rocco asked, breaking Charlie's concentration.

There wasn't much they *could* do. "I guess we'll just have to wait for my stepmom," Charlie said. And hope she could come up with an antidote for despair, he added to himself.

"There you are!" Andrew Laird barked when Charlie and Rocco walked through the door of the purple mansion. "Hello, Rocco. It's nice to see you," he added in a more civil tone. "Please excuse me while I yell at my son." Then he turned back to Charlie. "Where have you been? I need to leave for work! It's almost ten o'clock, and my first class started at nine-thirty. When Charlotte and I are both gone, it's your job to watch after your brother!"

Charlie had completely forgotten. "Sorry, Dad. I went downtown to see the new Tranquility Tonight store," he said. "I didn't think I'd be gone so long."

Andrew Laird's eyes lit up. "It's open?" he asked. "I might just stop by. I've been having the worst dreams lately, and—"

"Dad, no!" Charlie nearly screamed. Then he recovered his composure. "Remember what Charlotte's friend

Dabney told you? The tonic makes your breath smell like kitty litter."

Andrew Laird yawned and rubbed his eyes. "Might be worth trying it anyway," he said. "I can't go another twenty-four hours without a good night's sleep."

"Just wait," Charlie practically begged. "Wait for Charlotte to get home. She might get upset if you take anything without talking to her. Maybe she has something better to give you."

"Good point," Andrew Laird said. Nothing pleased him more than Charlie's newfound appreciation for his stepmother. "And if I'm going to have kitty litter breath, I should probably pass it by her first. Now I gotta run to work. Charlie, stick around the house today, would you?"

Charlie didn't even bother to argue. For the first time in days, there was nothing else for him to do but wait for something to happen—and waiting wasn't his specialty. He needed something to keep him from going crazy with worry. So he went out to the front porch and began tending to the plants. Rocco tagged along, and together they watered the herbs, repotted a passion flower, and gave the milk thistle a nourishing layer of cow dung.

At around ten-thirty, Jack joined them, still dressed in his pajamas. The three of them weeded, trimmed, and hoed. Few words were spoken. Charlie was too busy thinking through the situation. The people of Cypress Creek were lining up along Main Street to purchase a tonic that would turn them into Walkers. Thousands of goblins had gathered outside the Netherworld lighthouse—and they appeared to be waiting to invade Maine. ICK and INK seemed to be responsible for everything. But why? What was their plan? Try as he might, Charlie couldn't figure it out.

Just before noon, Rocco headed home for lunch. Charlie and his brother were tending to the Saint-John's-wort when Charlie heard someone coming up the drive. He turned to see a man in a pin-striped blue suit making his way toward the mansion. He had slicked-back hair and a fancy gold watch, and he smelled like he'd recently bathed in cologne. When the man greeted the boys with a wide, toothy smile, Charlie knew he'd seen the guy somewhere before. He stood up and brushed the dirt off his hands.

"Good afternoon, young man. I'm looking for Mrs. Charlotte Laird. Is she at home?"

"No," Charlie said curtly. He'd taken an instant dislike to the man. "She's out of town."

"You must be one of her stepsons." The man hadn't stopped smiling. "Let me guess. Charles? Am I right?"

"How did you know?" Charlie asked, surprised.

Before the man could answer, Jack appeared. "Hi," he said.

The man bent down and made a show of shaking the boy's hand. "And you must be Jack."

Jack looked over at Charlie and back at the man. "Who are you?" he asked bluntly.

"My name is Curtis Swanson." The name made Charlie's stomach churn. He'd seen the man's signature on several letters. "Your stepmother is a client of mine."

"You're from the bank," Charlie said.

"That's right!" Mr. Swanson exclaimed, acting as if Charlie had won the lottery. "I was hoping to have a word with your stepmother about an important business matter, but . . ."

"You look like the wolf," Jack said, recalling Charlie's nightmare.

"Excuse me?" Mr. Swanson asked, glancing from boy to boy, confused.

Charlie picked up a shovel and drove its sharp edge into the ground. "I told you. Charlotte is *not here,*" he said.

Curtis Swanson's smile was so wide that it almost seemed to wrap around his entire head. "Yes, and I heard you. So I'm just going to have a quick look around the property and take a few pictures before I go. Don't mind me!" He started off across the lawn, his eyes inspecting every inch of the building. "It's going to need some serious fixing up. And a new coat of paint to cover that purple," Swanson murmured to himself.

Charlie followed the man, Jack jogging alongside him. "Charlie, why is that guy just like the wolf from your dream?" Jack asked. "And what the heck is he talking about?"

Charlie knew the answer. He'd read the letters with Curtis Swanson's signature at the bottom. Swanson ran the bank that was trying to take their home away.

"No idea what they see in this place," Curtis Swanson muttered as he snapped photos of the front porch and the tower above.

"Who?" Charlie demanded. "What *who* sees in this place?"

"The people who intend to purchase this house," Curtis Swanson answered absentmindedly.

"Our house is for sale?" Jack asked.

"No." Charlie could feel the rage building inside him. "It *isn't*."

"Not officially," Swanson told Jack. "It won't go on the market until the end of the month. After we foreclose."

"What?" Jack asked, but the man was on the move again.

Charlie was on the verge of losing it, when a single thought popped into his head. It was an evil idea. But it was a chance to save the purple mansion. He hurried after the banker.

"By the way, Mr. Swanson, have you seen the new store that's opened up in town?" he asked. "It's just down the street from your bank, and the tonic it's selling seems to be really popular." He felt terrible recommending the tonic. But maybe it could do some good after all. Charlie could almost believe that turning a man like Curtis Swanson into a Walker would be a service to mankind.

Curtis Swanson glanced down at Charlie. "Are you talking about Tranquility Tonight? As a matter of fact, the gentleman who owns the store is one of the people who intend to purchase this house."

"The Shopkeeper?" Charlie blurted.

"Yes," said the banker. "I suppose he *is* a shopkeeper. He's moving to Cypress Creek soon, and I'm helping him and the girl find a place to live."

"What girl?" Charlie asked. It was the third time a girl had popped into one of Charlie's conversations in less than twenty-four hours.

Curtis Swanson didn't answer. Instead, he looked back up at the purple mansion. "They have their hearts set on this house. He's promised me a case of his special tonic when the deal is done."

"Don't drink the tonic," Jack warned him. "The stuff is poison."

Charlie could have throttled his brother. But when he saw Jack's expression, Charlie knew in his heart that the kid had done the right thing. Charlie couldn't let misfortune turn him into a monster.

"I'm sorry," said the banker. He crouched down so he could look Jack straight in the eye. "What was that you just said, young man?"

"He said don't drink the tonic," Charlie told the banker. "Now get off this lawn before I call the police. You're not going to take my house."

"I'm afraid I am, but there's no need to be rude about it," the man replied, completely unruffled. He tucked his camera phone into his pocket. "Now that I have what I came for, I'm happy to leave. And by the way, when you're a few years older, stop by the bank, and we'll get you pre-approved for your first credit card."

CHAPTER NINETEEN

THE HAND THAT MADE IT

Charlie and Jack spent the rest of the afternoon inside with the doors locked and the shades down. Shortly after the sun set, they heard a car in the drive. The boys left what they were doing and sprinted for the door. Andrew Laird came in the house carrying Charlotte's suitcase. He dropped it by the stairs, where it landed with a loud thump.

"Be super-nice to Charlotte," he whispered to Charlie and Jack. "She's had a really tough day."

Charlie's heart sank. Charlotte's meeting with the second publisher had been that morning. The publisher must not have wanted the book. The Laird family's last chance to come up with the money they needed to save the purple mansion was gone. Soon the Shopkeeper would buy their house. The Laird family would be evicted. The portal would fall into the bad guys' hands, and another child would call the mansion home. *The little girl*. Charlie's thoughts returned to her for the hundredth time that day. Who was she? Had she been kidnapped like the girl Meduso had seen in the lighthouse?

Charlie heard Charlotte's footsteps on the front porch stairs.

"So did you boys go into town this afternoon?" Andrew Laird asked loudly enough for his wife to overhear. He obviously didn't want Charlotte to think that he and the boys had been talking about her. "There sure are some weird folks wandering around Cypress Creek today. We just drove down Main Street on our way back from the airport, and it looks like some kind of zombie convention out there."

"Does that mean I'm too late?" When Charlotte finally appeared, she didn't look like herself at all. Her green eyes had lost their twinkle. Even her bright orange hair seemed duller.

"Yay, you're back!" Jack shouted, leaping into his stepmother's arms.

Charlie waited patiently. "You're not too late," he told Charlotte when it was his turn to hug her. "But things are happening really fast. Those people you and Dad saw are all from Orville Falls. They came here to build the new store."

The Cypress Creek branch of Tranquility Tonight had opened that morning. In less than twelve hours, they would start to see the damage that the tonic had done to their town.

Andrew Laird planted a kiss on the top of his wife's head. "I'll take your bag upstairs. Then I'll start getting dinner ready. Sound good to you?"

Charlotte gave her husband a weak smile. "Yep, sounds fine," she said, but Charlie could tell that she hadn't really been listening. As she spoke, her eyes roamed the mansion, taking in as much as they could. She knew that by the end of the month, the house that had been in her family for a hundred and fifty years would belong to someone else. Charlie didn't have it in him to tell her *who*. It was a serious problem, one that Charlotte didn't look ready to deal with.

"Great!" Andrew Laird was clearly trying to keep his wife's spirits up. "Then everyone meet me in the kitchen in twenty minutes. I'll have dinner on the table! Jack, you want to come help me?"

"Not really," Jack replied. "I want to talk to Charlotte."

"Jack." Andrew Laird lowered his voice. "I could *really* use your help."

"Oh, fine," Jack said, stomping off with a huff.

Charlie followed Charlotte into the drawing room.

"I'm sorry, kiddo," she said, dropping down onto one of the purple sofas.

"For what?" Charlie asked.

"I failed," Charlotte said. "I couldn't sell the book."

Charlie hated to see her like this. "You tried your best. Isn't that all that counts? What did the second publisher say?"

"She thought the Netherworld would make a great setting for a teen romance novel," Charlotte said. "She wanted one of the main characters to fall in love with Meduso."

"*What?*" It was so absurd that Charlie started to laugh. A few seconds later, Charlotte cracked up too. But her laughter didn't last long.

She looked around the purple drawing room, her eyes skimming over the books on the room's ceiling-high bookshelves. "You know, I used to play in here when I was little. I liked to climb those shelves. I had this weird idea that all of the best books were hidden on top, where kids couldn't reach them. Later on, I told my mother, and she confessed that she'd done the same thing." Charlie saw a tear trickle down Charlotte's cheek. "I really thought my book could save this place, Charlie. But I let our family down. And I let my family down too. A DeChant has lived in this house for the past one hundred and fifty years. Now it's going to be sold to another family."

Charlie took a seat beside her on the sofa. "Isn't there *something* we can do?" he asked. He wasn't ready to give up.

Charlotte tried to smile but didn't quite succeed. "I don't think we can save the mansion, Charlie. So let's focus on curing the Walkers," she said. "Where's the bottle of tonic that Bruce stole from the shop in Orville Falls?"

"Hold on," Charlie told her. Bruce had left a bottle of the tonic on Charlotte's desk in the tower room. Charlie ran up the two flights of stairs to the room, grabbed the little sapphire-blue bottle, and ran back down as fast as he could. Working to catch his breath, he handed the bottle to his stepmother and watched, hopefully, as she uncorked it and inhaled deeply. She grimaced at the smell.

"Did Medusa figure out what's in it?" Charlotte asked.

Charlie frowned. He wished he had an answer that Charlotte could use. "Medusa said that the main ingredient is despair."

"Despair?" Charlotte laughed. "But that's not an ingredient! You can't find an antidote to that."

"Medusa said the despair came from whoever made it."

Charlotte handed the bottle back to Charlie. "If that's what gives the tonic its power, then there's nothing I can do," she told her stepson.

"Maybe there is," Charlie replied. He wouldn't let her

give up. "Does this look familiar to
you?" He took out the lip balm that
Paige had found at her aunt Josephine's house. "A lady Walker had
it. The smell of it wakes her up
for a second or two."

Charlotte held the little container between her index
finger and thumb. "I made this," she said. "It's lip balm."

"Do you remember what ingredients you used?" Charlie asked.

Charlotte twisted off the container's cap and held the
balm up to her nose. Her forehead crinkled as she tried to
identify the contents. "It's the usual stuff. Beeswax. Coco-
nut oil. But this isn't one of my regular scents," she said,
giving it another sniff. "It's honeysuckle. It must have been
a special order."

"You made it for a person named Josephine," Charlie
said, realizing that he didn't know her last name.

"Josephine. Is she a pretty blond woman?" Charlotte
asked. "A few years younger than me?"

"That's the one," Charlie said. "She's Paige's aunt."

Charlotte's eyes twinkled for the first time since she'd
arrived home. "I remember Josephine!" she exclaimed.
"She was in the shop this spring. She told me she'd come
to town to look after her niece. I should have realized she
was Paige's aunt. They look just alike!"

"Josephine visits sometimes when Paige's mom is sick," Charlie said. He didn't need to say any more. Everyone in Cypress Creek knew that Paige's mom was sick a lot.

"Ah," said Charlotte solemnly. "Paige's mom must be the sister Josephine told me about."

"What did she say?"

"Well, we started talking, and Josephine told me that she and her sister grew up in Cypress Creek. They're both a bit younger than I am, so I never met them during the time I lived here. When I told Josephine that I'd inherited the purple mansion from my grandmother, she laughed and said that she and her sister had discovered a special hiding spot under the honeysuckle vines that grow along the mansion's fence. She said the smell of honeysuckle always made her think of those days."

"So that's why you put honeysuckle into Josephine's lip balm."

"I thought it would help keep her spirits up while she was here," Charlotte said. Then she smiled sadly and put her arm around her stepson. "But there's nothing in that lip balm that's going to help us, Charlie. It's made of very ordinary stuff."

"But it wakes Josephine up for a few seconds whenever she smells it!" Charlie argued.

"Wait—you're saying that Josephine is one of the

Walkers?" Charlotte looked stricken. She'd only just made the connection.

"She's the aunt that Paige is helping in Orville Falls."

Charlie watched as his stepmother crumpled. "Well, there's our explanation," she said. "It's not the lip balm that's waking Josephine up. It's the memory of her sister. And I can't put *that* into a bottle."

CHAPTER TWENTY

WE ASKED SO NICELY

Charlie went to bed in a terrible mood. It got worse when he fell asleep and found himself sitting in an office at the Netherworld bank.

"Well, hello there," said the wolf on the other side of the desk. He grinned at Charlie and flashed a perfect row of razor-sharp teeth. A scrap of blue denim was stuck between two incisors. The beast had recently eaten.

Fear surged through Charlie's body, but he refused to move from his seat. The Nightmare wanted him to run away—and he wasn't going to give the wolf what he wanted.

"It's too bad you weren't here in time to join me for lunch," the wolf said. He took a toothpick out of his desk. "Your stepmother was absolutely *scrumptious*."

"This is only a nightmare," Charlie said out loud to remind himself. He'd been to the Netherworld many times, but his own scary dreams still had the power to terrify him. The Nightmare creatures knew how to put on a good show, and their attention to detail was impeccable. He could see Charlotte's handbag in the wastepaper basket and one of her favorite shoes sticking out from beneath the wolf's desk.

"*Is* it only a nightmare?" The wolf slid out of his seat and slunk across the room on all fours. He sniffed at Charlie. "So it is," he said, sounding quite disappointed. "What a shame you aren't here in the flesh tonight. I've heard that children your age make delightful desserts."

"You don't fool me," Charlie sneered. "You've never eaten anyone. I'm having a nightmare about a hungry wolf because I'm worried that the bank will take away our house."

The wolf sprang back into his seat and grinned at Charlie from across the desk. "So you know how our system works," he noted with what sounded at first like real admiration. Then his voice grew dark. "But that doesn't change the fact that Mr. Swanson and his bank really *will* take the house."

That wasn't what Charlie wanted to hear at all. He crossed his arms. "There could still be time to save it," he fought back.

"Are you sure?" the wolf asked. "The way things are looking right now, by the beginning of August, your enemies will be living in the purple mansion. Every human in Cypress Creek will be hooked on Tranquility Tonic. The hole out there will have swallowed your entire Netherworld town. And do you know what the very best part is?" With both of his paws on the desk, the wolf looked ready to pounce at any moment.

"What?" Charlie asked defiantly.

"Your little brother is going to take the blame. Everyone here thinks he's responsible."

"But that doesn't even make sense!" Charlie insisted. "Jack's only nine years old!"

The wolf shrugged. "Be sure to tell my fellow Nightmares that when they find your brother," he said. "And in case you're wondering, Charlie Laird, they *will* find your brother." He pointed out the office window.

Charlie looked and saw flyers taped to every lamppost and tree. He couldn't read them from where he sat, but he could tell that each featured a picture of the same boy.

"Go ahead. Have a look," the wolf urged him. "I'm through with you for the moment. I have paperwork to do."

Charlie left the bank. Outside, the walls of the building were covered with the same flyers that Charlie had seen from the window. In the center of each was a photo of Jack, along with the words:

WANTED FOR CRIMES AGAINST NIGHTMARES
DON'T LET THE PROPHECY COME TRUE!
FIND THE BOY!
SAVE THE NETHERWORLD!

The wolf hadn't been lying. The Nightmare creatures had turned against Jack. A loud crack came from behind him. Charlie didn't just hear it—he felt it in his bones. He turned in time to see a crevasse open up through the middle of the square. It was only a few inches wide. He could step right over it. Nothing bigger than a mouse could have fallen inside, but Charlie knew that it was just the beginning.

He was about to leave, when he caught a glimpse of something unusual out of the corner of his eye. There was a new flyer on the wall. It hadn't been there when he'd turned away.

If you try to stop us, Charlie Laird,
we'll turn your brother in.
ICK & INK

He recognized the handwriting. It was the same cursive script he'd seen on the OPEN sign at the Orville Falls Tranquility Tonight store.

"Hello?" he called out. The flyer couldn't have appeared out of thin air. Even in the Netherworld, that wasn't how things worked. Someone must have put it there while his back was turned.

Charlie felt eyes on him, and the sensation made his skin crawl. The hairs on his arms stood on end, and a feeling of dread spread over his body. It was the same horrible feeling he'd had the night before, when he'd caught someone watching him through the window of the purple mansion. But this time Charlie noticed a peculiar smell in the air. It was a mixture of fragrances—tea leaves, sea salt, and lavender soap. Together, they smelled strangely *human*.

Charlie opened his eyes and immediately flipped on his bedside lamp. He was back in the Waking World, but he still sensed he was being watched. The feeling was horrible. Charlie hadn't felt so scared in months. But he knew he couldn't let it get to him. He forced his legs over the side of the bed.

The hallway outside his room was still and silent, but it wasn't quite dark. A thin strip of light shone from beneath the bathroom door. Someone was inside. He was about to

investigate, when the door to his parents' room opened.
Charlotte, half-asleep and dressed in her nightgown, walked
the short distance to the bathroom and opened the door.

"Psssst!" Charlie said, but it was too late. She'd already
shut the door behind her. Two seconds later, he heard
a scream and Charlotte burst out of the bathroom. She
screeched again when she saw Charlie—and he shrieked
in reply.

"They've been here!" Charlotte half whispered, one
hand over her heart. "We have to search the house."

"I'll wake up Dad," Charlie said.

"No," Charlotte said. "Don't do that! Not yet!"

"Why not?" Charlie asked.

Charlotte bit her lip. Her eyes shot back to the bathroom
door. Charlie cautiously pushed the door open. There was
no one there.

"I don't see anything," he told his stepmother.

"You're not looking," she told him.

He moved farther into the bathroom. That was when he
noticed it. A message written in soap on the mirror above
the sink.

> You should have come.
> We asked so nicely.
> Now we've found you.
> ICK & INK

"Charlotte? Honey? What's going on? Is everyone okay?" It was Andrew Laird's voice in the hallway.

Charlie grabbed a washcloth and quickly wiped the message off the mirror.

"We're fine, sweetheart," Charlie heard Charlotte say. "Charlie and I just heard noises and ended up surprising each other, that's all."

Charlie stepped out into the hall. "I thought there was someone inside the house," he said. "I'm just going to have a quick look around."

Andrew Laird raised an eyebrow. "Mind if I join you?" he asked. "You can be the brains. I'll be the muscle."

"And I'll be the eyes and ears," Charlotte said. "I'm coming too."

Charlie and his parents canvassed the entire mansion. Charlie volunteered to check the tower, charging up the stairs before his dad could have a look. When he arrived, the portal was sealed and the room was empty.

Downstairs, there wasn't a single window unlocked or door left open. Nobody was hiding under any of the beds or inside any of the closets. By the time they reached the kitchen, every inch of the house had been searched.

"Well," Andrew Laird said at last. "I think it's safe to go back to bed."

"My nerves are still a bit rattled, honey," Charlotte said. "I think I'll stay down here and have some warm milk."

"Me too," said Charlie, though there was nothing he found more revolting than the idea of warm milk.

"Suit yourselves," said Charlie's dad. "I'm going to get some sleep."

As soon as they heard Andrew Laird's footsteps on the second floor, Charlotte leaned in and whispered, "They were here! ICK and INK!"

"I got a message from them too," Charlie said. "Right before you got yours."

"Where did they leave it?" Charlotte asked. "In your room?"

"No, in the Netherworld." Then Charlie realized what that meant. ICK and INK had left a message for him in the Netherworld just minutes before they'd left one for Charlotte in the Waking World. There was only one way to get from one place to the other so quickly.

Charlotte gasped. "They came through our portal."

"But that's not possible!" Charlie insisted. "I thought the only ones who could go through our portal were me and Jack." Then Charlie remembered that Bruce had found the portal open—and neither Charlie nor Jack had opened it.

"If ICK and INK's lighthouse has a portal," Charlotte said, "maybe they're able to pass through our portal too."

Charlie looked up at the ceiling. "We should lock the

door to the tower. That will keep them out of the rest of our house."

"You really think that's going to do much good?" Charlotte asked.

Charlie sighed. Charlotte was right. If ICK and INK had made a tonic that turned people into Walkers, it seemed unlikely that they'd let a single locked door stand in their way.

∽ CHAPTER TWENTY-ONE ∽

STORMY SKIES

"Charlie!" Jack was shaking him. Charlie was hoping the little boy would go away. He'd been up with Charlotte half the night. "Charlie. Charlie!"

"What?" Charlie finally shouted, sitting up so suddenly that his brother nearly fell on his butt with surprise. "It's seven-thirty in the morning!"

"I know, but you gotta get up. Dad made pancakes, and he wants to have a family meeting before he goes to work. Plus, Alfie's on the phone." Jack tossed the phone onto Charlie's sheets and hightailed it out of the room.

Charlie picked up the device. "Alfie? Have you looked at your clock? It's seven-thirty in the morning."

"Get up and get over here!" Alfie shrieked, and Charlie held the phone away from his ear. "It's terrible! We've got to do something right away!"

"Calm down," Charlie ordered, heart thumping. "What happened?"

"It's Stormy! They got to her!"

"Stormy Skies?" Charlie asked. "The weather lady? The one you have a crush on?" He was out of bed in an instant and flying down the stairs toward the television in the purple mansion's drawing room.

"She's a *meteorologist,*" Alfie corrected him for the two hundredth time. "Or she used to be. Now she's just a Walker." Alfie's voice broke on the last word.

In the drawing room, Charlie found the remote control wedged between two couch cushions. He pressed the *on* button and turned the TV to channel four, where an ad for mattresses was playing.

"I checked the news this morning—strictly to see what was going on with world politics, of course—and there she was, pointing at complex weather systems and grunting like a gorilla," Alfie wailed. "We have to do something, Charlie. We have to save her!"

"Take it easy, Alfie," Charlie said. "I know you love Stormy, but—"

"I do *not* love Stormy!" Alfie cut him off. "It's just, if something happens to Stormy, how will anyone know what the weather will be?"

"It's summer, Alfie," Charlie said. "The weather is hot. Every day. Hot."

The commercial playing on the television ended, and channel four returned to the news. Suddenly Charlie's eyes were glued to the television, where Stormy Skies was supposed to be giving a morning weather update. The makeup people at the television station had done their best, but they couldn't disguise the fact that there was something very, very wrong with the station's meteorologist. Charlie

watched Stormy's face grow larger as she moved off her mark and shuffled toward the camera. Then an enormous bloodshot eyeball appeared as the weatherwoman tried to look through the lens.

Andrew Laird poked his head into the drawing room. "Charlie? We're going to have a family meeting in a couple of minutes. It's time to get off the phone."

Charlie knew what the meeting would be about. His father and stepmother were announcing that the Laird family would lose their home at the end of the month. But Charlie hadn't given up yet, and he refused to listen. Fortunately, he had the perfect excuse on the other end of the phone line.

"Sorry, Dad," Charlie said. "There's an emergency I need to take care of right away."

"Another emergency?" Andrew Laird asked. "How does a twelve-year-old kid have an emergency at seven-thirty on a Wednesday morning in July?"

Charlie heard the slapping of Charlotte's slippers on the floorboards. She arrived at her husband's side, looking utterly exhausted. Her eyes landed on the television, where Stormy Skies was now sniffing at the camera lens. Charlotte took the remote control from Charlie and switched the TV off. "We need to let Charlie go," she told Andrew.

Before his dad had a chance to argue, Charlie had put the phone back up to his ear.

"Hang tight, Alfie," he said. "I just gotta throw on some jeans and I'll be over right away."

Of course Alfie's emergency was nothing more than an excuse to get out of the house. There wasn't much Charlie could do for Stormy Skies. But he figured he should console his friend in person. So he hopped onto his bike and headed east. Charlie had barely ridden two blocks before he saw the first evidence of the tonic at work. Mr. Sturgill, who taught eighth-grade math during the school year, was out in front of his house. He was dressed in sopping wet Star Wars pajamas and attempting to drink from one of the sprinklers on his front lawn. A few doors down, Charlie saw an elderly woman in a wedding gown washing her car.

It wasn't until he passed a big brick house with a sweeping green lawn bordered by hedges that Charlie Laird felt compelled to stop his bike. It was Ollie Tobias's house. He noticed something large and white moving among the plants in one of the flower beds near the porch. He parked his bike and walked across the lawn to investigate. As he drew closer, he could see that it was Mrs. Tobias in her croquet costume, digging a hole in the dirt with her hands.

"Are you okay, Mrs. Tobias?" Charlie asked hesitantly.

The woman's head snapped around. She bared her teeth and snarled until Charlie backed away.

Charlie bounded up the Tobiases' porch steps and rang the doorbell. He could hear a clamor coming from inside. He rang the bell a second time, and the housekeeper opened the door. He could see that she too had sampled the tonic. Someone had given her a pirate hat, along with a black mustache and goatee. She stared at Charlie with a vacant expression.

"May I speak to Ollie, please?" Charlie asked.

The woman stood speechless in the doorway, so Charlie took matters into his own hands. "Ollie!" he shouted.

There was more noise. Then Ollie appeared, wearing pink dishwashing gloves, a plastic shower cap, safety goggles that he must have stolen from school, and an apron that read HOT STUFF. In one hand he held a large wooden paintbrush that was dripping with glue and covered in feathers.

"Hey, Charlie," Ollie welcomed him happily. "How's it going?"

"What are you doing?" Charlie asked.

Ollie looked down at his own rather unusual outfit and grinned. "Mom's a little bit out of it today. So I figured I'd do some redecorating."

Despite the seriousness of the situation, Charlie couldn't resist. "Can I see?" he asked Ollie.

"Sure," the boy said, leading him toward what had probably once been the house's formal living room.

The decorative pillows were all unzipped, and the feathers inside had been dumped into a pile in the center of the room. Ollie was painting the walls with carpet glue and then covering the glue with pillow feathers. The result was weird and wonderful, Charlie thought. The room felt just like a warm, cozy nest. The kid had talent as a decorator, though it seemed extremely unlikely that his mother would agree.

"I'm gonna work on the dining room next," Ollie announced. "I told my mom that I wanted to change a few things, and for the first time, she didn't even try to stop me."

"Your mom drank the tonic, didn't she?" Charlie asked. "And so did the housekeeper. Why didn't you?"

"I did," Ollie told him. "As a matter of fact, my mom gave me a double dose."

"And?" Charlie asked.

"And nothing," Ollie said with a sigh. "Still had the same bad dream."

He was immune to the tonic, Charlie realized, just like Poppy, the girl in Orville Falls.

"I need you to come with me. You got a few minutes?" Charlie asked him.

Ollie stuck his head out an open window. His mother was standing on the porch, covered in dirt. "Hey, Mom, is it okay if I hang out with Charlie for a while?" His mother just stared at him with a blank expression. A thin stream of drool trickled out of the corner of her mouth. Ollie grinned. "Great! Looks like I got all day."

Alfie must have been watching for help to arrive. He ran outside to meet Charlie and Ollie the second they turned the corner onto his street.

"Stormy just climbed up onto the anchor desk! We've got to stop this madness before she gets fired!" he shrieked. When it quickly dawned on him that Charlie wasn't alone, Alfie pulled himself together. "Hi, Ollie," he said. He shot Charlie a quizzical look that seemed to ask, "What's *he* doing here?"

Charlie put a hand on Ollie's shoulder. "Allow me to introduce you to our secret weapon," he said.

"I'm a secret weapon?" Ollie asked, as if his greatest dream had just come true. "Awesome! What do I get to do?"

Alfie looked concerned. "I don't think you want to use the words *Ollie* and *weapon* in the same sentence," he said.

"In this case, it's just a figure of speech," Charlie assured him. "Ollie took a double dose of the tonic last night. His mom had some too. She's a Walker now—but Ollie spent the morning redecorating the living room."

"Hey!" Ollie said. "That's my mom you're talking

about! I'm the only one who gets to call her a— What did you just call her?"

"Never mind. I'm sorry," Charlie replied sincerely. Ollie's mom may have been a Walker, but she was still his mom.

Alfie had started examining the subject. He lifted Ollie's hand and took the boy's pulse. "You say you had a double dose of Tranquility Tonic? And you feel just fine?" he asked skeptically. "No confusion? No drooling? No shuffling?"

"Nope," Ollie replied, doing a little jig to prove how much control he had over his feet.

"And he dreamed last night too," Charlie said.

"Then it's true!" Alfie hopped up and down with glee. "He really is immune!"

"What does that mean?" Ollie asked.

"It means that something inside your body is protecting you from the tonic! Come in, come in." Alfie grabbed Ollie's arm and practically dragged him into his house.

Alfie's room looked like a cross between a mad scientist's laboratory, a doctor's office, and a robotics factory. Charlie watched Ollie's eyes light up as he took it all in, and Charlie knew they wouldn't be able to leave Ollie alone for a second. There was no telling what the kid might do with Alfie's experiments and machinery. After steering his guest clear of anything fragile, toxic, or flammable, Alfie cleared a spot on the bed and told Ollie to have a seat. Then he grabbed a pen and slipped a fresh sheet of paper into a clipboard.

"I need to ask you a few questions in order to determine the source of your immunity," he told Ollie. "Some of them might feel a little personal."

"Cool!" said Ollie.

Charlie grinned while Alfie frowned. "Okay. Are you currently on any medications?"

"Yep," Ollie said.

"Great. Which ones?"

"I get purple pills in the morning, orange pills at night, and blue pills before bed."

Alfie looked up from his clipboard. "Do you know the names?"

"Nope," Ollie said.

Alfie seemed a bit daunted, but he persevered. "Okay, then. Have you ever been hospitalized?"

"Yep," Ollie said.

"What for?"

"Which time?" Ollie asked.

"You've been hospitalized more than once?" Alfie asked.

"Sure," Ollie said. "Haven't you?"

"No," Alfie told him. "Can you tell me what you were hospitalized for?"

Ollie looked thrilled that someone had asked. "Well, when I was two, I used to hide in the clothes dryer. One day the housekeeper accidentally turned on the dryer while I was inside it, and I broke my arm."

"Okay," Alfie said, scribbling a quick note.

"Then, when I was three, I swallowed a bunch of miniature My Little Ponies, and when they wouldn't come out the regular way, they had to be removed."

Charlie winced. He didn't dare ask how they had been removed.

"Is that it?" Alfie said.

"Nope," Ollie said. "When I was three and a half, I ate some poisonous mushrooms that I found in the yard. When I was four, a giant dog attacked me after I tried to ride it. When I was six, I parachuted off the roof of my house, but the chute didn't open. When I was seven, I wanted a pet jellyfish, so I tried to catch one at the beach. When I was nine, I tried welding. And last year, I had to go to the emergency room after I ate my mom's bath beads."

Charlie noticed that Alfie had stopped taking notes. "You're how old?" Alfie asked.

"I'll be twelve in September," Ollie replied.

"And you seem like a pretty smart kid."

Ollie smiled sheepishly. Charlie had heard from several

reliable sources that Ollie got straight As every year. That was one of the reasons he'd never been expelled.

"So why would a smart eleven-year-old eat a bunch of bath beads?" Alfie asked, mystified.

Ollie shrugged. "They just smelled really amazing, and it seemed like a good idea at the time. My doctor says I have poor impulse control. That's what the blue pills are for, I think."

Alfie looked over at Charlie. "This is hopeless," he said. "There's no way to figure out what might be giving Ollie immunity. It could be anything—the pills, the poisonous mushrooms, the jellyfish venom, the bath beads."

"Whatever is helping Ollie, he's not the only one who's got it," Charlie said. "That girl Poppy was immune too. And she didn't seem like the type who'd go around jumping off roofs or eating bath beads."

"We're going to have to talk to her," Alfie said. "We need to figure out what the two of them have in common."

Charlie thought of the girl who'd risked everything to stay in Orville Falls to take care of her family. Try as he might, he couldn't imagine Poppy having anything in common with the dog-riding delinquent on Alfie's bed.

✍ CHAPTER TWENTY-TWO ✍

THE SECRET INGREDIENT

When the three boys arrived at the purple mansion, Charlie set off in search of his stepmother. He found her in the kitchen, where four pots of bizarre-smelling goop were bubbling on the stove. Charlotte was moving from one to the next, smelling and stirring and sipping.

"Where's Dad?" Charlie asked. He needed to make sure they could talk in private.

"He took Jack to the supermarket," Charlotte told him in a cheerful tone. "I asked them to pick up a few extra supplies."

Charlie stared at her. She was far from the defeated person Charlie had left behind an hour earlier. Something had happened in the time he'd been gone. He was just about to ask, when his friends interrupted.

"Hi, Mrs. Laird. Whatcha making?" Ollie asked. He dipped a finger into a bowl of a white, creamy substance and stuck his finger into his mouth.

"Hi, Oliver," Charlotte said, looking a little confused to see him. "I'm trying to find a way to unclog people's brains. By the way, that stuff you just licked off your finger is foot cream. And you're very lucky it's edible."

"It's delicious! I bet feet wouldn't get such a bad rap if more of them tasted like this," Ollie said. "This foot cream is almost as tasty as that poison ivy stuff you made."

Charlotte grimaced but didn't comment. "Hi, Alfie," she said instead. "How's the Channel Four meteorology department?"

Alfie turned bright red and shot a withering glance at Charlie.

"What?" Charlie responded defensively. "I had to tell her why I was going over to your house at the crack of dawn!"

"There's nothing to be ashamed of," Charlotte assured Alfie. "When I was your age, I had a crush on the guy who read out the lottery numbers. His name was Bob Gruber." She sighed dreamily. "I still remember him fondly."

Alfie's face turned even redder. "I assure you, Mrs. Laird, my interest in Stormy Skies is purely scientific."

"Yeah, it's a little bit chemistry and a whole lotta biology," Charlie said. Ollie giggled, and Charlotte bit her lip to keep from laughing. Alfie did not look amused. "But Stormy's not the reason we're here. Alfie and I think we may have a key to the antidote."

Charlotte dropped her spoon into the pot she was stirring and wiped her hands on a tea towel. "You do? Me too! What's yours?"

"Well, Ollie here is half of it," Charlie said. "The other half is in Orville Falls. We need you to give us a ride."

"I can't drive you anywhere right now," Charlotte said. "That's my big news. We have a guest visiting from out of town."

"We have a what?" Charlie asked. No one had mentioned anything to him about a guest.

"Hi, Charlie. Remember me?" A girl stepped into the kitchen wearing one of Charlotte's old robes. She'd obviously just gotten out of the bath, because her skin was pink from scrubbing. Her freshly washed hair was a startling red, and curly coils of it seemed to shoot in every direction.

"Whoa," breathed Ollie.

Charlie stared at the girl. He knew her somehow, but he couldn't remember where they'd met. The girl blushed, embarrassed by the attention.

"You guys know Poppy, don't you?" Charlotte said, returning to her work at the stove.

"Hold on—that's *Poppy*?" Charlie asked his step-mother. He would never have recognized the girl in a million years. The last time he'd seen her, she'd resembled a small troll. "What's she doing in Cypress Creek?"

Poppy huffed. "I'm standing right here, Charlie. You can ask *me*." She waved a hand in front of his face to get his attention. "I'm here because you told me to come to the purple mansion if I ever made it to Cypress Creek. I would have been here sooner if I'd known you were Charlotte's stepson."

It was all way too weird to be a coincidence. "How do you guys know each other?" Charlie asked.

"Poppy's mom used to bring her to my shop," Charlotte explained. "And I have a soft spot for kids with gorgeous curly red hair." She gave Poppy a little wink. "She makes me remember what it was like to be a kid, with my whole crazy future in front of me."

"But how did you get here from Orville Falls?" Alfie asked Poppy. "Did you walk the whole way?"

"My family was sent here to help at the new Tranquility Tonight shop," Poppy said. "When I saw the mansion on the top of the hill, I decided to come up and say hello."

"Poppy's lucky. The tonic doesn't seem to affect her," Charlotte said. "So we might be able to find a way to stop it. Maybe there *is* some hope after all."

Charlie threw his hands up. "I know!" he exclaimed.

"That's why we wanted to go to Orville Falls—to find *her*. Ollie's immune to the tonic too. They've got to have something in common, something that's protecting them both."

"Do you have any idea what it could be?" Charlotte asked.

"Nope, but we're going to find out," Charlie replied. He nodded to Alfie. "You ready to get started? Poppy, maybe you should have a seat."

Ollie rushed over with a chair for her, a crazed grin on his face.

"What exactly are you going to do to me?" Poppy asked nervously as she sat down.

Alfie took his clipboard out of his backpack. "I'm just going to ask you a few questions to see if there's anything

in your medical history that you and Ollie might share. First question: Do you take any medications?"

"No," Poppy replied.

Alfie nodded and looked down at his list. "Have you ever eaten poison mushrooms?"

"What?" Poppy asked.

"I'll take that as a no." Alfie scribbled a note.

Poppy looked up at Charlie. "These are some really weird questions," she said.

"They're going to get even weirder," Charlie warned her. "Ollie's led a very interesting life."

Alfie cleared his throat. "Have you ever been stung by a jellyfish, attacked by a giant dog, or eaten bath beads?"

Poppy gazed at Ollie in wonder. "You've eaten bath beads?"

Ollie nodded. "The instructions said—and I quote—'Add bath beads to warm running water and stir until completely dissolved,'" he told her. "Nowhere did it say 'Do not eat.'" Then he shrugged. "Besides, I figure you gotta try everything once."

"He's kidding, right?" Poppy asked.

"I'll take that response as a no," Alfie said.

"You know, I'm not sure Ollie and I have much in common," Poppy said primly.

Suddenly Charlie knew the answer. They did have something in common: Hazel's Herbarium. Poppy had visited the shop with her mom. And Charlotte had treated Ollie for poison ivy.

"Hold on a second. When was the last time you had poison ivy, Poppy?" he asked.

Poppy gave the question some thought. "Kindergarten, maybe?"

Charlie's spirits sank a little. Hazel's Herbarium hadn't been open when Poppy had been in kindergarten. So there was no way that Charlotte's poison ivy ointment was what she and Ollie had in common.

Then he had another burst of inspiration. "Did you ever use any of the stuff that your mom bought at Hazel's Herbarium?" he asked.

"Sure," Poppy said. "Charlotte's homemade toothpaste is the best. She makes it for me special whenever I go to the shop."

Suddenly the connection became clear. "Ollie, you used Charlotte's poison ivy ointment. Poppy, you used her homemade toothpaste. And every time Paige waves Charlotte's lip balm under her aunt's nose, Josephine seems to wake up a bit." He turned to Charlotte. "There must be a common ingredient in those three things! Whatever it is could be the antidote!"

Charlotte was already shaking her head. "But there isn't, Charlie!" she insisted. "Other than water, there isn't one single thing that those three products share."

"Nice try, though," Alfie offered. His and every other face in the room had fallen. They'd come so close to finding an answer.

"Wait," Charlie said. Medusa had told him that the tonic's power came from the hand that made it. "There is something that all three of those things have in common."

"What?" Charlotte asked.

"They were all made by *you*," he told her. Charlotte must have added something to them without even knowing she'd done it.

"I don't understand. What difference does that make?" Alfie asked.

"Charlotte told me that she made the honeysuckle lip balm to keep Josephine's spirits up while her sister was sick. And I know for a fact that when she made Ollie's ointment, Charlotte was looking forward to her trip to New York. And she just said that seeing Poppy always makes her remember what it was like to be young, with her entire future ahead of her."

"Yeah. I still don't get it," Alfie said.

"Charlotte mixed something into each of those products—something strong enough to fight the despair in the Tranquility Tonic."

"I did?" Charlotte couldn't seem to believe it.

"Yep," Charlie told her. "I think you added *hope*."

CHAPTER TWENTY-THREE

THE TRAP

There was an eviction notice on the front door of Hazel's Herbarium. Charlie tore it down and crumpled it up.

"Come on, you guys," he said, switching the shop's lights on. "We've got work to do."

Alfie and Ollie filed in behind him, eager to get started. Alfie had a box of garbage bags. Ollie was clutching a handwritten list. They were there to get supplies. Charlotte planned to mix up a big batch of antidote, using every ingredient in the toothpaste and poison ivy ointment. While she believed Charlie's theory that the antidote's most important ingredient would be hope, Charlotte wasn't going to leave anything to chance. She'd also asked them to bring every bottle of valerian root on the shelves in the shop. It would put the Walkers to sleep long enough for her anti-dote to do its work.

The boys filled three garbage bags with oils and extracts and jars of gloopy substances that even Charlie couldn't identify. But when Alfie went to collect the large glass can-ister labeled HOARY MUGWORT, he discovered it was com-pletely empty.

"What should we do?" he asked.

"I guess we should head back to the mansion," Charlie said with a sad shake of his head. "Hoary mugwort was the most important thing on Charlotte's list."

"We're giving up?" Ollie asked.

"No way!" Alfie looked shocked. "We're really just going to go home?"

"What else can we do?" Charlie grinned and opened the front door of the shop. "The only hoary mugwort bush in town is behind my house."

Once they were out on the street, Charlie led his team toward the purple mansion. Almost all of the shops on Main Street were empty. But one, a few blocks away, had drawn a crowd. A line of people were still waiting to get the tonic, and a few of the customers who'd already visited were lingering outside in a daze. A tall Walker at the edge of the crowd seemed to take an interest in the boys.

"Let's hurry," Charlie whispered. Then he turned to Alfie. "I think I just saw Winston Lindsay."

They booked it back to the purple mansion in record time and arrived to find Charlotte in a whirlwind of activity. The second the boys appeared in the kitchen, she began pulling bottles from trash bags and organizing ingredients— all while humming a little tune to herself. She was back to being weird, witchy Charlotte, Charlie thought. Whatever happened, he hoped that would last forever.

Alfie and Charlie were given herbs to chop, while Ollie and Poppy were put to work scrubbing pots. Charlie saw them talking as they stood side by side at the sink. Judging by their intense conversation, they'd found something else that they had in common.

As soon as the herbs were chopped and deposited into little glass bowls, Charlie's stepmother began issuing new orders.

"Charlie and Alfie, I need six cups of hoary mugwort leaves. Three cups of mint. A dozen dandelions and a handful of feverfew."

"Poppy and I are finished with the pots," Ollie said. "Should we go outside to help them?"

"Nope. You guys are staying here with me," Charlotte said. "I overheard the two of you talking about your nightmares. Have a seat at the counter. I'm going to go get my markers."

Charlie wished he could stay and watch Charlotte draw their nightmares, but the antidote needed hoary mugwort. He sent Alfie out the front door to search the lawn for dandelions while he went out the back door with a bag. He was still plucking leaves off the silvery bush by the fence when Alfie raced around from the front yard, a dozen limp dandelions gripped in his fist.

"There are Walkers at the bottom of the hill!" he exclaimed, gasping for breath. "One of them is Winston Lindsay. He must have followed us here from town."

The blood in Charlie's veins ran cold. He grabbed his sack of hoary mugwort leaves, and together he and Alfie barreled through the mansion's back door.

"Charlotte!" Charlie said. "The Walkers are at the bottom of our hill."

Charlotte was on her feet in an instant. "Lock the doors!" she yelled as she ran to the windows at the front of the house.

Charlotte might have sprung into action, but Poppy and Ollie seemed not to notice. They sat at the kitchen counter, staring at a piece of paper that Ollie held in his hands. Charlie walked up behind him to see what had captured their interest. It was one of Charlotte's drawings. This one showed a little girl wearing a navy-blue pinafore with a crisp white shirt underneath. A red tie peeked out at the collar. Her bobbed hair was a deep auburn and was parted on one side. The outfit she wore reminded Charlie of pictures he had seen of his great-grandmother when she was a  child. But the eyes in Charlotte's drawing weren't those of an ordinary girl. They held far too much anger and sadness for a child of her age.

"Who is that?" Charlie asked. He couldn't seem to pull his gaze away from the picture. "I think I've seen her somewhere before."

"It's the little girl from our nightmares," Ollie replied. The laughter had disappeared from his voice. Ollie Tobias sounded terrified.

"*Both* of you dreamed about the same kid?" Charlie asked.

"Yeah," said Poppy. "And my brother dreamed about her too. That's why my dad bought the tonic for us. This girl kept showing up in our nightmares, and we were both too scared to go to sleep."

"I think I saw her here in Cypress Creek too," Ollie whispered. "When I was awake. She's real. I swear it."

There was a banging at the front door. Ollie shrieked and fell off his stool, and the picture fluttered to the floor, where it landed in a puddle of goop. Charlie helped Ollie first, then retrieved the illustration. But it was already ruined.

"Who's there?" he heard Charlotte yell at the front door.

"It's me!" Andrew Laird shouted from the other side.

"And me!" Jack shouted too. "Why'd you lock the door?"

Charlotte unlocked the dead bolt and threw her arms around her husband. "Charlie said he saw some men lurking outside."

"I'm sure he did," Charlie's dad said, putting down his shopping bags. "They must be expecting a full moon tonight, because there sure are a lot of strange people out on the street today."

Charlie hurried to the front porch and looked out over the railing. He could see three men and a woman loitering at the end of the mansion's drive. All of them were Walkers.

"I think we better get to work," he told Charlotte. He had a feeling that the Walkers were there for a reason. And it couldn't be a good one.

Hours later, after the sun had set and the streetlights had come on, the Walkers were still there at the bottom of the drive. But there were more of them now. The original four had quickly turned into eight. And the eight had become sixteen. Now there were at least twenty Walkers out on the street. They weren't doing anything yet. Just standing and drooling—and waiting to receive their orders. But there was no way for Charlie's friends to leave with the Walkers that close, so Charlotte had declared it a sleepover party. She told Jack to take his father to the living room and keep him busy. The less Andrew Laird knew, the better. Charlie's job was to keep an eye on the Walkers and sound the alarm if it looked like they were about to attack.

Charlie and Ollie had stationed themselves at one window. Poppy and Alfie had chosen to guard the other. From his post, Charlie could hear the goop in Charlotte's giant cauldron bubbling and spitting. Charlotte had warned them that the stuff needed hours to cook. It wouldn't be done before eleven o'clock. Until then, there was nothing to do but sit quietly in the dark drawing room, watching the Walkers congregate outside the purple mansion.

"Hey, look! It's my mom!" Ollie exclaimed. He pointed to a woman in a dirt-streaked white outfit who was making her way toward the rest of the group. Sure enough, it was Mrs. Tobias, dressed in her croquet costume. She'd even brought along the mallet.

"Sorry," Alfie said.

"Don't feel sorry for me," Ollie said with a snicker. "Feel sorry for the guy who sold her the tonic. He's going to be in a world of pain when my mom wakes up. She's a genius when it comes to revenge."

Charlie heard footsteps on the stairs to the second floor—and they were far too heavy to belong to anyone but Andrew Laird. Charlie took a look at Alfie's watch. It was past ten. He hoped his dad was finally going to sleep.

The door to the drawing room cracked open, and Jack stuck his head inside. "Big guy just took a bunch of valerian root and he's going to bed," he whispered. "What's happening out there on the street?"

"I think they're waiting for a command or something," Charlie said.

Jack slipped into the room and went over to the window where Ollie and Charlie were watching. "How many are there?" he asked, pressing his forehead to the glass to get a better look. "Whoa. That's a whole *bunch* of Walkers!" He looked at Charlie, fear in his eyes. "What are we going to do if they attack before the antidote is done?"

"I have no idea," Charlie answered truthfully.

"Do you think we should bring in some backup?" Jack asked.

"You got anyone in mind?" Charlie joked grimly.

"Hey! Look!" Alfie said, drawing Charlie's attention back to the window. "I just saw a kid down there with the Walkers. Think it might be someone from school?"

"What did he look like?" Charlie asked.

"I didn't see much," Alfie said. "But it looked like a girl."

Ollie said he'd seen the little girl from his nightmares in

Cypress Creek. Was it possible that the girl in question was mingling with the crowd of Walkers at the bottom of the hill? "Where did you see her?" he asked. "Show me!"

Charlie nervously scanned the crowd of Walkers but didn't see anyone who could have passed for a kid. "Did you see her, Jack?" he asked, but there was no answer. "Jack?" he called out. A terrible thought entered Charlie's head before he could even turn around.

"I think I heard him go upstairs," Poppy said from her spot near the window on the other side of the room.

In a split second, Charlie was on his feet and running for the tower. He should have taken his brother's suggestion more seriously. He had a pretty good idea of where Jack went and sure enough, the portal was still open when Charlie reached the octagonal room at the top of the stairs. Jack had gone to the Netherworld for backup.

Charlie stepped through the portal and into the Netherworld's version of the Lairds' purple mansion. His brother hadn't needed to imagine a nightmare. Things were scary enough as they were. Charlie raced down the stairs and found Jack standing in the foyer of the mansion. He was holding a sheet of paper in his hands. As Charlie drew closer, he could see it was one of the WANTED signs with Jack's face on the front. It was a moment Charlie had hoped would never come.

"Somebody slipped this under the door," Jack said with

a nervous grin. He showed Charlie the flyer. "It's got to be a joke, right?"

"Jack—" Charlie couldn't find the words. How did you tell a nine-year-old that the creatures he thought were his friends had turned against him?

"I mean, the Nightmares don't really think I'm the kid from the prophecy, do they? The one who is going to destroy their world?" Jack's smile was fading.

"I doubt all of them think that." It was the best Charlie could offer. And it clearly wasn't good enough for Jack.

"Well, I'm gonna find out," he said. Before Charlie could stop him, his brother had opened the door.

Just like the purple mansion in the Waking World, the Netherworld's black mansion sat on a hill. The first thing Charlie saw when Jack opened the door was the hole that was on the verge of devouring downtown. The second thing Charlie noticed was the ogres stationed near the tree in the mansion's front yard. There were five in all, and one looked a lot like Shrek.

"Orog!" Jack called out to the giant. Charlie could hear the relief in his brother's voice.

The ogres didn't turn around at first. Their spines stiffened and they sniffed at the air.

"He's here in the flesh," the one called Orog told his companions. Then he turned and waved to Charlie's brother. "Jack!"

Jack was heading for the yard where the ogres were waiting for him. There was something about the way they were
standing—so still and so rigid—that made Charlie wonder
what they were up to. His brother was almost to the edge
of the porch when Charlie spotted the rope. The end was
in one of the ogres' hands. From there, it stretched upward,
toward the tree's branches. It was well camouflaged, and
Charlie couldn't see where it went, but he figured it had to
be part of a trap. The ogres weren't throwing a welcome
party.

A burst of speed helped him catch up to Jack the instant the little boy was about to step off the mansion's
front porch. Charlie snatched Jack's shirt and pulled him
backward, just as a net fell from a tree branch overhead. If
Jack had taken one more step, he would have been caught.

For a moment, it was almost as if he *had* been. Jack
looked at the net. Then he looked at Orog. The confusion
on his face made it clear that he was struggling to put the
two together.

The anger rose so quickly in Charlie that he couldn't
stop it from spewing out. "Jack was your friend!" he bel-
lowed at the Shrek-looking ogre. "He helped you, and this
is how you choose to repay him? You should be ashamed."
If Charlie had stood any chance against five giant ogres, he
wouldn't have stopped at shouting.

"He's a criminal!" the ogre yelled back from across the

lawn. "He's been smuggling stuff through the portal in that mansion!" Charlie could tell that the creature wasn't particularly bright.

"If Jack was coming here to smuggle stuff that would destroy the Netherworld, why would he waste so much time teaching a dumb oaf like you how to be scary again? Hmmm?" Charlie demanded.

"But the prophecy . . . ," the ogre began. His words trailed off as he worked it out in his head. He no longer seemed to be so certain.

"The prophecy is a lie," Charlie said. "My brother and I have been busting our butts to keep that hole from getting any bigger." He gestured toward the abyss that was now creeping up the side of the hill. "As of this moment, we're the Netherworld's best hope." He put his arm around his little brother. "We're going back to the other side now to try to finish the job. And unless you really are as dumb as you look, you won't lift a finger to stop us."

The two boys turned and walked back toward the front door. Charlie held his breath, waiting to hear the pounding of footsteps on the floorboards behind them. But they didn't hear a sound. Only once they were inside the mansion, with the front door closed behind them, did Charlie breathe a sigh of relief.

Jack stared at the door. "I really thought they liked me," he said in a small voice. "But they didn't, did they?"

Charlie looked down at the boy beside him. He hated to see his brother so low. "I'm sorry, Jack."

"You always act like I drive you crazy," Jack added. "But you stood up for me."

"I'm your brother," Charlie said. "I was just doing my job." The instant the words were out of his mouth, he knew it wasn't the right thing to say.

"Yeah." Jack sighed. "And I know it's a job you don't like. It's too bad you had to get stuck with it."

Jack started up the mansion's stairs, his shoulders slumped and his head hanging.

"Jack," Charlie called out to him. "I didn't mean it like that!"

"I know how you meant it," Jack said, looking back when he'd reached the landing. The sadness on his face was almost too much to bear.

⚘ CHAPTER TWENTY-FOUR ⚘

TWINS

"Where have you two been?" Charlotte asked. She looked crazed.

Charlie glanced at the clock on the stove. He and Jack had been in the Netherworld for less than thirty minutes. And yet somehow everything seemed to have changed while they'd been gone. Charlie could hear the windows rattling and fists banging on the front and back doors.

"The Walkers are attacking!" Ollie exclaimed, looking like he might burst with excitement. He and Alfie had raided the cleaning supplies. They'd gathered all of the spray bottles and were dumping their contents into the

sink while Charlotte filled the empty bottles with antidote.

"Good thinking," Charlie said, taking a bunch of bottles out of the sink and delivering them to Charlotte, who
was working by the stove.

"It was Ollie's idea," Alfie said. "The kid's kind of a genius." It was the first time Charlie had heard Alfie use the
word to describe anybody besides himself. Ollie grinned
from ear to ear as he poured a bottle of cleaner down the
drain.

Then they heard the sound of glass shattering in the
drawing room.

"They're coming through the windows!" Alfie shouted.

Charlotte slid two spray bottles of antidote down the
counter to her stepsons. "Go get 'em, boys," she said.

Charlie looked over to see his brother standing by his
side. He grabbed a bottle for himself and
passed another to Jack. "I'll get your
back if you get mine," he told the boy.
"Deal?"

"Sure," Jack agreed halfheartedly,
a sad little smile on his lips.

Together, they marched toward
the front lines, prepared to do
battle with the drooling Walker
mob.

Shattered glass littered the drawing room floor. Aggie the cat stood in front of the window, her back arched and fangs bared at the Walkers outside. Mrs. Tobias was the first through the window. It was her trusty croquet mallet that had broken the glass. With her lipstick smeared across her face and mascara ringing her eyes, she resembled a rabid raccoon.

Aggie leaped onto the woman's back, and her claws dug into Mrs. Tobias's croquet shirt. But the woman didn't seem to notice. While the cat continued its attack, Mrs. Tobias pushed Jack out of her path and headed straight for Charlie, her arms stretched out in front of her and her fingers straining to reach his neck.

It was the antidote's first test, and there was no guarantee it would work. Charlie lifted his spray bottle with both hands, aimed the nozzle right at Mrs. Tobias's pointy little nose—and pulled the trigger. Nothing happened. The bottle had jammed. Mrs. Tobias's hands were around his neck. Her pink talons were on the verge of puncturing Charlie's flesh, when her grip weakened and her fingers slipped away. Charlie saw her legs wobble, and then she collapsed into a heap on the floor.

"Gotcha," Jack said. He blew imaginary smoke from the nozzle of his spray bottle.

Charlie dropped down beside the unconscious woman. He pressed two fingers against Mrs. Tobias's neck and sighed with relief. He could feel the steady beat of her pulse. She was fast asleep. "It worked!" he announced.

"Sure it did. What were you expecting?" Jack said. He pointed at the nozzle of his spray bottle. "By the way, you have to turn the top here until it says ON."

Charlie opened his mouth to respond, but Ollie chose that moment to burst into the room, a spray bottle in each hand. "Ha! You bagged the first Walker! And look at that! It's my mom!"

He grabbed one of his mother's legs. "Help me out here, guys. We gotta get her onto one of the sofas. None of us will ever hear the end of it if Theresa Tobias wakes up on the floor."

Charlie and his friends put twenty-five Walkers to bed that night. When they were done, there were sleeping bodies all over the yard. One by one, all the Cypress Creek Walkers were loaded into Charlotte's Range Rover and driven home, where they were left to sleep off the antidote in their own front yards. When Charlie and Charlotte finally returned to the purple mansion, the lights were off. It was well past three in the morning, and even Jack had gone to sleep.

As Charlotte's car turned into the driveway, its headlights briefly illuminated a dark figure lurking in the shadows on the front porch. Tall, wide, and dressed in black from head to toe, the creature wore a hood that hid most of its face.

"Do you see that thing?" Charlie asked.

"Get ready," Charlotte told him. She threw the car into park and yanked up the emergency brake. "Looks like we have another visitor."

Charlie grabbed a spray bottle that was filled with antidote and slid out of the car. As he drew closer to the figure on the porch, he saw two bright yellow eyes watching him from beneath its hood. Then a clawlike hand reached out and snatched up a field mouse as it scampered across the floorboards. Soon, Charlie heard the crunching of bones. He let out a sigh. No human being could move so quickly—or chew so loudly.

"Ava?" he called out.

"Yepth," the Harpy replied with her mouth still full.

Charlie dropped the bottle of antidote to his side. He'd almost forgotten that there was still one Nightmare creature in the Waking World. Then Charlie heard the Harpy swallow. "Pardon me. I'm famished from the flight."

"Ava!" Charlotte hurried up the porch stairs to greet her. "Come inside and tell us everything you've learned while I fix you something to eat."

"Don't make a fuss over me," Ava said shyly. "There's plenty of fresh food running around tonight."

Charlie would much rather have moved indoors, but he

couldn't wait to hear the Harpy's report, even if it meant listening to the chomping of rodent bones. And Charlie had updates for the Harpy too. Thanks to Charlotte's antidote for the tonic, the Walker invasion would soon be over, and hopefully the Netherworld hole would disappear. The tonic's creators were at large, though, and if they had the ability to pass through portals, they remained extremely dangerous. As soon as all of the Walkers were cured, finding ICK and INK would be Charlie's top priority.

"So did you locate the lighthouse?" Charlotte asked Ava as she took a seat on the porch railing.

"Yes," Ava said. "You were right. It was on a bleak rocky beach in Maine, miles away from the nearest town. There were no trees to perch in, or buildings that could shelter me. I had nowhere to hide during the day, so I was able to visit only at night."

"And did you see anyone?" Charlie pressed, his excitement growing.

"It took a while, but I finally did," Ava said.

"ICK and INK," Charlotte whispered.

Ava shook her head. "There was only one human inside," she said. "The night I arrived, I flew past the windows, but I couldn't see into the shadows. The next night, the clouds cleared for a few minutes, and the moon was out. I passed by the bottom window and I saw her."

"Her?" Charlie asked.

Ava nodded. "Yes," she said. "It was a young girl. Around the same age as you."

Charlotte gasped, but for some reason Charlie wasn't surprised. It was almost as if he'd been expecting to hear it.

"ICK and INK must have kidnapped a child," Charlotte said.

Ava looked confused. "No. The girl wasn't guarded. She lived there, alone in the lighthouse. If she'd wanted to escape, she could have done so at any time."

Charlotte's brow furrowed. "I don't understand," she said. "If the only person in the lighthouse was a little girl, where were the people who've been smuggling the tonic into the Waking World?"

"I wondered the same thing," Ava said. "Then last night, a truck arrived. The girl opened the lighthouse door for three men, who loaded the truck with crates that had been stored inside the building. Each of the crates was filled with little blue bottles."

They'd thought all along that the tonic was being smuggled into the Waking World through the lighthouse, and now they had irrefutable proof. But that didn't answer the questions that had been bothering Charlie—where were ICK and INK? Who was the girl all alone inside? And why was she helping the smugglers?

A disturbing idea was forming in Charlie's head. He couldn't stop thinking about the girl who'd appeared in

Ollie's and Poppy's nightmares. The girl Meduso hadn't been able to rescue from the lighthouse. The girl Curtis Swanson had seen with the Shopkeeper—and the human presence Charlie had sensed in his last bad dream. "Ava, did the girl you saw in the lighthouse have auburn hair?" he asked.

"I'm sorry," said the Harpy. "I don't know this word . . . *auburn*."

"Hold on for a second." Charlie rushed into the house and returned with a sheet of paper and a fistful of Charlotte's markers. He handed the art supplies to his stepmother. "Draw the girl again, the one Ollie and Poppy described," he said. "The one they say they saw in their nightmares."

"What?" Charlotte asked in confusion.

"The picture you drew earlier fell into a puddle. Can you draw her again? Please?"

Charlotte sighed and got to work. As soon as she had a rough sketch to share, Charlie took the paper and held it up for Ava to see.

"Is this what she looked like, the girl in the lighthouse?" he asked.

"Yes." The Harpy nodded emphatically. "That's her."

Charlie spun around to face Charlotte. "I don't know which one it is," he said, tapping the paper with his finger. "But the girl you just drew is either ICK or INK. I think there are two of them, and I think they're twins. That's why it seems like they're everywhere—at the lighthouse and in people's nightmares. Ollie even thought he saw one of them here in Cypress Creek."

"But how can ICK and INK be a couple of kids?" Charlotte asked. "They stalked me and your mother twenty-five years ago."

Charlie didn't know the answer, but he suspected that ICK and INK were far older than they looked. According to Medusa, the lighthouse they'd built in the Netherworld had been around for at least eighty years. ICK and INK might have been children once, a long time ago, but the twins were no longer young.

They also kept some unusual company, Charlie thought, remembering the last time he'd seen the Netherworld lighthouse. He'd looked through the telescope in Medusa's cave and seen the building surrounded by goblins who'd broken the laws of the Netherworld by crossing the border.

"Did any goblins come out of the lighthouse in Maine while you were watching?" he asked Ava.

"Goblins?" Ava and Charlotte both repeated in surprise.

"The last time I saw the Netherworld lighthouse, there were thousands of goblins gathered outside it," Charlie explained. "Medusa thought they were waiting for ICK and INK to open the door so the goblins could pass through the lighthouse's portal and into the Waking World."

"Does that mean Maine is about to be invaded by goblins?" Charlotte gasped.

"No," Ava assured her. "Maine is safe."

"How can you be so sure?" Charlie asked. "How do you know that ICK and INK won't open the lighthouse door?"

"The door won't open because the lighthouse burned down," Ava said. "It happened last night. There was nothing left."

It took a few beats for the horror to sink in. Charlie looked over at Charlotte, who seemed to be stunned speechless. "So the portal in the lighthouse is gone?" Charlie asked.

"Everything is gone," Ava replied.

"What about the little girl?" Charlotte asked.

"She escaped," Ava said. "Right after she set the building on fire."

❧ CHAPTER TWENTY-FIVE ❧

HOME, SWEET HOME

It didn't make any sense. Why had ICK or INK burned the lighthouse down? Charlie lay awake in the dark, turning the question over in his mind. He was completely exhausted. Sleep should have arrived the instant his head had hit the pillow. Instead, he kept thinking about the sisters.

Charlie had pieced together parts of their story. The twins must have smuggled the tonic into the Waking World. No matter how old they really were, they looked like a couple of kids, which meant ICK and INK couldn't just open a shop themselves. So they'd teamed up with the

Shopkeeper and made him the face of the business. Then
ICK and INK must have spent weeks building demand for
Tranquility Tonic by terrorizing the citizens of Orville
Falls in their dreams.

Now the twins were after the purple mansion. With the
lighthouse gone, they needed the mansion's portal to go
back and forth between worlds. And there was no doubt
that ICK and INK knew about the portal in the tower
upstairs. Charlie was convinced that they'd already been
using it.

But why burn down the lighthouse before they got
their hands on the purple mansion? And why disappoint
all those goblins who'd been waiting to cross over into the
Waking World? Was destroying the lighthouse all part of
some plan? Charlie wondered. And what *was* that plan?
Why were the twins doing their best to destroy three
worlds?

When sleep finally settled upon him, Charlie found
himself back in the Netherworld, standing on the lip of
the giant hole that had swallowed part of his town. As he
stared into the abyss, Charlie thought of the despair that
filled every bottle of Tranquility Tonic. That was what had
eaten everything away, leaving only a bottomless pit. As he
stood there, Charlie realized that he knew exactly what it
would feel like to fall inside. In the months after his mother
had died, he'd been consumed by that same darkness and

despair. It was like there had been a pit of sadness in his heart.

What had happened to ICK and INK? In order to make the tonic, they too must have known unspeakable sorrow. Which meant that, as wicked as they were, they deserved Charlie's pity. If their despair was powerful enough to spawn an abyss, it must have been too much to endure.

As Charlie stood at the hole, the edge seemed to move. He watched in wonder as it inched toward the tips of his toes.

"It's still growing," a voice behind him confirmed. "We haven't stopped it yet."

Charlie spun around to see Jack stepping out from behind a tree. "Have you been following me?" Charlie asked.

"No!" Jack insisted. "I was just . . ."

Charlie saw the fear on the little boy's face, and he knew that his brother was being honest. "You were hiding." He was sure of it as soon as he said it out loud.

Jack nodded. "I don't want to run into one of *them*." Charlie's heart broke a little to hear such a thing. The boy who'd made friends with half the creatures in the Netherworld was now reduced to hiding from them.

"Did you come through the portal?" Charlie asked. "Are you here in the flesh?"

"No," Jack told him. "I'm just having a really bad dream."

Charlie walked over to his brother and put an arm around him. "Then there's nothing to be afraid of," he told Jack. "Remember what Mom told me? If we stick together, two will be stronger than one."

"I just don't understand, Charlie." Jack's voice had gotten smaller. "Why do the Nightmare creatures think I want to destroy them?"

Charlie had never wanted to kick an ogre's butt more than he did at that very moment. "They're scared," he said. "And sometimes when you're scared, you do stupid things. But as soon as we stop the hole, things will go back to the way they were."

"I don't want everything to be the way it was," Jack said miserably. "All I want to do is go home."

The brothers crept through the empty streets of the Netherworld Cypress Creek, toward the mansion that sat on top of the hill in the center of town. It seemed like the best place to pass the night and wait for their nightmares to end. But it wasn't long before Charlie began to regret that they were making the trip. Everywhere he looked, Jack's face stared out from

WANTED flyers that were taped to the town's windows, streetlamps, and walls.

When the boys finally reached the forbidding black mansion, Jack was a nervous wreck, and Charlie was eager to get him inside and out of sight. But the front door was locked. The back door wouldn't open either, and all of the downstairs windows appeared to be sealed.

"What's going on?" Jack asked.

"No clue," Charlie admitted. He left the front porch and walked out onto the barren brown yard. With his head tilted back, he scanned the building, searching for some other way inside. When Charlie's eyes reached the tower, they went wide with surprise. Someone was standing in one of the windows. It was a girl in a blue dress and a white shirt. A red tie peeked out from beneath the collar. Her auburn bob was parted on the side, and though he couldn't see her eyes, he knew from Charlotte's drawing that they were a deep, dark brown.

It was either ICK or INK. The sister who'd burned down the lighthouse had last been seen in Maine and was now at large in the Waking World. The other sister was here at the Netherworld

mansion. Whichever one it was, she was clearly sending Charlie a message. The Lairds might have put a few Walkers to rest, but they hadn't saved their house. If Charlie didn't do something, the purple mansion would belong to the evil twin sisters by the end of the month. Now that the lighthouse was gone, they needed it more than ever.

Charlie heard Jack's footsteps. His brother was coming to join him on the lawn. "Indy!" the little boy shouted. "Indy, what are you doing up there? Let us in!"

A shiver ran down Charlie's spine. "You know that girl?" he asked his brother.

"Sure," Jack said. "Her name's India. I have no idea what she's doing in our house, though. She lives far away at the end of the world."

When Charlie looked back up, he saw the girl lean forward toward the window. A round patch of condensation appeared on the glass, and the girl used the tip of her finger to write five letters in the fog. *IZZIE.* She drew a line beneath the word for emphasis. Then she disappeared.

"What's that supposed to mean?" Jack said.

Charlie understood. "I think it means that's not your friend Indy. It's her sister, Izzie. They're twins." Charlie bent down to look Jack in the eye. "How did you meet Indy anyway?"

Jack shrugged. "She just showed up one night while I

was here," he said. He still had no idea what was going on. "We hung out for a little while. She said she heard there was a human in Cypress Creek, so she came to say hi. I think she used to be human too."

"But she's not anymore?" Charlie asked.

Jack shrugged. "I don't know what she is," he said. "I don't know anything about her, except I think she's really lonely."

Charlie looked down at his brother. "I need you to be completely honest with me, Jack. Did you tell Indy about the portal in the purple mansion?"

"No! I swear I didn't! Indy already knew," Jack insisted. "What's going on, Charlie? Why are you asking me all of this?"

"You sure made some interesting friends here in the Netherworld," Charlie said. "Your friend Indy and her sister also go by the names ICK and INK."

CHAPTER TWENTY-SIX

UNDER THE TOUPEE

The morning after the epic Walker battle, Andrew Laird tiptoed into the kitchen. "A strange woman is sleeping on the couch in the drawing room," he whispered.

"Oh, that's just my mom," Ollie said. He was standing on a chair in front of the stove, wearing an apron and stirring a batch of antidote that was bubbling inside Charlotte's biggest cauldron.

Andrew Laird stared at Ollie and then glanced over at his wife. Charlotte grinned nervously and shrugged.

"When Mrs. Tobias came to pick up Ollie, she said she had a really bad migraine," Charlie explained. They'd spent at least half an hour crafting the story. "Charlotte told her to go lie down, and she ended up falling asleep."

"Oh," his dad said. "So who broke the window in the drawing room?"

"We got a little rowdy last night, and there was an accident," Charlie answered, again prepared. "Don't worry. We're being punished. Charlotte's put us all to work."

"And what exactly are you working on?" his dad asked.

The kitchen had been turned into a factory. Every spray bottle, water gun, and plant spritzer in the house had been commandeered. A raid of the garage had produced a paint sprayer and a bag of balloons. Alfie, Charlie, and Jack were filling the bottles and balloons with antidote. Poppy cleaned the containers while Charlotte and Ollie prepared the next batch.

"Ummm," Charlotte said, unable to answer her husband's question. She'd been up all night, and her brain wasn't fully functional.

"We're making plant food," Jack piped up.

"Interesting delivery methods," Andrew Laird said. "I never would have thought of water

balloons." He grabbed a banana, pulled back the peel, and took a bite. "Say, did you guys hear anything strange last night?" he asked through a mouthful of fruit. "That valerian root really knocked me out, but I swear it sounded like there was one heck of a party outside."

"Nope," Charlie answered for all of them. "We didn't hear a thing."

"Okay, then. Good." Andrew Laird swallowed and cleared his throat. "Listen, Charlotte. I think tonight's the night for that family meeting we've been planning. We can't keep putting it off. How does six o'clock sound?"

"That sounds great," Charlotte replied distractedly. "Can't wait."

"You can't?" Andrew Laird looked like he was wondering if his wife had gone crazy. "Well, then I guess I'm off to work." He waited for a proper goodbye from his family, but the antidote factory couldn't stop production. There was an entire town to save.

"Bye, Dad!" Jack shouted without looking up from his work.

"Have a great day, honey," Charlotte said, hastily blowing a kiss.

"You too," Andrew Laird said, but no one was listening. He shook his head in confusion and left the room.

By ten a.m., Charlotte's Range Rover was jam-packed with spray bottles of every imaginable variety. There was barely enough room for Alfie, Ollie, Jack, Poppy, and Charlie. When they stopped to pick up Rocco, it took five minutes to figure out how to squeeze him inside.

There was no traffic on the road to Orville Falls. It was as if the mountain village had been completely forsaken by the rest of the world and abandoned to the Walkers. Even the forest animals seemed to be keeping their distance. The entire ride passed without anyone spotting a single deer, rabbit, or skunk.

Charlie and the gang met their first resident on the edge of town. As the Range Rover passed the rustic wooden sign that said WELCOME TO ORVILLE FALLS, a burly teenage Walker dressed in camouflage barreled out of the forest. Charlotte hit the brakes.

"Who's got this one?" she asked.

Charlie's heart was racing, but Rocco was grinning from ear to ear.

"May I?" Rocco asked the car. When he got the thumbs-up, he picked out a Super Soaker water gun. As the teenager rushed toward the car's open window, Rocco aimed and fired. A stream of antidote hit the teen right in the forehead and flowed down over his nose and mouth. In an instant, the kid's legs went limp, his eyes closed, and he fell to the ground in a great camouflage heap.

"Nice work, Rocco," Charlotte said. "Now two of you get out there and put that kid to bed."

Charlie and Alfie hopped out of the car and dragged the teenager to a soft clump of grass on the side of the road. Alfie dug into his pocket and pulled out a small chocolate, which he left on the kid's chest, like a hotel room mint. Then the boys scrambled back into the car. The plan had gone like clockwork.

"Woohoo! Only a few thousand more to go!" Alfie yelled, then added a quick "Sorry" when he realized exactly how daunting that seemed.

The team took down twelve more Walkers on the way to Paige's aunt Josephine's house. Poppy's and Ollie's aims turned out to be almost as good as Rocco's, so the three of them acted as sharp-sprayers. Jack was a whiz with the water balloons, and he almost never missed his mark. When the Walkers fell asleep in safe spots, the car drove past. But when they landed in the street—or fell face-first into a puddle—Charlie and Alfie would hop out of the car and drag them to safety. It had to be done, but it took precious time.

While Charlie and Alfie were moving one such sleeper to safety, they were attacked by a kid dressed in the blue uniform of the Orville Falls Comets. He appeared out of nowhere, launching himself at Charlie with such force that he almost seemed to be flying. One solid head butt was all the kid managed to land before he was drenched with antidote by Poppy, Ollie, Rocco, and Jack. Charlie could feel his cheekbone swelling from the head butt, but the pain didn't bother him. He was completely focused on getting where they needed to be.

It was almost noon by the time the Range Rover finally reached their destination—Paige's aunt Josephine's house. The rest of the kids stayed in the car while Charlotte and Charlie trudged through the now nearly chin-high weeds in Josephine's yard.

After Charlie gave the emergency knock, Paige opened the door and took one look at their happy faces. "You did it!" she exclaimed. The hug she gave Charlie was what he'd been looking forward to all morning.

"Thanks in part to you," said Charlotte. "Josephine's lip balm helped us figure out how to make the antidote."

"What was inside the lip balm that almost woke Josephine up?" Paige asked.

"Hope," Charlie said.

"*Really?*" Paige asked, eyebrow lifted skeptically. "*Hope?*"

"And a little bit of honeysuckle," said Charlotte.

"Come on," Charlie said, grabbing Paige by the wrist. "If you don't believe it, you'll just have to see the antidote in action."

He led the way to Josephine's bedroom, where the three

of them found Paige's aunt sitting up in bed just as she'd been the last time Charlie had visited.

Charlie pointed a bottle of antidote at Josephine and gave her a spray. Within seconds, Josephine's eyelids began to flutter, and then they closed.

Paige bent down and studied the tiny droplets of antidote on her aunt's skin. "It looks like water. Do you think it's really going to work?" she asked nervously.

"Your aunt will be fine," Charlotte said confidently. "But the antidote isn't the only reason."

"What do you mean?" Paige asked.

Charlie watched a smile spread across his stepmother's face. "You know, the day your aunt came into my shop, she told me that her sister was ill." Charlotte looked over at Paige. "But now that I think of it, she seemed to be far more worried about her young niece."

"Me?" Paige asked. Charlie could tell by the look on her face that she was wondering where Charlotte's story was going.

"Does Josephine have any other nieces?" Charlotte asked.

"No," Paige replied.

"Josephine told me that things get really hard for you when your mother is ill. And I told her that I knew you were going to be fine. Do you know how I knew?" Paige shook her head, and Charlotte continued. "Because I could tell that you have the most important thing a person can have—someone who loves you and will always look out for you. And that's how I know that Josephine's going to be okay too. She has someone to look out for her, Paige. She has *you*."

The room was silent, and Charlie saw Paige's lower lip quivering. He was about to reach out for her, when someone spoke up.

"What just happened? Why am I soaking wet?" His eyes were instantly drawn to Josephine, who was yawning and wiping her face with the sleeve of her nightgown.

"Josephine!" Paige shouted. She leaped onto the bed and hugged her stunned and soggy aunt.

"I'll get a towel!" Charlie offered, rushing for the bathroom. As he grabbed a towel from the rack, he noticed a painting tucked away in the corner. He suddenly recalled seeing it hanging on the living room wall when he and Paige had first visited Josephine. When he'd first come across it, Charlie had assumed it was a picture of a girl gazing at her reflection in a mirror. Now Charlie knew there were two auburn-haired girls in the picture. The painting was a portrait of ICK and INK, watching each other across an open portal.

He pulled out the painting and carried it back to show the group. "Look what I found in the bathroom!" he exclaimed.

Paige let go of her aunt and glanced over her shoulder. "Oh, *that*," she said with disgust. "I left it in there so I wouldn't have to look at it." Then she quickly turned to her aunt. "I'm sorry, Aunt Josephine. I usually love your art, but that picture really creeps me out."

The valerian root in the antidote seemed to be dragging Josephine toward sleep. Charlie could see the woman's eyelids drooping with exhaustion. But when she caught sight of the artwork, she let out a weak yelp.

"Do you know these girls?" Charlie asked quickly before Josephine could fall asleep.

Josephine let out a big yawn before she answered. "One of them was with the Shopkeeper when he came to the newspaper office and he gave me a bottle of the tonic," she said, and rubbed her eyes. "I thought she was his daughter, but she was really in charge. And the other one . . ." Josephine's voice trailed off.

"I don't understand," Paige told Charlie. "What are you guys talking about? There's only one girl in that picture."

"No, there are two—ICK and INK. They're the masterminds behind the tonic, and they're twins," Charlie announced. He'd expected the revelation to astound Paige. But his friend didn't bat an eye. "Why aren't you surprised? You just found out that the bad guys are evil twin girls!"

"Why would I be surprised?" Paige asked haughtily. "Girls can do anything. Now if you don't mind, can you put that hideous thing away?"

Charlie turned the painting around and propped it

against the wall. By the time he'd turned back, Josephine was fast asleep.

Paige glanced down at her aunt and leaped up in alarm. "Why are her eyes closed?" she asked frantically.

"She's resting," Charlotte explained. "I added enough valerian root to the antidote to put a rhinoceros to sleep. I didn't know how long it would take the stuff to work, so I thought it would be a good idea to let the Walkers sleep through their recoveries."

"How long will it take for my aunt to wake up?" Paige asked.

"We gave it to some Walkers in Cypress Creek last night," Charlie told her. "The first one was still asleep when we left, and she'd been out for at least eight hours."

"Perfect," Paige said as she tucked her aunt in. "That should give us enough time before Josephine wakes up."

"To do what?" Charlie asked.

Paige pointed at the painting that was leaning against the wall. "To go kick those brats' butts."

Back outside, the Range Rover was surrounded by sleeping Walkers of all shapes and sizes. Their bodies were twisted together and piled on top of each other. But each and every one of their faces wore a blissful smile.

"They just kept coming down the street!" Ollie called from the car. "Where the heck were they all going?"

"Tranquility Tonight is a few blocks away," Paige informed him. "They were probably heading to the shop to stock up on tonic."

The line. Charlie hadn't factored it into their plans. Suddenly he knew how to cure all of the Orville Falls Walkers. At one point or another, they'd all need to go to the shop. The only thing he and his friends had to do was be there to ambush them. Charlie marshaled his troops.

"Grab as much antidote as you can," he ordered. "We're heading downtown. It's time to put Tranquility Tonight out of business."

The announcement was met with a loud cheer and a thud as another Walker was felled by Poppy's impressive aim. She and the rest of Charlie's little army stayed busy as they marched downtown, splattering Walkers with antidote.

"That's fifty-nine by my count," Jack announced as one of his water balloons drenched a Walker less than a block from the tonic shop. "How many more do you suppose we have left?"

They turned a corner and found the answer. Hundreds upon hundreds of Orville Falls citizens were lined up in the street. None of the Walkers seemed to care about Charlie's water-gun-wielding army. They were too battered and exhausted to do anything but wait in line for their next bottle of tonic.

"Whoa." Charlotte gulped. "I hope we have enough antidote for everyone."

"I say we find out," Ollie said with a crazed smile. His trigger fingers were twitching.

Spray guns were readied and Super Soakers were pumped. Jack and Ollie had their antidote aimed at the last two Walkers in line, when Charlie heard the sound of a car racing through the otherwise empty streets.

"Quick!" he shouted at his friends. "Get in line." It was the only moving car Charlie had encountered in Orville Falls since his first trip to town, and there was no telling who might be behind the wheel.

Charlotte and the kids all squeezed into the line and did their best to look dazed until the car had passed. It was a black Mercedes with a license plate that read ABCC1.

The meaning popped into Charlie's head. "Amalgamated Bank of Cypress Creek," he muttered out loud. The Mercedes belonged to Curtis Swanson.

"That car was from Cypress Creek?" Paige whispered back. "Where do you think it's going?"

"I know exactly where it's headed," Charlie said, turning to his friend. There was only one possible destination—the Shopkeeper's castle. Swanson was going to see his clients about the purple mansion, and there was a chance

ICK or INK might be there. "You still itching to kick some butt?"

Paige cracked her knuckles. "Absolutely."

"Can you guys handle all the spraying without us?" Charlie asked Charlotte, who'd been standing in line behind him.

"Where are you two going?" she asked, and Charlie realized he'd never told his stepmother about the castle.

"There's a weird building just outside of Orville Falls . . . ," Charlie started to explain, struggling to find the right words to describe one of the creepiest places on earth.

"We call it Kessog Castle," Poppy interrupted. "Some crazy hermit built it way back when. The Shopkeeper lives there now."

"*Kessog* Castle?" Charlotte caught Charlie's eye. It was the first time Charlie had ever heard the castle's name.

A lightning bolt streaked through Charlie's brain. "Wasn't ICK and INK's lighthouse in Maine called—"

"Kessog Rock," Charlotte confirmed. "If ICK and INK are initials, the *K* must stand for *Kessog*."

"And I'd bet almost anything that at least one member of the Kessog family is with us here in Orville Falls today," Charlie said.

Charlie and Paige left their friends behind at Tranquility Tonight and raced for the castle at the edge of the forest, taking every shortcut they could find. Sure enough, Curtis Swanson's car was parked in the drive, and they arrived just in time to see the banker knock on the castle's front door. A Walker let him in with a grunt, and a minute later Charlie and Paige quietly opened the door and tiptoed in behind them.

The torch-lit foyer was empty. There was no way to tell which direction the banker had gone. The fear was building inside Charlie, and every one of his senses was on full alert. He could hear the crackle of the torches. He spotted a spider climbing one of the walls. Then he caught a whiff of something. With his nose in the air, he tracked the scent.

"What are you doing?" Paige whispered. "What do you smell?"

"Curtis Swanson's disgusting cologne," Charlie said.

Paige followed Charlie as he cautiously ventured down the same path they'd taken on their first visit to the castle. When they heard footsteps coming down the hall, Charlie and Paige ducked into the room where they'd first met Poppy and ran for the wardrobe. They clambered inside it and pulled the door shut just as two people entered the room.

"I hope it's those evil brats," Paige whispered. "Just let me know when it's time to get down to business."

But it wasn't ICK and INK.

"Have a seat, Mr. Swanson." The Shopkeeper's voice creaked like a rusty hinge. "I trust you had a pleasant trip?"

"I did, thank you," replied Curtis Swanson. "Though I did see some rather remarkable things on the way here."

"For instance?" asked the Shopkeeper, feigning surprise that anything strange could possibly happen in Orville Falls.

"For instance, there are people sleeping along the side of the road right outside town."

"Sleeping?" The Shopkeeper's word came out quite gruffly.

"Yes," Swanson confirmed. "And I saw a bunch of children with water guns waiting in line at your shop."

"*Water guns?*" the Shopkeeper repeated. He wasn't amused. "I haven't been out yet today. I'll have to pay a visit to town right after you leave. So perhaps we should quickly get to the subject at hand. The DeChant house—is the deal done?"

Charlie's stomach fell. Paige must have sensed his discomfort. Charlie felt her hand on his shoulder.

"It will be," Curtis Swanson assured him. "The paperwork is all in order. And my sources tell me there's no chance that the Laird family will be able to find the money to save it. But I'm afraid that the mansion is legally theirs until the end of the month."

"That is not fast enough," growled the Shopkeeper. "My employers say they need the house immediately."

"I can't just *give* them the mansion, sir," Swanson said with a nervous laugh. "But the end of the month is only a few days away—"

"A few days is too long! We won't get our reward until they have the house!"

The shriek was so loud that it rattled Charlie's eardrums.

"Sir—" Swanson tried to calm the Shopkeeper.

"I have guests arriving! Lots of guests!" The voice no longer sounded human. It was the screech of an enraged animal. "They won't be allowed to come until the job is done and the mansion is secured!"

"I'm sorry—" Curtis started again.

But the Shopkeeper couldn't be pacified. "I'm tired of pretending! I've been wearing this ridiculous hairpiece for weeks! Do you have any idea how much it itches?"

"Sir, *please* . . . ," Curtis Swanson begged. "Why do you need the mansion so quickly?"

"Why? I do not ask *why*! I serve my masters. My masters are wise and my masters are vengeful. My masters want that purple mansion and they want it *now*! So get me the purple mansion."

It was too much for Charlie. He had to take a peek. He opened the door a crack and saw Curtis Swanson. This time the banker wasn't smiling. He was staring in sheer horror at the angry creature before him.

The Shopkeeper had torn off his toupee and thrown it onto the ground. His suit jacket had ripped down the seams, revealing a metal back brace that he removed and hurled across the room. Without it, the creature's spine curved, and a much more obvious hump appeared.

The disguise had been so simple, and yet so effective, Charlie realized. He should have known from the start that the Shopkeeper was a goblin.

"Who's making that racket?" demanded a new voice.

"What's the greasy human done now?" asked another.

"Holy moly," Paige muttered under her breath.

There was no longer one goblin in the room. There were three. Charlie remembered the day they'd met Poppy. She'd told them that the Shopkeeper had helpers who kidnapped anyone in Orville Falls who refused to take the tonic. But she'd never seen the bad guys, and now Charlie knew why. All three bad guys looked almost exactly the same.

"Get out of here!" the first goblin screamed at Curtis Swanson. "And don't you dare return until the mansion is ours!"

CHAPTER TWENTY-SEVEN

HOPE

Charlie and Paige sprinted back downtown from the castle on the hill as if they were being pursued by every last one of their very worst Nightmares. As they neared Tranquility Tonight, Charlie saw that his friends were still busy spraying the Walkers lined up outside the shop. In all the time that Charlie and Paige had been gone, fewer than half of the Walkers had been put to sleep. Charlie watched Ollie, Jack, and Rocco give a Walker a thorough dousing. The man collapsed into a heap, his nose buried in another Walker's armpit. As the boys moved on to the next Walker, Charlotte, Poppy, and Alfie arranged the previous man's body in a more comfortable and dignified position. There were hundreds of Walkers laid out in a neat row on the ground, but there were hundreds more to go.

Charlie headed straight for Charlotte, who was looking thoroughly exhausted.

"Charlie! Did you see ICK and INK at the castle?" she asked as he closed in.

"Goblins," Charlie panted. He bent over, hands on knees, to catch his breath.

"Goblins?" Charlotte's eyes went wide. "Are you saying ICK and INK are goblins?"

"No." Charlie shook his head. "The goblins work for ICK and INK. They're helping the twins buy the purple mansion."

Charlotte looked stunned by the news. "They're *what*?"

"I'm sorry." Charlie drew in another deep breath. "I should have told you sooner, but I was hoping one of the publishers would buy your book and I wouldn't have to give you the bad news. ICK and INK are planning to buy the purple mansion as soon as the bank forecloses."

Charlotte gasped. "They destroyed their own portal, so now they're going to take ours!" Her knees seemed close to buckling, and Charlie reached out a hand to steady her.

"What should we do?" Charlie asked. "If ICK and INK get their hands on the mansion, who knows what they'll let through the portal. Cypress Creek could end up being goblin central."

"There's only one thing we can do now," Charlotte replied, her voice cracking. "We'll have to burn down the mansion before they can buy it. It's the only way to stop them from using the portal."

There were tears welling in Charlotte's eyes. Charlie could tell that she meant it. She'd burn down her own beloved home before she would let the town be overrun by goblins.

An idea flickered in Charlie's mind. His thoughts turned to the girl Ava had seen setting the Waking World building ablaze, and the goblins who'd been waiting on the other side. Had ICK or INK burned the lighthouse down so the goblins would be stuck in the Netherworld? If so, what did that mean?

The ringing of a phone kept Charlie from finishing the thought. He glanced over to where the other kids were still hard at work, and saw Ollie fish a phone out of his pocket. A look at the caller ID brought a grin to Ollie's face.

"Hey, Mom!" Ollie answered. "How ya feeling?" Charlie exhaled a breath he hadn't realized he'd been holding. If Mrs. Tobias was phoning her son, she was the second Walker they knew of to be cured by the antidote. "You're not going to *believe* how much fun you had last night."

Then Charlie saw Ollie's impish grin melt into an expression of confusion, then horror. Within seconds the boy was booking it toward Charlotte.

"Mrs. Laird! Mrs. Laird!" he cried. "My mom's on the phone, and there's something really wrong with her. Just listen to this!" Ollie hit the speaker button on his phone.

"Mmrake murumph mwa mwamff!" shouted a garbled voice on the other end of the line.

If Charlie hadn't known better, he would have guessed he was listening to an angry monkey with a mouth full of bees.

"Are you sure that's your mom?" Charlie asked. His heart was sinking fast.

"I'm positive!" Ollie insisted. "What's going on? I thought she was cured!"

Charlie looked to Charlotte. Every drop of blood appeared to have drained from her face. "It sounds like the antidote didn't work for your mother," she told Ollie. "All the valerian root I put in it may have knocked her out for a while, but when she woke up, she was still a Walker. Everyone we sprayed last night fell asleep, but that doesn't mean they were cured."

But the tonic couldn't be a total dud, Charlie assured himself. He'd seen with his own eyes what it had done for Paige's aunt. "What about Josephine?" Charlie asked. "The tonic saved her! So why didn't it work for Mrs. Tobias?"

Charlotte shook her head. "I don't know."

She sounded totally defeated, and Charlie understood

why. It looked as if all of their work had been wasted. But something told him that the battle wasn't quite over. Charlotte, however, seemed to have lost the will to fight.

"I tried my best," she said. Her voice was flat, and her bloodshot eyes stared off into space. "I really did. But look where it's gotten me. My book was rejected, the purple mansion is being sold, and now this. I give up. There's nothing else I can do."

"Come on, Charlotte—" Charlie started to argue, but there wasn't time to make his case.

"Goblins!" Alfie shrieked. Charlie's eyes instantly darted in the direction of the castle. Three goblins were stomping toward them. They wore the tattered remains of their Shopkeeper suits, but they'd removed the rest of their human disguises. Their backs were hunched, their heads were bald, and one had an index finger jammed up his nose.

"There were *three* Shopkeepers?" Poppy screeched. "I should have known!" Charlie could see the little differences between them, but anyone who'd never met a goblin would have assumed they were identical. Identically terrifying.

The grizzled, potbellied creatures approached, and Charlie and his friends drew in closer around Charlotte.

The goblins kept coming. They didn't stop until the one in the lead was nose to nose with Charlotte. "We heard we had visitors," he snarled. "What do you think you're doing in our town?"

Charlie and his friends waited for Charlotte's answer. If anyone was going to show a goblin who was boss, it would be her. But when she opened her mouth, nothing came out but an exhausted sigh.

"We've been curing your victims!" shouted Jack, who hadn't heard the news about Mrs. Tobias. "It's not going to be *your town* anymore."

The goblin peered down at the boy. "Curing them?" He laughed. "These humans aren't *ill*. They don't need a *cure*." He walked over to one of the Walkers—a large, hairy man in lumberjack plaid—and playfully pinched the gentleman's cheek. "Just look at this one. He's perfectly content! Do you see any suffering? Do you see any tears? No one in this town feels *bad*."

Charlie's eyes passed over people in the Tranquility Tonight line. The goblin was right. "They don't feel bad, because they don't feel anything at all," he said.

"And they have our employers to thank!" the goblin said.

"The tonic is evil," Paige spat. "And so are ICK and INK."

"Ignorant brat! The tonic is bliss!" the goblin yelled, his anger growing. "You would understand that if you'd been forced to live your entire life underground as we have—or if you'd been abandoned in a lighthouse at the end of the world. If any of you spoiled humans had ever known true fear, you'd welcome the oblivion the tonic brings!"

"It's destroying the Netherworld," Jack argued back. "All the Nightmares are in danger."

"Why should we care?" the goblin said. "They've tortured ICK and INK for years, and they banished me and my fellow goblins from their land. Being swallowed by a giant hole is exactly what the Nightmares deserve!"

"And do ICK and INK know that the tonic isn't just destroying the Netherworld, that it's destroying the Dream Realm too?" Charlie asked, and the head goblin smirked.

"Of course they know!" the goblin replied. "The hope humans find in the Dream Realm is worse than the Netherworld's fear! What could be crueler than *hope*? You wait and you wish and you dream, and nothing ever happens. That's why ICK and INK made the tonic, to rid the Waking World of hope *and* fear. We goblins helped them produce it. We were the only ones who were strong enough to visit the lighthouse. And as a reward we shall rule the Waking World."

Charlie suddenly understood. In return for the goblins' help, ICK and INK had promised to let them pass through the portal. But the twins hadn't held up their part of the bargain. "You've been tricked," he told the goblin.

"What are you talking about?" the goblin snapped.

"The goblins who've gathered at the Netherworld light-house will never make it to the Waking World," Charlie said. "One of the twins burned down the lighthouse on this side. The portal is gone. ICK and INK were never going to allow your kind to rule our world."

Anger flashed in the head goblin's eyes, and he turned, falling into a huddle with his comrades. Their voices rose and fell as they argued in their horrible language, until at last the head goblin turned back to Charlie. "The light-house is not the only portal," he said. "Surely our benevo-lent masters have simply, as you humans say, changed the location of the party."

The lightbulb that went off in Charlie's head at that moment was as powerful as the lighthouse lantern. When he started to laugh, everyone gaped at him as if he'd gone mad. But the goblins had given him the clue he'd been looking for. He knew what would cure the Walkers.

"You just found out that you've been double-crossed," Charlie said. "But you still have hope! No matter what hap-pens, you can't get rid of it!" He marched over to the Walk-ers who were still obediently waiting in line. "It makes no difference what ICK and INK put in that tonic. It couldn't possibly destroy *all* hope. There's still a tiny piece inside all these people. And soon it's going to spring back to life."

"Ridiculous," the goblin snorted. "These humans have

been drinking the tonic for weeks now. In a day or two, its effects will be permanent. There's nothing you can do to change that."

"You're wrong," Charlie said confidently. "I'll make their hope grow, and they'll all be cured. All I have to do is figure out the magic words."

"Magic words!" The goblins cackled.

"Charlie . . ." Charlotte sighed and shook her head.

Charlie ignored the goblins and walked back to Charlotte. "I know how you cured Josephine," he said. "It wasn't the antidote. It was what you said to Paige while Josephine was listening."

Charlotte didn't look at all convinced. "What did I say?" she asked skeptically.

"I remember!" Paige exclaimed, and Charlie could see that she'd figured it out too. "You told me that Josephine would be just fine because I was looking out for her. My aunt must have heard it."

"See?" Charlie said. "Magic words." He looked over at Ollie. "When you came into Charlotte's store for the poison ivy ointment, did Charlotte say anything special to you?"

Ollie nodded. "When no one was listening, Charlotte whispered that my mom was tough on me 'cause she cares, and she said that I was lucky to have someone who loved me that much."

"And you?" Charlie asked Poppy.

Poppy blushed. "Some kids at school kept making fun of my hair. I asked Charlotte if she had anything in her shop that would turn it brown, and she told me that one day soon my red hair would bring me the kind of attention I'd *want* to have. I try to remember that whenever I'm feeling down."

Charlie stood in front of his stepmother. He should have known what she was capable of doing. Her "magic" had saved him once too. "Your words protected Ollie and Poppy from the tonic because they stayed with them and gave them hope. They cured Josephine too. Somehow you know what scares people the most—and you know just what to say to help them get past it."

"But I've barely said anything at all!" Charlotte argued.

"A little hope goes a long way, Charlotte," Charlie said. He realized then that it was time to pay her back. "Even if we have to burn down the mansion to protect the portal, you and me and Jack and Dad will all be together. That's the most important thing, don't you think?"

Charlotte nodded and wiped a tear from her eye.

"We've got your back, Charlotte," Jack added. "Right, Charlie?"

"That's right," Charlie agreed, giving his little brother a wink.

"Is this disgusting display of human emotion over?" the head goblin sneered. He was looking a little less confident.

"Not yet," Charlie told him. "Prepare yourselves for a revolting grand finale." Facing the line of Walkers, he cupped his hands around his mouth. "People of Orville Falls!" Charlie yelled at the top of his lungs. "I want you to know that you are all going to be okay! We are here to help you get back to normal. None of us will give up until you are!"

In the silence that followed, Charlie waited for a sign. Half a minute ticked past, but nothing happened. Charlie saw the goblins grinning, and his friends beginning to fidget. But he wasn't worried at all.

"Take your time!" Charlie shouted at the citizens of Orville Falls. "We're not going anywhere! We know why you all started drinking the tonic. We know about your nightmares and the little girl you saw in them. When she was around, you felt hopeless and alone, like there was no one who could help you. But those were just bad dreams, and if you face them, you'll beat them. There *are* people who can help you, and we're here! We are not going to leave a single one of you behind. It doesn't matter how long it takes, we'll get through this together."

The only sounds were the whistling wind and the caw of a single crow. Then someone yawned loudly. A boy in a filthy blue soccer uniform stepped out of the line. He yawned again and rubbed at his eyes with his knuckles. "Hey!" He stumbled toward Rocco. His legs must have still been weak, but the smile on his face was proof he'd been cured. "Aren't you that kid from Cypress Creek? Remember me? Kyle, from the Orville Falls Comets? I thought you'd forgotten all about us. But you didn't! You came to help just like you promised!"

Behind the soccer kid, a lady sniffled. A man cleared his throat. Somebody farted, which made someone else laugh. The Walkers were slowly returning to life.

"What did I tell you?" Charlie spun around triumphantly to face the goblins. But they were no longer there. He caught sight of the three of them right before they hightailed it around a corner at the end of the block.

"The goblins are making a run for it!" Rocco shouted, fully prepared to take off after them.

"Don't bother chasing them," Charlie told his friends.

"Why not?" Jack asked. "Do you know where they're going?"

"Nope," Charlie admitted. "But I know where they're going to end up."

CHAPTER TWENTY-EIGHT

THE HERO

After their victory, Charlie's army disbanded. Paige and Rocco stayed in Orville Falls, where they hunted for Walkers in need of the cure. The rest of the crew headed back to Cypress Creek, where Ollie and Poppy set off in search of their parents, while Alfie rushed to the local television station to personally cure his beloved Stormy Skies.

Charlie, Jack, and their stepmother had gone straight to the purple mansion—and up the stairs to the tower.

"Are you sure the goblins are going to come here?" Charlotte asked once the three of them were standing in front of the portal.

"They can't stay in Orville Falls," Charlie said. "The whole town will be looking for them. But they can't go anywhere else either. They're on the run. They have nowhere to go. No place to stay. No—"

"Storage sheds filled with cat food and lightbulbs," Jack offered.

"Exactly," Charlie said. "Pretty soon they're going to figure out that they have to go back to the Netherworld. And I have a feeling that we don't want to get in their way when they arrive at the mansion and start looking for the portal."

"Are we going to let them go through?" Jack asked.

"Yep," Charlie said. "We'll just make sure that justice is waiting for them on the other side."

"You mean Medusa?" Charlotte asked.

"She can arrest the goblins as soon as they get to the Netherworld," Charlie said. "All I need to do is go get her."

"By yourself?" Charlotte asked.

"No, Charlie," Jack said firmly. "I won't let you."

"I have to go alone," Charlie explained. "Charlotte can't get through the portal anymore, and you're still on the Netherworld's Most Wanted list."

"That's why I'm the one who has to do it," Jack said. "Going back to the Netherworld is my very worst nightmare. I've got to face it."

"But if you go, I can't go with you," Charlie warned him. "One of us has to stay here to protect the mansion."

"I know," Jack said. "I'll go alone."

"Aren't you scared?" Charlie asked his brother.

Jack nodded.

Charlie put an arm around his brother. "Good," he said. "Because every time you're scared, you have a chance to be brave. Think you can do it, Jack?"

Jack nodded again.

"Then go," Charlie said, stepping aside. "Be our hero."

Charlie watched his little brother close his eyes as he conjured his worst nightmare. The portal opened. Charlie could see half the Netherworld from where they stood. And in the distance, on top of a mountain, was Medusa's cave.

Jack glanced up at Charlie and Charlotte with a scared little smile. Then, without a word, he stepped over to the other side.

Hours passed, and Jack didn't return. Charlie watched his stepmother pace back and forth across the tower. She made the trip so many times that he was sure she'd wear a hole in the floorboards. Charlie, on the other hand, had started off perfectly confident. But as the minutes dragged by, he felt his conviction draining away. He couldn't help but worry that he might have sent his own brother to his doom.

Jack was still missing when the goblins showed up as expected. Charlie and Charlotte heard them on the porch three stories below. Charlie was glad he'd left the down-stairs doors open. There'd been no point in locking them. Nothing would have stopped the desperate creatures from finding a way inside. The goblins had taken their sweet time getting to the mansion. They were probably equipped with everything they'd need to force their way into the house, from weapons to a battering ram.

Charlie and his stepmother scrambled down the stairs from the tower and into Charlotte's bedroom below. They hid there, under the bed, while the goblins stomped all the way upstairs.

A brief silence followed as the goblins searched for the por-tal. Then the smashing and crashing and thumping began.

"Guess they can't find what they need," Charlie said, and grinned. Closed, the portal looked like an ordinary wall.

"Yeah," Charlotte agreed. "But they're going to tear the whole place down searching for it. And what's going to happen if Jack gets back while they're up there?"

"You're right," Charlie said, scooting out from under-neath the bed. He'd been hoping to avoid another unpleas-ant face-to-face with the goblins. But now there was no other way. "We have to be there for Jack."

When Charlie and Charlotte arrived at the tower room, they found it in shambles. The floor was covered with a salad of dried herbs and shards of the glass jars that had held them. And there were holes in all eight walls. Charlie stood in the tower doorway, watching the three goblins wrestle each other across the room. He could only guess, but the bruises on their foreheads seemed to explain the holes in the walls. They must have tried to crash right through them.

"You told us to trust them!" one goblin screeched at another.

"They've left us trapped on this side!" the second one shouted.

"How dare you question ICK and INK!" the third goblin exploded. "When they arrive to open the portal, I will make sure they know that you've both been disloyal!"

Charlie cleared his throat, and the goblins finally caught sight of their visitors. They scrambled to their feet.

Charlie addressed the third goblin. "You still trust ICK and INK? After everything that's happened?"

"They're the *prophecy*," the goblin spat. "Our kind has been waiting for them for a very long time."

Charlie shook his head. *The prophecy*. "Looks like you're going to have to wait a while longer," he said.

"It doesn't matter how long we must wait," the goblin answered. "Destiny cannot be stopped."

Suddenly the wall behind the goblins began to fade, then disappear. Where there had once been beaten-up plaster, there was now an entrance to another room in another tower.

"It's open!" the two other goblins cried.

"What did I tell you?" the first goblin said triumphantly. "ICK and INK have arrived."

Charlie saw it coming before the goblins, and jumped out of the way as a large object shot through the portal and into the tower. It knocked over a goblin and slammed into Charlotte's desk, then fell to the ground. Once the missile had stopped, everyone could see it was a kid. But it wasn't ICK or INK. It was Jack, his face white and his chest heaving.

Charlie dropped down to his knees. "You okay?" he asked his brother.

All Jack could do was nod and point. Charlie turned to see the goblins going for the portal. They were so intent on making it to the other side that they didn't notice what was waiting for them until it was too late. They stopped in their tracks, knocking into each other as they did. The portal was blocked by Nightmares, all of them panting as if they'd just ended a race. Half of the Netherworld must have chased Jack back to the mansion. It was clear from their expressions that the last thing they'd expected to find on the other side of the portal was three goblins.

The goblins turned tail and rushed for the tower door, but Charlotte was too quick. She'd gotten there first and locked it.

"Back up, goblins, or the glasses come off!" Charlie heard someone command. The Nightmares on the other side of the portal parted and allowed Medusa to slither into view, one hand raised to her sunglasses. Dabney the clown and Ava the Harpy followed her through the crowd and took their places at her side. "Goblins, you are hereby under arrest for crimes against the Netherworld, the Dream Realm, and the Waking World. Cuff them," Medusa told the clown.

"My pleasure, Madam President," Dabney said with a giggle.

Dabney grabbed two of the goblins, and Ava took the third. Once the creatures had been escorted out of the tower, Medusa slithered up to Jack.

"You showed remarkable courage today," she told the boy. "I've never seen anything quite like it. Running through the Netherworld with half its creatures chasing after you—just to get a message to me. I didn't think you'd make it, but here we are. Three villains were captured because of you."

Jack beamed. "Thank you," he said, his voice still hoarse. "But I wasn't the only—"

"Hey," Charlie interrupted his brother. "Don't be modest. I would never have done what you just did."

"No, but you would have done something else just as good," Jack said.

"Doubt it," Charlie shot back.

"Okay, okay," Charlotte said with a playful huff. "You guys stop arguing about who's more awesome."

"I'd say you have *two* rather exceptional stepsons," Medusa told Charlotte.

"And I'd have to agree," Charlotte replied, grinning from ear to ear.

Medusa put an arm around each of the boys. "Would you mind if I borrow them both for a little while?"

"Not at all, as long as they're back by six o'clock, when their father gets home," Charlotte said, and Charlie looked up at her in confusion. "Remember the family meeting?" she reminded him.

Charlie nodded. How could he forget?

Trying not to think about the bad news that would be waiting for him at six, Charlie passed through the portal and into the Netherworld, his brother by his side. Dabney and Ava had already taken the goblins down the stairs of the nightmare mansion, and Jack and Charlie were alone in the tower with Medusa.

"I know it feels like we've won, but it's not over yet," Charlie told the gorgon. "ICK and INK are still on the loose. One of them burned down the lighthouse to keep the goblins from passing through the portal and into the Waking World. I don't know why, but I guess it must have been part of their plan. Now one of the girls is here, and the other one is somewhere in the Waking World."

"Yes," Medusa said. "And we must catch them. You know, I never imagined there was any truth to that prophecy. It's still hard to believe that ICK and INK are human children."

"You're sure they're really human?" Charlie asked. "They may look like ten-year-olds, but they're at least eighty years old."

"They were human once," said Medusa. "That much I know for sure. The Netherworld lighthouse collapsed last night, and my troops found something in the rubble. It's from your world, not ours."

Medusa reached into the pocket of her suit jacket and pulled out a photo. The paper it had been printed on was creased and yellowing around the edges. But the black-and-white picture was still clear. It showed twin girls in identical old-fashioned dresses smiling at the camera. Charlie flipped the photo over and found an inscription on the back.

Isabel Cordelia Kessog
India Nell Kessog
Orville Falls, 1939

ICK and INK. Charlie stared at the girls' happy faces. What could have turned two little schoolgirls into the monsters who'd almost managed to wipe out three worlds?

"Indy and her sister both look so sweet," said Jack.

"Keep the photo," Medusa told the boys. "But put it away. Right now we have a celebration to attend."

As Charlie tucked the picture into the back pocket of his jeans, he heard the roar of a crowd outside.

Jack jumped at the sound. "What was that?" he asked nervously.

"The creatures of the Netherworld are waiting," said Medusa. "They just saw the goblins who nearly destroyed our land. Now they need to see who was responsible for saving us all. Go," she urged them.

The Laird boys made it as far as the front door. Then Jack came to a stop.

Charlie gave his little brother a nudge. "You first," he said.

"I'm not sure I want to," Jack said.

"Why not?" Charlie asked him. "Are you scared?"

"No, I faced my fear. But they thought I tried to destroy the Netherworld," Jack said, his face twisting into a frown. "I don't want to be friends with them anymore."

"They made a mistake, Jack. Sometimes people—and Nightmares—do that. It won't be any fun for you to stay mad at them. And don't forget, you have lots of friends in the Waking World," Charlie reminded him. "And you'll always have me."

"Yeah, but you made it pretty clear that you're not my friend," Jack said, looking down at his feet. "You're my *brother*."

"Yep," Charlie said. "I'm your brother. And that means it's my job to be your friend for the rest of your life."

"Yeah, your *job*," Jack muttered.

"The best job ever," Charlie told him.

"You mean it?" Jack asked, a grin lifting the edges of his mouth.

"Yep," Charlie said. And he did.

Charlie opened the door for his brother. In the distance, he could see what was left of the hole that had almost swallowed the Netherworld. The formerly bottomless pit was now no bigger than a fishing pond. A hush fell over the crowd when Jack stepped outside onto the porch. Thousands of Nightmares surrounded the mansion. They stared at the boy, and for several long seconds, Charlie wondered if he'd made the wrong call. Then a little creature hopped up onto the porch and climbed on top of a rail.

"Is that how we say hello to a hero?" Bruce shouted down at the crowd. "Come on, Nightmares! Lemme hear what you got!"

That was all the encouragement they needed. The Nightmares went wild.

CHAPTER TWENTY-NINE

FULL RECOVERY

Charlie wished he could have stayed in the Netherworld. But at six o'clock, he and the rest of the Laird family were gathered around the kitchen table for the family meeting that Charlie's dad had called.

"I'm afraid we have some very bad news," Andrew Laird began.

"But at least now it won't be the end of the world!" Charlotte added merrily. Charlie appreciated the effort to keep things lighthearted, but it was time to get serious. He'd helped save the world, and now he needed to find a way to save his house.

Charlie's dad didn't know what to make of his wife's outburst. He cleared his throat. "Your stepmom and I have been having some financial difficulties lately, and it seems—"

The doorbell rang, and Jack jumped up to get it.

"Let it go," Andrew Laird ordered impatiently. "We've put this meeting off for too long. It can't wait any longer."

Jack reluctantly returned to his seat at the table.

Andrew Laird took a deep breath and then set it free. "As I was saying—"

The doorbell rang again, and Charlie's dad sat back with his arms crossed.

"Let me get it," Charlie offered. "I'll tell whoever it is to go away."

He ran to the door and pulled it open. On the other side stood Ollie Tobias and his mother. Both of them were dressed for croquet. When Charlie saw Ollie's straw hat and suspenders, he gulped.

"Where's your stepmother?" Mrs. Tobias demanded before Charlie could even say hello.

"She's in the kitchen, but she's—"

Mrs. Tobias squeezed past Charlie and headed straight for the kitchen. Ollie gave Charlie a helpless shrug. "That woman's never understood the meaning of the word *no*," he said.

"So I guess you found her," Charlie said.

"Yeah. Mom was standing in line at the Cypress Creek

tonic shop when I got back to town. I told her that I love her, and I promised not to eat any more bath beads. When she woke up, I took her home. And guess what! She loves what I did with the living room!"

"That's great, but why is she here?" Charlie asked. "Why does she want to see Charlotte?"

Ollie smiled mischievously. "Maybe you should go find out," he said.

Charlie ran back to the kitchen to find Mrs. Tobias planting a kiss on Charlotte's cheek. "I am *so* sorry to disturb you," she told Charlie's stepmom. "But I wanted to thank you for . . . for . . . for whatever it is that you did. Ollie says you and your stepson are the ones who came up with the cure for my . . . condition."

Charlotte cast a nervous glance in her husband's direction. "It was my pleasure, Mrs. Tobias," she said. "I'm glad you're feeling better."

"Not just better," the woman announced. "Better than ever!" She opened her handbag, pulled out an envelope, and thrust it into Charlotte's hands. "I hope this is enough to thank you."

Charlotte tried to hand the envelope back. "Oh, I wasn't expecting payment, Mrs. Tobias," she said.

"But why not?" asked Mrs. Tobias, refusing to accept the envelope. "How do you expect to run a successful business if you don't accept payment for your services?"

"*Please*. Don't argue with her, Mrs. Laird," Ollie advised.

"I added a little extra for taking care of Ollie while I was ill," Mrs. Tobias added with a smile. "I hope he minded his manners."

Charlotte gave Ollie a wink. "He was a perfect angel," she said. "He's welcome back anytime."

"*See?* I told you, Mom. I've turned over a whole new leaf," Ollie insisted, though his mischievous grin said otherwise.

"Well, then I guess Mrs. Laird must have worked another miracle last night." She held out a hand to Charlotte. "Thank you. My apologies for disturbing your family. I hope you don't have plans this evening. You may have a few other guests popping by. I'm afraid I have a very big mouth."

With that, Mrs. Tobias headed for the front door with her son in tow.

"What are you waiting for?" Jack said as soon as the family was alone again. "Open it!"

Charlotte hesitantly ripped open the envelope. Her eyes widened at the sight of the check inside.

"How much is it for?" Charlie asked.

"A lot," Charlotte answered. She gave her husband a peek at the check, and his eyes widened too.

"What on earth did you do for that woman?" he asked.

"Sprayed her in the face with a water gun," Jack said with a cackle.

"And then made her son say he loves her," Charlie added.

"Excuse me?" Andrew Laird asked.

Then the doorbell rang again and Jack sprinted off to answer it.

"Hey, Charlotte!" he shouted. "Alfie's here. And he brought Stormy Skies to see you!"

"Since when do you know the weatherwoman?" Andrew Laird asked in amazement.

Charlotte gave her husband a peck on the cheek. "I'm full of surprises," she told him.

There were at least a dozen other visitors to the Laird house that night. Stormy Skies hung around for more than an hour, happily telling anyone who would listen about the brave young meteorology fan who'd appeared out of nowhere to rescue her. By the time Alfie's parents came to take him home, he and

Rocco had snapped more than a hundred selfies with the indulgent weatherwoman. Poppy DuBose and her family stayed for a dinner of kale casserole and left with a year's supply of Charlotte's homemade toothpaste. As the evening wore on, the Lairds opened their door for people they barely knew, and a few people they didn't recognize at all. But everyone came bearing envelopes, and Charlotte reluctantly accepted payment for her services.

When the guests were gone, Charlie and Jack cleaned up the dishes while Charlotte counted her earnings.

"You sure did treat a lot of people over the last few days," Andrew Laird said.

Charlotte smiled. "I guess you could say there was something going around."

"Do you think you made enough to pay the mortgage?" Charlie heard his dad ask softly.

"Not quite," Charlotte replied. "But it will certainly help with the move."

The very next morning at eight a.m., the Lairds' doorbell rang again. Charlie opened it to find Paige and Josephine grinning from ear to ear.

Josephine bent down and kissed Charlie on the cheek. "Thank you," she said. "I always told Paige you were a hero in the making."

"Now stop blushing and go get Charlotte!" Paige exclaimed. "We just saw something that she's gotta see."

"I'm here!" Charlotte was coming down the stairs in her nightgown and robe. Charlie knew it wasn't a good sign. His stepmom was usually at the herbarium by eight. "But I'm not dressed yet."

"Doesn't matter." Paige grabbed her hand.

Paige and Josephine practically dragged Charlotte downtown, with Charlie nearly jogging to keep up with them. When they reached Cypress Creek's Main Street, they found a line that stretched for blocks. In the middle of the line was the original Walker, Winston Lindsay. He'd brought the entire Orville Falls Comets soccer team.

"What are they waiting for?" Charlotte asked. "The goblins are gone and the Walkers are cured. Tranquility Tonight should be closed."

"They're waiting for *you*," Paige told her. "See where the line ends?" She pointed down the street.

Charlie rolled up his sleeves. "Looks like Hazel's Herbarium is back in business."

And he knew that meant the purple mansion was safe. The victory felt even richer when Charlie spotted Curtis Swanson of the Amalgamated Bank of Cypress Creek standing across the street from Hazel's Herbarium, watching in awe as the line continued to grow. Everything had changed overnight, and even Curtis Swanson seemed to know it. When he glanced in Charlie's direction, Charlie offered the banker a wave. Swanson was responding with a rather unconvincing smile, when he seemed to catch sight of something behind Charlie. In an instant, the man's face had gone white and he'd rushed away. Charlie checked over his shoulder but saw nothing frightening, just a single red balloon floating through the sky.

ᴥ CHAPTER THIRTY ᴥ

THE BIG QUESTION

Charlie sat beside his mother on the front porch steps of her Dream Realm house. In the distance, they could still see faint, wispy traces of the Nothingness cloud that had once seemed so threatening. Charlie had just come from a tour of the Dream Realm's Orville Falls. There wasn't much there yet, just a fountain and a few trees. The progress was slow, but Orville Falls was being rebuilt.

Charlie's mother had listened to his story. She told him how proud she was, and how happy she was that the purple mansion was safe. But then she went quiet for a minute. "I still can't believe that ICK and INK were little girls," she finally said. "They must have been so lonely in that light-house. Maybe Charlotte and I should have paid them a visit."

"ICK and INK were little girls in the 1930s," Charlie replied. "We have no idea what they are now. All we know is that they're really dangerous. Charlotte and I are doing our best to keep them from using our portal."

"But the lighthouse's portal is gone, and the purple mansion's portal is secured?" his mom asked.

"Yep," Charlie said. "We added three dead-bolt locks to the tower door, and we sealed both of the tower windows shut."

"Which means ICK and INK are trapped for good on the other side."

"No," Charlie said. "One of them is in the Waking World. She disappeared after she set fire to the lighthouse. The last time anyone saw her, she was in Maine. The other sister is somewhere in the Netherworld."

"So they're apart?"

Charlie nodded. "And we're going to keep it that way."

"Are you sure that's the right thing to do?" his mom asked.

Charlie hadn't been expecting that. "What are you talk-ing about?"

"Well, I guess I keep thinking about their tonic's secret ingredient," Veronica Laird said. "It came from them—but it wasn't anger or hatred, was it?"

"No," Charlie said. "It was despair."

"And now we know that despair has a cure," his mom said. "ICK and INK are sisters. They need each other the way you need Jack, and he needs you."

Charlie was baffled by the direction their talk had taken. He had thought she would be glad to be rid of her old stalkers. "But, Mom, ICK and INK nearly destroyed three worlds! They turned thousands of people into Walkers— and they almost let goblins into the Waking World!"

"But *why*?" his mother asked. "Why would they do such things? Have you ever asked yourself that?"

Charlie started to respond, then shut his mouth. She was right. They'd stopped ICK and INK, but they'd never figured out why the twins had created the tonic. What were they trying to do?

"Look up there." Charlie's mom pulled him from his thoughts. She was pointing at the Dream Realm's version of the Lairds' purple mansion. Standing on the front porch was a handsome man with black hair and an old-fashioned suit. "Do you know who that is?"

Charlie grinned. "It's Silas DeChant," he said. "He built the purple mansion. I was hoping I'd meet him here someday."

"So you remember the DeChants' story?" his mom asked.

"Of course!" Charlie said. "When Silas let darkness take

over his life, he left his friends and family and came here. But the darkness only got worse when he was all alone, and he ended up opening a portal to the Netherworld."

"Ah, see?" his mother said. "You told the story without even mentioning its real hero."

"Who was the real hero?" Charlie asked.

"The *heroine* of the story was Silas's fiancée, Abigail. When he abandoned her, she could have despised him. She had every right to, after all. They were supposed to be married, and Silas just up and left town. But instead of hating him, Abigail asked *why*. She tried to understand what had made Silas leave—and then she set out to find him. What do you suppose would have happened if Abigail hadn't found Silas?"

"The portal he created would have stayed open, and Nightmares could have come through to this side," Charlie said.

"That's right," his mother told him. "So Abigail DeChant may have saved the world, just by asking *why*. Now, let me ask you again, Charlie. Why did two little girls try to destroy three worlds?"

Charlie thought for a moment, before he answered. "I have no idea," he said. "But I suppose I'd better try to find out."

EPILOGUE

Summer break had reached an end, and the first day of eighth grade had arrived. Charlie grabbed a seat in his homeroom class just as the first bell rang.

"Hello, everyone," said the woman in black at the front of the room. "My name is Ms. Abbot. I teach seventh- and eighth-grade history, and this is my homeroom."

There wasn't much need for introductions, Charlie thought. Everyone in Cypress Creek knew all about Ms. Abbot. She'd arrived in town in the middle of August, dressed like she was going to a funeral. Charlotte seemed to be one of the few people in town who'd managed to speak with her. She said Ms. Abbot was perfectly normal. She came from New York, where dressing in black from head to toe was considered quite chic, and not necessarily a sign of evil proclivities.

"Do we have anyone else who's new to Cypress Creek Elementary this year?" Ms. Abbot asked the class.

A hand shot up at the front of the class.

"And what's your name?" Ms. Abbot inquired.

"India, ma'am," said the girl in a British accent. "But you may call me Indy for short."

JUST WHEN CHARLIE LAIRD THOUGHT IT WAS SAFE TO GO TO SLEEP, NIGHTMARES STRIKE AGAIN!

Jason Segel and Kirsten Miller won't let
a kid get any rest. Look for book three
in the Nightmares! series.

NIGHTMARES!

THE LOST LULLABY

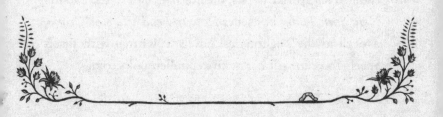

ABOUT THE AUTHORS

JASON SEGEL used to have nightmares just like Charlie, and just like Charlie, he's learned that the things we're most afraid of are the things that can make us strong . . . if we're brave enough to face them. Jason likes acting, writing, making music, and hanging out with his friends. Sometimes he writes movies. Sometimes he writes songs for movies. Sometimes he stars in those movies and sings those songs. You might know him from *The Muppets* and *Despicable Me*. Your parents might know him from other stuff. *Nightmares! The Sleepwalker Tonic* is his second novel and the sequel to the *New York Times* bestseller *Nightmares!*

KIRSTEN MILLER grew up in a small town just like Cypress Creek, minus the purple mansion. She lives and writes in New York City. Kirsten is the author of the acclaimed Kiki Strike books, the Eternal Ones series, and the *New York Times* bestseller *How to Lead a Life of Crime*, as well as the Nightmares! novels, cowritten with Jason Segel. You can visit her at kirstenmillerbooks.com.